THE CHESIL BEACH MURDERS

Rachel McLean writes thrillers that make your pulse race and your brain tick. A proud indie author who manages her own publishing company, she has sold millions of copies digitally and hundreds of thousands in print, regularly topping the bestseller lists. She is the author of the Dorset Crime novels and five spin-off crime series, with beloved characters appearing in multiple series. In 2021, she won the Kindle Storyteller Award with *The Corfe Castle Murders*. She divides her time between Birmingham and Dorset and lives with her wife, three children and two cats Cagney and Lacey.

ALSO BY RACHEL MCLEAN

Dorset Crime series

The Corfe Castle Murders
The Clifftop Murders
The Island Murders
The Monument Murders
The Millionaire Murders
The Fossil Beach Murders
The Blue Pool Murders
The Lighthouse Murders
The Ghost Village Murders
The Poole Harbour Murders
The Chesil Beach Murders
The Beach Hut Murders
...and more to come

RACHEL McLEAN

THE DORSET CRIME SERIES BOOK 11

THE CHESIL BEACH MURDERS

ACKROYD PUBLISHING

Ackroyd Publishing

ackroydpublishing.com

Printed and bound in the UK by CPI Group (Uk) Ltd, Croydon CR0 4YY

Illustration by Maria Burns

rachelmclean.com

CHAPTER ONE

Anika's breath caught in her throat as she adjusted her camera's focus.

Perfect conditions. And she was out here on her own. How come no one else had looked at the weather forecast and seen it would be like this?

In her camera viewfinder, St Catherine's Chapel rose ahead of her, at the top of its hill outside Abbotsbury. Beyond, the sun was rising in a blaze of reds and oranges.

It was gorgeous.

She fired off some photos then moved up the hill to get closer to the chapel. The best viewpoint up here was in the air, but use of drones was restricted; you had to get someone from English Heritage to accompany you for that. And this was a spur of the moment visit.

Anika knew what she was doing. She could get an angle that would include the walls of the castle in the foreground, the Fleet and Chesil Beach beyond in the background, and the sunrise resplendent above it all.

This was worth waking early for. Not as early in October as it would be in the summer, thank God.

She stopped after entering the fenced area surrounding the chapel and took more photos, stopping to change lenses partway through. There was a spot where the shadows would be at their most distinct, around the side of the building.

She walked round, holding onto her camera and watching the rough ground. When she reached her spot, she looked up.

What the hell?

There was someone in the alcove she was heading for, the spot where the light hit the chapel walls in a way that made for fantastic close ups. A man, or it looked like a man, was slumped against the wall.

Another photographer, out here early and dozing off from lack of sleep?

Or someone who'd come out for the lacklustre sunset the night before and decided to stay for the dawn?

No. That would be foolish up here, even protected by that alcove.

She shivered and moved closer.

"Hello?"

No answer. The man didn't move. He was dressed in a black coat, heavy and old-fashioned. His head was slumped downwards and she couldn't see his face.

"Hello?" she repeated. "Are you alright?"

Nothing.

Anika took a breath. This was making her feel uneasy. She'd heard a rumour that people slept up here sometimes, but only in the summer.

"Alright, mate," she said, trying to sound breezy. "Time to wake up. You're not the only one after a good photo."

Nothing.

Oh, hell.

Was she going to have to wake him?

As she approached, she caught a smell. The smell of dirt, or decay. She sniffed the air and stopped moving.

Death?

"Are you OK?" she said.

Don't waste your breath, she told herself. *He's completely out of it.*

She felt sick now, the smell combined with the dread. Should she get closer, or was that too risky? What if he got nasty, if disturbed? What if...?

There were so many what ifs. But she couldn't just leave him up here.

Anika turned her head away and took a deep breath. She clamped her lips shut and turned back to the man.

She took one step forward, two, three.

No point in trying to talk to him again.

She reached out, her hand stopping before she made contact.

That smell.

But she couldn't leave him.

"Are you alright?" she said. "Can I help?"

Do it.

She took a final step and reached further so she was touching his shoulder. She gave him a shake.

The man's head lolled. The bottom half of his face become visible.

Anika's breath caught in her throat.

His mouth...

It was a gaping hole. Did he not have teeth?

She let out a whimper, then put her hand to her own mouth.

Don't be sick.

She shook his shoulder again. He moved in a way that felt... wrong.

Oh, hell.

She grabbed her phone and dialled 999.

So much for the sunset. This poor bastard was dead.

CHAPTER TWO

DC Tina Abbott leaned over the bed and kissed her sleeping husband.

Mike stirred, rolling onto his back and stretching his arms. He looked up at her, blinking. "T. What time is it?"

She smiled. "Seven thirty. Sorry, love, but it's time for you to get up."

He groaned. "I know, I know."

Tina straightened, adjusting her suit jacket. It had fit just fine before her pregnancy with Daisy, but now it stretched across the shoulders. Did she need to lose weight? Or did she have more important things to worry about?

"Louis is downstairs, eating oat cakes in front of the TV," she told Mike.

Mike yawned. "Let me guess. Bluey?"

Tina chuckled. Their son Louis, who'd just turned three years old, was obsessed with the Australian cartoon. If she let him, he'd watch it from the instant he woke up to the moment he went to sleep again. She was worried he dreamed about Bluey.

"What about Daisy?" Mike asked.

"I put her back in her cot, just to contain her till you got up." Daisy was crawling now, and could move around the house faster than Tina believed possible for a six-month-old.

He eased himself up. "Sorry, love. OK, I've got it. You go to work." He grabbed her hand and pulled her towards him, giving her a deep kiss.

"What's that for?" she asked.

He shrugged. "Good luck. Hope you enjoy your first day back."

She raised an eyebrow. "I will. I mean, I'll miss you and the kids, of course. But yeah, I will."

Mike heaved himself out of bed and called out in a babyish voice. "Right, Daisy-do. Daddy's coming." Tina heard giggling from Daisy's bedroom.

With the help of Mike's questionable DIY skills, they'd divided their old bedroom in two so that each of the children had their own space, and now they were in the smaller room Louis had previously occupied. It was a squeeze, but it was better than having to move house.

The doorbell rang.

"I'll get it," said Tina. She clattered down the stairs and flung the door open.

A man stood on the path outside the house, holding a bouquet of flowers so big it looked like it might eat him alive.

"Tina Abbott?" he asked.

"That's me." She reached out for the flowers, checking the card. It was in an envelope, no obvious indication of who'd sent it. But she had a pretty good idea.

"These are for you," the man said. "Congratulations on whatever it is. Must be pretty big."

She gave him a sardonic smile. "First day back at work after having my second baby."

"Oh," he replied. "Not that big."

She gave him a look and closed the door.

Mike was at the bottom of the stairs, Daisy in his arms. "Look, Daisy, what's Mummy got?"

Tina hauled the flowers into the kitchen, losing a few petals as she dragged the huge bouquet through the doorway. She dumped them into the sink. There was no way they had a vase big enough. These would have to be split between multiple vases, pint glasses, jugs, anything they could find.

"There's only one person who'd have sent those," Mike said.

Tina nodded, opening the envelope.

To my wonderful detective daughter, good luck back in the force. With love from Mum.

"Annie," Mike said.

Tina gave him a smile. "Yep."

"Well, it was good of her to think of you."

She raised an eyebrow. "This is just that bit too much thinking."

"It's Annie. What d'you expect?"

She frowned. "Can you deal with this? I really need to get to work."

"Of course, love. We'll sort it, won't we, Daisy?"

The baby blew a raspberry on his cheek. He wiped off the saliva with a grimace then kissed the top of her head.

"One moment, Daisy-do. Don't look." Mike pulled Tina towards him and gave her another kiss. Daisy shrieked.

Tina waggled her eyebrows at Daisy, then tickled the girl's tummy. "Right," she said, "I'm off." She popped her head round the living room door and blew a kiss at Louis. He glanced round, irritated to be distracted from his favourite show.

"Have a good day, Louis," she said. "Don't miss me too much."

He said nothing.

Tina sighed. Was he turning into a teenager already?

No. Teenagers didn't watch Bluey... did they?

CHAPTER THREE

DCI Lesley Clarke squinted into the low sun as she turned into the access road leading to Dorset Police HQ at Winfrith.

This route was all too familiar now. For four years she'd commuted here, first from Wareham and then from Boscombe in Bournemouth. Now she was making the slightly longer journey from Southbourne. It meant an hour's drive, but it also meant living right by the sea and the wildness of Hengistbury Head.

Some things were worth tolerating.

Her hands gripped the steering wheel tighter as she approached the gates to the car park, anticipating another day of managing her two DIs.

DI Jill Scott, in charge of the Cold Cases Team, was fine. She got on with her job. Sure, she sulked a little every now and then when there wasn't enough for her team to do, but she didn't give Lesley any trouble.

And when her team didn't have an active case on, she was happy to let Lesley borrow people and move them across to the other team. Something that made Lesley's job much easier.

Today, Tina Abbott would be returning to work. Tina was a

member of the Major Crime Investigations Team, and her husband Mike, who was now going on parental leave in Tina's place, was a member of Jill's Cold Cases Team, so the balance would probably work out.

Lesley parked her car and slumped back in her seat.

Jill was one thing. DI Hannah Patterson, in charge of the MCIT, was entirely another.

Recruited to head up the MCIT when Lesley had been instructed to pull on her big girl pants and act like a 'proper' DCI, Hannah had resented her posting almost from the start. She rubbed her team up the wrong way, contradicted Lesley at every turn, and definitely didn't get along with Jill.

Lesley wanted to think this might just be a personality clash, but her copper's instincts said otherwise. Hannah, she was coming to realise, was a bad influence on everyone around her.

She opened the driver's door and sighed. Maybe today was the day she'd have that conversation with Hannah. The one where she told the DI to start behaving nicely towards her colleagues. Where Lesley overcame her unease around Hannah, and just did her damn job as the woman's senior officer.

Just as she was about to swing her legs out of the car, the passenger door opened and a man slid in.

Lesley put her hand to her chest. What the—?

She turned to him, and the tension in her body eased.

"Sir."

Superintendent Anthony Carpenter closed the passenger door and turned to her.

What the hell was he doing?

Carpenter was in the habit of summoning her to his office. Occasionally – very occasionally – he came down to her office if there was something pressing, or something that involved the rest of the team. But coming out here to the car park...

Shit. Something must be really wrong.

"What is it?" she asked, hearing the tension in her voice.

He looked at her, his expression tight. "You've got trouble, Lesley."

She took a breath. "What kind of trouble, Sir?"

"One of your team seems to have it in for you."

Lesley had a pretty good idea who he was talking about. But she had to check.

"Who?" she said.

He shook his head. "I'll need you in my office in five minutes. There's a PSD officer in there already."

Shit.

Lesley looked at the Super. What had Hannah said about her? Was this something to do with DC Johnny Chiles coming back?

Shit.

She should never have listened to Dennis. She should have let Johnny languish in the Met, like she'd intended in the first place.

She straightened in her seat. "Sir," she said, "I'll be with you in five minutes."

"Good." He opened the passenger door and had all but jumped out before she'd even had the chance to find out which of her team supposedly had it in for her.

CHAPTER FOUR

Tina walked into the new MCIT team room, surprised by how uneasy she felt.

She'd forgotten that since her maternity leave started, the old HQ building had been emptied out, and everybody was in this sleek glass structure now. It felt like coming back to a different job.

She'd struggled to find the right corridor and had felt unsettled by all the new faces, people who nodded and smiled but clearly didn't recognise her. Hopefully, rejoining the team would help with some of that.

As she closed the door behind her, Meera stood up from her desk, turning towards her, and smiled.

"Tina," she said. "Welcome back."

"Thanks."

Tina turned at the sight of movement in the corner of her eye. "Well, I never," she said. "DC Johnny Chiles. What brings you back here?"

He grinned at her. "Hasn't Mike filled you in?"

"Of course he has." She beckoned him towards her. "Come here and give me a hug, you old bugger."

"Not so much of the old, thanks," he said. "I'm not the one who's just had a baby."

She raised an eyebrow. "I thought you had two of them now."

He pulled away from the hug and smiled. "We should get together sometime, take them on a play date."

She wrinkled her nose. "Really? You want to spend our time together on play dates and not solving cases?"

He laughed. "Same old Tina Abbott."

Meera was hovering behind him. "Hi, Tina," she said.

Tina gave her a smile. "Hi, Meera. Sorry, I was rude. It's nice to see you."

The two of them hadn't worked closely together before. But Meera had worked with Mike, and he thought she was a good copper. She'd been instrumental in solving the murder of Fran Dugdale, who'd been found in Tyneham Village a couple of years earlier.

"It's good to be back," Tina said. "What's been going on in my absence?"

Johnny retreated to his desk. It was covered in photos: him and Alice, his wife; him and Alice and the kids; the kids each on their own; the kids all together; the kids with Alice; the kids with what looked like grandparents.

This wasn't the same Johnny Chiles she remembered from four years ago, the Johnny Chiles who'd mysteriously transferred to the Met with very little in the way of notice or explanation. There hadn't even been a leaving do.

Still, Tina was a detective. She'd find out what he'd been up to soon enough.

The door opened and a man strode in, looking agitated. "Where is she?" he asked.

Tina stepped back. This was DS Nathan Strunk, the newest member of the team. He'd been a PSD officer in the past, working for Robert Collingwood, the man who'd killed DCI Mackie. Tina knew she shouldn't hold that against him. Mike had told her that Strunk hadn't known anything about what Collingwood was up to.

But still...

"Sarge," she said, as she stepped forward. "I'm back from maternity leave."

He turned to her, blinking. "Ah right, yeah, OK." He turned back to Meera and Johnny. "Anybody seen the DI? Hannah? Where is she?"

Tina swallowed. She'd heard about DI Hannah Patterson. Truth was, she'd been relieved not to find the woman in the team room when she'd arrived.

"Something wrong, Sarge?" she said.

He shook his head. "You don't need to worry. It's your first day. But I can't find the DI. Anybody know where she is? Has she been in this morning?"

Meera shrugged. "Sorry, Sarge, I haven't seen her."

"Me neither," said Johnny. "Do you want me to give her a call?"

Nathan gave him a look. "What d'you think I've been doing for the last half hour?"

Johnny cast his gaze downwards. "Sorry, Sarge."

Tina watched them. The room was full of tension. No one seemed at ease. And why was the DS so worried about the DI not being here?

Was this what it was like in the Major Crime Investigations Team now?

CHAPTER FIVE

Carpenter's PA, Carla, gave Lesley a bright smile as she approached the suite of offices reserved for the high-ups on the top floor of the shiny new HQ building.

"Morning, DCI Clarke."

Lesley forced a smile in return. "Morning, Carla."

Maybe a smile from Carla meant that things weren't quite so bad. Or just that Carpenter hadn't told her what was going on.

Was that somehow worse?

"Is he in?" she asked.

Carla nodded. "He's expecting you."

Of course he is. She approached the smooth oak door and knocked.

"Lesley, is that you?" came the super's voice from inside.

"Yes, Sir." She brushed her fingers through her hair and pushed her shoulders back, then opened the door.

Carpenter was inside, sitting at his desk. On one of the chairs opposite it sat a woman she didn't recognise. She wore a dark maroon suit and a pinched expression.

Lesley gave her a nod. "Morning."

"Morning," the woman replied, barely making eye contact.

Lesley turned to Carpenter. "You wanted to see me, Sir?"

Pretend the conversation in the car didn't happen.

He leaned back in his chair. "I did. Take a seat." He nodded towards the second of the two chairs opposite his desk.

In the corner of the room, by the full-height windows that looked out onto the car park, was a set of easy chairs. But it seemed they weren't using those today.

Lesley took the seat that had been indicated. "Is there something wrong, Sir?"

"There might be."

OK. But why isn't he getting to the point?

He glanced at the woman in the maroon suit. "This is Detective Chief Inspector Zara Weathers from the Professional Standards Department."

Lesley felt her stomach clench, even though she'd known this was coming.

So this *was* about Johnny.

"Sir," she said, "if it's—"

He raised a hand. "Stop, Lesley. You need to hear this out."

Lesley cleared her throat, wishing that she'd taken a moment on the way up to get herself a bottle of water. She'd been trying to drink more of it lately, part of the health kick her wife Elsa was encouraging her to try out.

"Of course," she said.

The woman was still silent.

Lesley placed her hands in her lap, trying not to show her stress. Was she sweating?

Come on, woman, she told herself. She'd been through worse than this. She'd taken down notorious killers and organised crime bosses. She'd dealt with David bloody Randle in Birmingham, for God's sake.

Carpenter placed a hand on a sheaf of papers on his desk. It was face down, but his gesture told her it was important. He glanced down at it, then looked at her.

"There's been a complaint made against you," he said.

She nodded: *no surprise.*

Witnesses made complaints all the time, suspects, too, particularly those who'd been subsequently cleared. They thought it would amplify their innocence if they could blame the police for everything that had happened. She could deal with this.

But then, if a complaint had been made by a witness or a suspect, PSD wouldn't be here.

"Can I ask who made the complaint, Sir?"

He shifted his fingers on the paper, his gaze still on her. "One of your team."

He'd already implied that. But that meant this couldn't be about Johnny.

Unless...

"Are you going to tell me which member of my team?"

The PSD woman shifted on her chair. Lesley wanted to tell her to fuck off, but that wouldn't get her anywhere.

Carpenter leaned back, drumming his fingers on the mysterious document. "DI Hannah Patterson."

"Hannah." *As expected.* "And can I ask what the nature of the complaint is?"

"You'll be receiving the full details in writing as soon as we're done here. But in short, it's a complaint of bullying and harassment. Both against members of your team, and against witnesses."

For God's sake.

"On what grounds, specifically?" she asked.

He took a breath, glancing at the PSD woman. "It's all in the paperwork."

Lesley nodded. "And where is DI Patterson now?"

He raised an eyebrow. "You're not to speak to her."

"I know that, Sir. I just—"

"She's phoned in sick. Her doctor has signed her off with stress."

Lesley clenched her teeth. *Stress, my arse.*

"Very well, Sir," she said, keeping her voice even. "Is that everything?"

He cocked his head. "I'll want to be keeping close tabs on you while this is going on. In particular on your relationship with the other members of your team."

"Of course, Sir," She glanced at the PSD woman. "What can I expect in terms of the formal process?"

The woman leaned forward. "There will be an interview," she said, "with you, with DI Patterson, with any other officers involved."

Involved? Had someone else complained about her?

No. They just wanted to get witness reports.

"We'll be seeking witnesses, of course," the woman continued. What was her name again? Watson? Withers?

Lesley closed her eyes. *Weathers. DCI Zara Weathers.* Not that she'd ever heard of her.

"Of course," Lesley replied.

Play along. Go with the process. They'd soon work out that this was a malicious complaint. If anybody in her team was guilty of bullying and harassment, it was Hannah, with the way she treated the officers beneath her.

She turned to the super. "Right, Sir. Thank you."

The phone rang on his desk. He frowned. "I told Carla not to."

"I think you should pick it up," said DCI Weathers. "If it's come through despite your instruction..."

He grunted and picked it up. "Carla," he snapped. "What is it?" Lesley watched as he listened to his PA on the other end. "And you're absolutely sure there's nobody else who can take responsibility?" he said.

Another pause. "No, of course," he said after a moment. "Not for you to know."

He put the phone down.

"Sir," Lesley said, "there's something wrong?"

He eyed her. "It looks like you've got a case. A body has been found on Chapel Hill, above Chesil Beach. One for the MCIT."

The MCIT. Headed up by DI Hannah Patterson. Who was currently off sick.

With supposed stress.

Lesley looked back at him. "And with DI Patterson off sick..."

He nodded. "You're SIO, Lesley."

She nodded. "Of course." She started to rise. "Can I...?"

He nodded. "I'm watching you, Lesley. You'll need to allocate time to help DCI Weathers here, as well as running this case."

"I will."

"Don't fuck it up, Lesley. Just... don't fuck it up."

CHAPTER SIX

JILL LOOKED up as the door to her office crashed open.

Nathan Strunk stumbled in, panting.

"Nathan," she said, "you OK?"

He placed a hand on her desk, resting his full weight on it. His face was red.

"What's up, Nathan?" she said. "Is everything alright?"

He shook his head. "It's Hannah, the DI. Have you seen her?"

She frowned.

Jill tried to avoid seeing Hannah unless she absolutely had to. She knew that it wasn't the best approach, in the long term, and that she needed to work on their relationship and make strides to improve it. But every time she contemplated it, she simply decided to put it off to another day.

"Sorry, Nathan," she said, "I haven't seen her this morning. Is there a reason I should have?"

He shook his head. "Sorry, Guv," he said. "This isn't your business."

"It looks like you've made it my business," she told him. "Sit down, get your breath, and tell me what's going on."

"Thanks."

Jill brought a bottle of water out from her bag, under the desk. She hadn't touched it yet, and Nathan was more in need of it than she was.

"Here," she said, pushing it across the desk. "Drink some of this."

He picked it up and guzzled at it greedily, then choked, spluttering half the water across her office.

She tried to hide her grimace.

"Sorry, Guv," he said. That was..." he looked down at the bottle, then at his trousers, which were damp. "Sorry, Guv." He took another swig, calmer this time, then placed the bottle on the table.

"OK," she said. "You're breathing properly again. Your brain should be running at something approaching a normal pace. Are you going to tell me what's up?"

He closed his eyes, then opened them again. "We've got a case," he said, "and I can't find the DI."

"You can't find DI Patterson?"

He shook his head. "She's not in her office. She's not in the DCI's office, nor is the DCI. She's not in the team room. I've looked in the canteen. I sent Meera to look in the ladies' toilets. Johnny's been out to the car park looking for her car. It's not there, Guv."

"OK," Jill said, "maybe she's just not in the building. Could she be working on a case? Could she be sick?"

He shook his head. "If Hannah was off sick, she'd call me. She always does."

Jill raised an eyebrow. "Is Hannah off sick a lot?"

He shrugged. "She suffers from migraines. She's been getting them quite a lot lately, leaving work early."

Jill nodded, wondering whether DCI Clarke knew about this. "OK," she said, "so tell me about the case."

He put his hand on the desk and clutched the bottle. "Chesil Beach," he said. "A photographer found a body. She was up there to capture the sunrise."

"Alright," Jill said. "Do we have an ID?"

He shook his head. "There's an argument going on between forensics and the English Heritage people. We don't have access yet."

Jill felt a smile pull at the corners of her lips. She could well imagine Gail Hansford dealing with some bureaucratic type.

"OK," she said, "so, in the absence of the DI, you need to speak to the DCI."

He leaned back in the chair. "You're right. But like I say, she's not in her office, either."

"Somebody needs to get over there," she said. "Establish a crime scene, make sure it's protected." She waved a hand. "I mean, I'm sure Gail's doing all that. But somebody needs to take charge."

She watched him. He was calming now, but there was still some agitation. She knew things weren't great in the MCIT, but why was he panicking like this?

"For starters," she said, "you need to find out who this body is. It could be a straightforward case."

He looked at her. "It could be a cold case."

"Evidence that the body's old?" she asked.

"Nothing on the 999 call. But..."

She shook her head. "So we've no reason to assume—."

"They're not all decomposed, your bodies," he said. "What about that one in Lyme Regis Harbour last year?"

She shrugged. "OK, so maybe it's one of ours. Do you want me to take it on as SIO?"

He looked at her, blinking. "Sorry, Guv. I'm being a bit useless, aren't I?"

Jill said nothing.

"Yeah, sorry, Guv," he repeated. "I'll track down the DCI, see what she says."

"And she might know where DI Patterson is," Jill added.

"You're right, yes." He stood and turned towards the door. His trousers were still damp, and his jacket was crumpled.

Jill had never seen Nathan like this. He had a reputation as a solid detective, somebody who turned up, got on with the job, didn't get emotional. This wasn't the man standing in front of her.

There was a knock on the door.

"Come in," Jill called, hoping it was Hannah, despite herself.

It wasn't Hannah; it was the DCI.

"Boss," Jill said. "Nathan was just about to go looking for you."

DCI Clarke eyed Nathan. "Is this about the body at Chesil Beach?" she asked.

He nodded.

"Good," the DCI said. "Come with me."

CHAPTER SEVEN

Jackie Kendall stamped the snow off her boots as she reached the red-painted cabin in Kolltveit where she and her partner, Yiannis, were living. It was cold here, bloody freezing in fact, but it was at the end of the road from Bergen in western Norway.

Miles from anywhere and, most importantly, not in the UK, Vera Kelvin would never find her here.

She unlocked the front door, using the two keys and the padlock like she always did, and called up the stairs as she entered. They lived on the first floor of this cabin, in a tiny apartment barely big enough for the two of them. Jackie rarely went out in case she was recognised, and Yiannis stood out around here, being the darkest-skinned person for miles. Claustrophobia had soon set in.

She put her boots in the cupboard and pulled out her slippers: thick, fluffy, warm. They weren't enough, but they were better than nothing. She called up the stairs again, "Yiannis, honey. It's me, I'm back."

Placing the bag of groceries on the floor at her feet, she pulled her hair back into a ponytail. It had grown while she'd been here; no point in risking being seen for something as unimportant as a haircut.

"Hey, love," came the call down the stairs.

Jackie picked up the shopping bag and trudged up the stairs, wishing that walking through snow wasn't such hard work. At the top, the door to their apartment lay open.

She smiled and planted a kiss on his cheek. "I got your favourite sausages."

He raised an eyebrow. "Who'd have thought a lad from Greece would end up with an obsession with Norwegian sausages?"

She laughed. "Come on, let's get inside."

Jackie didn't like leaving the doors open any longer than she had to. And at least with these temperatures, they never had to open a window. She was paranoid somebody might hear them from outside and note their English voices.

There'd been no sign of anybody following them since they'd left the UK. But still, after what Jackie had seen, and those text messages, she wasn't taking any risks.

"Anything happen while I was gone?" she asked Yiannis.

"The usual," he said. "I went out, hit the hot spots, took in a show. Had a slap-up dinner at a fancy restaurant. You know the kind of thing." He winked.

She smiled. "I'm sorry, honey. I know our life is dull here. And it's all my fault."

He shook his head, taking her hands in his. "It's not your fault, Jack. It's the fault of those bastard Kelvins. If they hadn't killed that man, if you hadn't been unlucky enough to stumble upon them... you wouldn't need to hide."

She gulped in a breath. "You're right. But we can't do this forever. Can we, Yiannis?"

A shrug. "Maybe the police will solve the case. Maybe the body will be found."

She felt her chest tighten. "I still don't think I'd be able to go home. Even then."

"No," he agreed, his voice careful, "but maybe we could live a fuller life here in Norway. I quite like it here." He held up the packet of sausages. "I mean, I have these, after all."

Yiannis was a good man. When Jackie had initially left Bournemouth for Cumbria, disappearing without telling him what she was doing or why, he'd mounted an online search for her. He'd been obsessed with tracking her down, and he'd refused to rest until he found her. She'd only learned of his tenacity when the detectives had come to speak to her in Cumbria. They'd been working a murder case, a body found in Poole Harbour. That body hadn't been hers, but she worried that the next one might be, or the one after that.

"Put the TV on," she said. "It stops my nerves from jangling."

Yiannis opened up their laptop. He'd set up a VPN when they'd arrived, allowing them to view British TV and websites without being traced. "International news?"

She shook her head. "Put the BBC on."

"Fair enough." He shrugged and flicked to the BBC.

"I want to see if there's anything in Dorset," she told him. "Bring up the local news."

He looked up from the screen to her face. "Are you sure? I really don't think this does you any good."

"We can't know if they've solved the case if we don't keep on top of the local news, can we?" she asked.

"OK." He sighed and navigated to the Dorset page on the BBC website.

She pushed him to one side and leaned in. He'd opened up a news report, a reporter talking to camera.

"That's her," she said. "Sadie Dawes. I spoke to her, told her to leave me alone."

"I know, love." Yiannis put an arm around her shoulder. "She can't bother you now."

Jackie grunted, her gaze on the screen. Sadie was on a beach. A pebbly one, not Bournemouth Beach, more familiar to Jackie, but Chesil Beach, miles to the west.

She frowned and turned the volume up. "Why is she on Chesil Beach?" she asked.

"Maybe they've finally worked out why the stones are ordered the way they are," Yiannis replied. She gave him a puzzled look, then turned back to the laptop.

"The police aren't yet on the scene," Sadie said, "but following a tip-off from a local man, we understand the forensics team are already up there. Unfortunately we'll have to wait a while to determine the identity of the body discovered by a photographer behind me on Chapel Hill earlier this morning."

Jackie narrowed her eyes. "They found a body."

Yiannis had his arm tighter around her. "You think it's him?"

She shrugged. "Could be anyone. I'm paranoid."

She'd been jumping at shadows ever since she'd witnessed the Kelvins killing that man in the garage of the house she'd been selling in Canford Cliffs.

"Turn it off, Yiannis," she said. "I don't want to watch it."

"You sure?"

"You heard her. They don't know who it is. I don't want to watch it."

CHAPTER EIGHT

Lesley entered the MCIT team room, Nathan right behind her.

She'd been blindsided by that meeting with Carpenter, and especially by the presence of the PSD woman. She was still fuming at Hannah, incensed by the hypocrisy of the woman. But then, Hannah had never been somebody she felt she could trust.

But right now, she had a case to run. Despite the worry about what Hannah had done, despite her fear of the consequences, a little bit of her was tingling with excitement.

She'd missed this, now she was running two teams, being a 'proper DCI' like she had been in Birmingham. That was her job. And it was fair enough. It was how DCIs were supposed to operate. But for four years, she'd run the MCIT on her own, with DS Dennis Frampton at her side. She'd loved it, and now she was about to do it again.

As for Dennis... well, she owed him a visit.

Johnny, Tina and Meera were all waiting as she entered. Tina stood up. "Boss," she said, "it's good to see you."

Lesley took a step towards her. "And you, Tina. How's the family?"

"Good. Mike's probably falling apart already, but he'll get used to it."

Lesley laughed. When Sharon had been small, she'd had no choice but to rely on childcare. Her job as a DI had been full-on, and her ex-husband Terry... well, he'd been in a world of his own.

Mike, it seemed, was a different kind of father.

"Well, it's good to have you back, Tina," she said. "And you have very good timing." She turned to the DS. "Nathan, can you fill us in on what you know so far?"

He nodded. "Everybody sit down," he said. "We need calm heads for this."

"Still no sign of the DI?" asked Johnny.

Nathan shook his head. "All I know is she's off sick." He looked at Lesley.

Lesley licked her lips. "She's taking some time off because of illness, and I'll be SIO on this case. OK with everyone?"

She eyed Nathan. Some detective sergeants would hope that with their DI off sick, they'd get to lead a major investigation like this, but DS Strunk didn't seem to be in any fit state to run a serious inquiry.

He nodded. Johnny was grinning, Meera smiling, and Tina nonplussed.

"Sounds good to me," said Johnny.

Lesley raised an eyebrow at him. "Everything sounds good to you, Johnny."

He laughed. "I'm just enjoying being back. I hated London."

"Really?" she asked. "I thought you enjoyed it."

A shrug. "Maybe at first. I mean, there were opportunities there that you don't really get down here. But, God, everything's so expensive. And the abuse... The public hate the Met, you know."

She nodded, unsurprised. "Anyway," she said, "Nathan, what do we know about this case?"

Nathan pulled his shoulders back. She hadn't noticed before how short he was; Johnny towered over him.

"Right," he said. "So, early this morning, a photographer found a body right by the St Catherine's Chapel, between Abbotsbury and the Fleet. She called 999. Forensics are now onsite along with local Uniform, and we need to get somebody out there soon. There's... well, there's been a delay, I guess."

"Don't worry, Nathan," Lesley said. "Now we know who's working on this case, we can get on with it. Do we have an ID yet?"

He shook his head. "As far as I know, nobody's even got near the body yet. It's not the easiest spot to access."

Lesley rolled her eyes. "Give me strength. They're never the easiest spot to access."

"Are we sure they're dead?" Meera asked. "Is it possible there's somebody there in need of medical assistance?"

Lesley turned to her. "You're right. Get on the phone to Gail, tell her to speak to local Uniform and inject a sense of urgency."

"No problem, boss." Meera picked up her phone.

"Right," Lesley said. "Johnny, I want you to start working on an ID."

"How can I do that when nobody's even seen the body?" he asked.

"Start with mispers. You never know, we might have somebody who's gone missing in recent days. If we can start narrowing things down, then once we do get to see this person, we'll have a head start."

"Fair enough."

Meera was still on the phone, speaking in hushed tones. Lesley looked at Tina. "Can you and Meera collate anything that's coming in from the scene? At least until we get there."

"No problem, boss. That all?"

"For now. I'm sure there'll be more very soon."

Tina gave her a nod. It was good to have the younger woman back.

Lesley turned to the DS. "And that's what we need to be doing. Nathan, I think you and I need to get over to Abbotsbury."

CHAPTER NINE

TINA LOOKED at Meera as the boss and the DS hurried out of the office.

"Is it normally like this?" she said.

Meera looked up from her screen. "Like what?"

"I don't know." Tina considered. "It feels tense."

Meera gave a mirthless laugh. "Welcome to the Major Crime Investigations Team."

"But it wasn't like this before I went on maternity leave," Tina said.

Meera leaned back in her chair. "Had the DI started before you went off?"

Tina nodded. "About a week before I left."

Meera took a long breath. "Yeah. It took her a couple of weeks to hit her stride."

"What stride?" Tina asked. "Is there something going on that I don't know about? Do I need to know about it?"

Meera shook her head. "Look. Hannah – that's what she insists we all call her, seems to think it makes her more approachable – Hannah's off sick right now. Maybe for a day or two, maybe for longer. I'm not surprised we're not getting any details. I don't know anything about her. I don't know if she's got a partner or kids. I don't even know where she lives."

Tina frowned. "She came in from Devon, didn't she? I remember the boss saying they had a run-in on a previous case."

Meera didn't look surprised. "Look. My recommendation is that you get your head down, do as you're told and avoid drawing attention to yourself."

Tina glanced towards Johnny, who'd been studiously ignoring their conversation. He was tapping away at his keyboard, leaning in towards his screen.

"Johnny," she said, "when did you come back?"

He turned to her with a smile. "Four months ago, Tina."

"And you're happier here, rather than in the Met?"

"Loving it," he said. "Alice loves being back in Dorset. We've got this cute little house only a couple of miles away from the sea, and my dad... Well, it's good to be able to help my dad out."

Tina had forgotten about Johnny's dad. Mike had told her he was a retired sergeant. Wasn't he suffering from... She couldn't remember.

"How is your dad?" she asked. "He wasn't very well. Am I right?"

"Sciatica," said Johnny. "He has good days and bad days, more good days now that he's got us to look after him. Alice is brilliant with him. She manages to fit him around the kids."

Tina smiled. She knew all about managing grandparents and a young family, although at least her mum was fit enough to take care of her two from time to time. "Good for her," she said.

He shrugged. "Not sure how it'll all work when she finds a job, but... Well, you work it out, don't you?"

Tina nodded. Mike had worked with Johnny for years. Tina had only worked with him for a short while. He'd barely mentioned Alice. It seemed things had changed. Johnny had changed.

"So you're happier here than in the Met, despite what Meera says about the atmosphere in the team?"

Johnny shrugged. "Yeah. I mean, I wish the sarge was still here, but I see him occasionally, and well, let's just say he keeps his hand in."

"DS Frampton?" Tina asked.

Johnny smiled. "He helps with cases. Advises, sometimes. Helped the boss track down the guy who killed Rowena Sharp... you know, the woman who washed up in Upton Lake?"

Tina nodded, then shivered. DCI Mackie had carried on 'helping out' with cases after his retirement. It hadn't ended well.

Johnny narrowed his eyes. "Don't worry, Tina. Everybody's okay. That bastard Collingwood went to prison, and he won't be out for a long time." He sniffed. "So... I've got an aerial photo of St Catherine's Chapel and the area around it. I'm trying to work out if there's anywhere we can expect to find CCTV, or where a vehicle might have come in and out."

Tina stood and went to his desk. She hadn't expected to find herself right at the beginning of a potential murder investigation on her first day back. Maybe it would distract them all from whatever else was going on.

"OK," she said. "Can you call the boss, see if she or the sarge can take a look while they're over there?"

He shrugged. "I think you should do that."

"Why me?"

Johnny looked up at her. "Because you're her favourite, silly."

"No, I'm not." Tina drew back. She glanced at Meera. "I'm not, am I?"

"I'm not saying anything," said Meera.

Johnny laughed. "The boss barely tolerates me. I'm pretty sure she wishes I'd never come back. But you? She's very glad to have you back."

Tina gritted her teeth. She wasn't sure how she felt about her colleagues thinking she was the DCI's pet. But one thing she did know: if the boss expected good things of her, she had to live up to those expectations. Regardless of what her new DI was like.

CHAPTER TEN

LESLEY LEANED back in the passenger seat as they turned off the A352 onto the road down to the coast. She'd let Nathan drive, preferring to conserve her energy, and wanting to give him an outlet for his. The man was in a state.

"Are you sure you don't know where she is?" he asked. "She hasn't called you? She's not working on a case I don't know about?"

"Nathan," she said, "you need to stop panicking. The DI is off sick. You know she's been suffering from headaches."

"Migraines," he said.

"Migraines," she admitted, not entirely sure if Hannah had been exaggerating. "Let's just leave her a bit of space to get better, eh?"

He shook his head. "It doesn't make sense. When she left the office yesterday, she was talking about a case she wanted to discuss with me this morning."

"Well," Lesley replied, "that's irrelevant now, isn't it? We've got this one."

He grunted. "I suppose so."

"Straight on here," she said at a roundabout with a lone shrub at its centre. Sometimes she missed the sculptures that adorned the centre of Birmingham's roundabouts. The flying planes at Spitfire Island. "This takes us to the Fleet. Otherwise you'll end up in Weymouth."

"You know this area well," he said.

She shook her head. "There's a sign, right there. But I've visited a couple of times with my wife, and there was that case on Portland Bill a couple of years ago."

"The organised crime boss splattered on the lighthouse bulb," he said.

"That's one way of putting it," she told him. "Not necessarily what I'd have said, but..."

"Sorry, boss," he said, "I'm not myself today."

"I can see that." She pointed. "Take that turn."

He veered off to the left, and they took a narrow lane. After maybe fifteen minutes, they crested the brow of a hill, and the Fleet appeared in front of them, the sea beyond it.

The view here was breathtaking. It was a cold October day, but the skies were clear, and the sea glittered. She could almost imagine it was June, just with a hell of a lot less traffic.

"I'll call into the office," she said. "See if there's anything we need to know before we arrive."

Meera picked up. "Boss," she said, "we're making progress."

"Good. What kind of progress?"

"They've allowed access. Gail and her team are onsite. You'll have no problem getting to the body. And I was wrong. It is a body."

"Not something you're all that happy about being wrong about, I imagine."

"No. Not much of a surprise, though."

No. But at least they had access. "Any more on a potential ID?" Lesley asked. "Has Gail found any forensics that might be of use to us?"

"I haven't heard anything since she was allowed access to the site," came the reply. "Sorry, boss."

"Not your fault, Meera," Lesley said. "What about the surrounding area?"

"It's pretty remote. We're still looking for places where there may have been witnesses, but no."

"We'll take a look once we're there. Hopefully our job's about to become a whole lot easier."

"Hopefully." Meera didn't sound convinced.

Lesley leaned her head back, gazing up at the roof of the car. Hopefully the case would pick up once they had access to the site, the crime scene. And hopefully the mood of the MCIT would pick up with it.

"OK, Meera," she said, "if you or anybody finds anything helpful, let us know."

"Will do, boss."

"And we'll tell you what we find here."

"Thanks, boss. So the DI won't be involved?"

Lesley clenched her jaw. How many times would she be asked this question? How many times would she have to lie?

"The DI is off sick, Meera," she said. "Don't you worry. I'm running the case, and I'm sure we'll have it cracked soon enough."

CHAPTER ELEVEN

Gail was standing behind her CSI van pulling out some equipment when Lesley and Nathan arrived at the crime scene.

Lesley got out of the car, leaving Nathan to lock it up. "Gail," she called, walking over to her friend.

Gail looked her up and down. "You're not going to get very far dressed like that," she said.

Lesley frowned. "Sorry?"

Gail gave her a smile. "Don't you remember when you first came to Dorset and you realised you couldn't wear those skirt suits and attend crime scenes?"

Damn. After spending most of the last year behind a desk, Lesley had reverted to the kind of clothes she'd worn in her last job in Birmingham. She'd had to replace some of those old suits – too many fancy dinners with Elsa meant most of them didn't fit any more, and besides, they were looking a bit shabby – all of which meant that she'd come to the crime scene wearing a mid-blue skirt suit and a pair of two-inch heels.

"You've not even got any boots with you?" Gail asked.

Lesley glanced back at the car. "We came in Nathan's car. Mine are in my boot."

Gail chuckled. "Well, you'll have to do the best you can." She pointed down at Lesley's feet. "But those shoes won't last the day."

Lesley looked back at Nathan, who was walking his way from the car. "Don't suppose you've got any spare walking boots in your car?"

He lifted his feet one after the other. "I do, boss, but I'm wearing them, see, and they're a size ten."

Lesley wrinkled her nose. She was a size six. *No chance.* The two-inch heels would have to take their chances. "OK. Gail, this case is more important than my outfit. Let's get to it."

Gail gave her a mock salute. "Glad to hear it. So are you SIO on this?"

Lesley gave her a curt nod. "I am."

"Not DI Patterson?"

"Hannah," Lesley looked at Gail for a moment. She could confide in her friend, but not with Nathan standing next to her. "She's off sick," she continued, trying to sound casual.

Gail gave her an inscrutable look. "I don't imagine anybody's heartbroken about that."

Lesley frowned, wondering where that had come from. Was Hannah as obnoxious to the CSIs as she was to the other officers?

And she had the nerve to claim Lesley was the bully.

She sighed. Hopefully, that PSD woman would figure out what was what. "It's me in charge," she told Gail. "Can you tell me what you've found so far?"

"Not much," Gail said. "The body's nestled into an alcove in the side of the chapel. Slumped over, not sure how he got there."

"You think he was killed there, or taken up after death?" Lesley asked.

Gail shrugged. "No idea yet. It's a photography hotspot, if he'd been there for long someone would have seen him."

"And someone might also have seen him being taken there."

Gail nodded. "Let's hope so."

"Yes, please," Lesley replied. "Are pathology here yet?"

"No sign of them. Press are, though." Gail pointed.

Just a short distance away, by a press van, Sadie Dawes stood with a man Lesley didn't recognise. The man held a camera, which Sadie was speaking into.

"Heaven help us," Lesley said. "How did that woman manage to get here before me?"

"No idea," said Gail, "but she's already put out a broadcast about the discovery of the body."

Fuck. "OK," Lesley said. "I'll need to speak to Carpenter, make sure she's reined in."

"Really?" said Gail with a raised eyebrow. "You want to curtail the freedom of the press?"

Lesley gave her a mock slap on the arm. "Don't get me started."

Gail smiled back at her. "Thought not. Right, let's go and have a look at this body."

CHAPTER TWELVE

Lesley picked her way across the damp ground. Luckily, Gail had found a route that didn't involve trudging through the tall grass, which she imagined would be impossible in these shoes.

It had rained heavily over the last week, and her heels were sinking into the earth. But she tried not to let the state of her shoes worry her. These were brand new, bought on a shopping trip to Southampton with Elsa. They didn't exactly coordinate with a white forensic suit and blue overshoes.

Lesley sighed. Maybe now she was managing cases again, she'd abandon the smart outfits and go back to her walking trousers and boots. Those godawful trousers her daughter Sharon had bought her when she'd arrived in Dorset. But however much she hated the clothes, that had been her outfit when she was at her happiest, when she'd been running cases with Dennis and not managing two teams from behind a desk.

As they rounded the chapel, she spotted two white-suited CSIs working around the body.

She turned, thinking through how someone might have got the body here. Assuming it was brought here after death.

"Have you seen the woman who found the body?" Lesley asked Gail.

Gail turned briefly to her, not breaking stride. "She's at the abbey café in the village. They've been plying her with cups of tea. Somebody needs to go and talk to her as soon as possible."

"Are Uniform with her?"

Gail nodded. "Yeah, but all they can do is sit with her. You need to see the body first, then maybe you can work out how to go about questioning her."

Lesley gave Gail a quizzical look. "You telling me how to do my job now?"

Gail flushed, then smiled. "Sorry. I'm used to... Never mind."

Lesley eyed her. *Used to what?* Or who, more likely. "Well, at least we've got access to the site now," she said.

Gail had turned to the front, her pace brisk. Lesley stumbled occasionally, but even with Gail, she didn't want to draw attention to her lack of preparation.

They arrived at the body, where Gail finally stopped walking. Gavin, her unfeasibly tall second-in-command, was bent over the shape. He straightened, stretching out his back.

"Alright, Gail," he said. "Lesley."

Lesley gave him a nod. "Gavin. How's progress?"

Gail's other colleague, Brett, squatted beside the body. He was taking photographs of the face. Lesley picked her way towards him, Nathan following. Nathan reached out over the body, his hand outstretched. Brett gave Nathan a quizzical look, then removed his glove to shake the sergeant's hand.

"DS Nathan Strunk," Nathan said. "Good to meet you."

"Brett Dobell." He glanced at Gail. "From the CSI team."

"I gathered that." Nathan smiled.

"Anything useful yet, Brett?" asked Lesley.

Brett looked up at her, lowering the camera for a moment. "This gash on his face, I don't think it's from the time of death."

"But without pathology here yet..." Lesley said.

He shrugged. "I know I'm no pathologist, but I've seen plenty of bodies, haven't I, Gail?"

Gail grunted. "We've all seen plenty of bodies, Brett."

"So what are you saying?" Lesley asked him.

"Look at the line of the wound down his face."

Lesley looked past the technician at the victim's face. The man was slumped against the wall, twisted to his right, in the direction of the sea. The right side of his face faced upwards, exposing a wound running from his forehead almost to the corner of his mouth. It bisected his eye, which was closed.

Lesley peered in. "Has he lost an eye?"

Brett shook his head. "That's not the point. This wound. It's old. There's a section of it here, just above his eye, where it's been reopened. But I think the wound was there before he died. Some time before he died."

"OK," she said, "so any idea of the cause of death?"

Gail was standing next to her. "We haven't moved him yet," she said. "We can't ascertain anything until we do, and we need to get plenty of photos first."

Lesley nodded, straightening up.

"What about forensics?" asked Nathan. "Anything in the vicinity that might help determine when he was brought here, or who by?"

Gail eyed him. "Yeah. I found a wallet over there behind that fence." She pointed. "It's got a driving licence in, and it's a woman's, so she's clearly the person who brought it here."

Nathan's eyes widened. Lesley suppressed a smirk.

"I'm joshing you," Gail said. "No, of course we haven't found a bloody wallet. My life would be a hell of a lot easier if we did find things like that. But there are boot prints over there."

Lesley followed her outstretched hand. Sure enough, there were boot prints on the other side of the body. The forensics team had placed plates around the area for them to stand on, so the prints weren't disturbed.

"You'll be taking a cast of those?" Lesley asked.

"I certainly will," Gail replied. "You never know, we might be able to find our killer almost as easily as if they had left their wallet."

CHAPTER THIRTEEN

"But surely the boot prints could belong to this guy," Nathan said, pointing at the body. "Maybe he had an accident, committed suicide?"

Gail looked at him. "You think someone who's thinking of committing suicide is going to choose this place, when there are cliffs up at Portland, a couple of miles away?" She gestured southwards.

Nathan shrugged. "We can't rule anything out. There's no evidence yet that he's been murdered."

"And besides, look at his feet."

Lesley looked down at the man's feet. Sure enough, he was wearing trainers. She smiled, then frowned. Hopefully, once Nathan had got over the morning's panic, he would stop being a liability.

Gail grunted. "My money's on a man with a wound like that on his face getting himself into trouble quite frequently. I wouldn't be surprised if he's on your system, Lesley."

Lesley pursed her lips. "Let's hope so."

Her phone rang, and she pulled it out of her pocket: Jill.

"I want to take this, folks," she said. "Nathan, you stay with Gail and her team. Make a note of anything that comes in, and then we'll regroup." She held out her hand. "Give me your keys, I want to fetch something."

"No problem, boss," he said. Lesley trudged away from the crime scene, cursing the mud on her shoes again.

She'd left a scarf in the back of Nathan's car, and it might just help her feel a little bit warmer. Just a little bit.

"Jill," she said, answering the call. "Everything OK?"

"Yes, boss," Jill said. "How's the crime scene?"

"Well, there's good news and bad news," Lesley told her.

"Yes?"

"Good news is we've got access. Bad news is pathology aren't here yet."

"Pathology is stacked out right now," Jill told her. "I think Dr Bamford has been spending most of his time on clinical work."

"Really?" Lesley couldn't understand the mentality of anybody who'd rather work with the living than the dead. "He's not doing pathology work?"

"I don't know," Jill told her, "but you might want to call him and find out."

"I'll do just that. Anyway, you didn't call me to chat about the pathologist. What's up?"

"We've had a call, a potential cold case."

Lesley stopped walking. She was fifty feet away from the car, on a path now, and not just a bank of mud. Not that it made much difference.

"Right," she said. "Fill me in."

"The governor of HMP Exeter's been in touch with the assistant chief constable."

Lesley narrowed her eyes. "I thought you were going to tell me a decomposed body had been found."

"Cold cases don't always start like that," Jill said. "I've been researching."

"No," said Lesley. "You'll know more about that than me. Just tell me what's happened."

"So, the governor contacted the ACC to let him know they might have evidence in what might turn out to be a cold case."

"There's a lot of 'mights' in there."

"Often true, with these cases."

Lesley grunted. "What cold case is this?"

"It's from 1993. Frank Kelvin."

Lesley felt her jaw tighten. "Frank Kelvin. You're sure?"

"Perfectly sure, boss."

"Right."

Frank Kelvin had been the brother of Arthur Kelvin and the son of Vera Kelvin. He'd disappeared in 1993, while the police were looking for him in connection with a drug supply investigation. At the time, they'd assumed he'd buggered off abroad. Probably living the high life on the Costa del Sol right now.

Or maybe not.

"So what's this evidence?" Lesley asked.

"There's an inmate at Exeter, name of Lucas Parsons. He's after a sentencing deal in exchange for information about what he claims was the murder of Frank Kelvin."

Lesley clutched the phone tighter. "Murder? We sure about that?"

"That's what he says."

She narrowed her eyes. "He could just be making it up, trying to curry favour."

"I did consider that," said Jill, "but I think we should check it out. If the prison governor thinks it's enough to contact the assistant chief constable, then..."

"You're right," Lesley said. "OK, you take a member of your team to the prison, interview this Parsons bloke, and let me know if you think it's got legs."

"Will do, boss. And... if this turns out to be a cold case, I'll need resources."

Lesley frowned. "We'll work that one out when we come to it.

We've potentially got two concurrent cases, and I'll have to spread resources across the teams."

"Understood, boss." Jill didn't sound happy.

Under normal circumstances, a recently discovered body would take priority.

But if they could find out more about Frank Kelvin...

"Just let me know when you've spoken to that prisoner," Lesley said. "I'll see what I can do."

CHAPTER FOURTEEN

Jill put the phone down just as a knock came on her office door.

"Come in," she called.

The door opened and Meera slid inside, closing it behind her and standing against it.

Jill softened. "Hi," she said. "Everything alright?"

Meera shook her head. "I just wanted a break from the MCIT team room."

Jill leaned forward in her chair. "Is Hannah back?"

Meera sighed, then approached the chair opposite Jill's desk. She pulled it out with a grinding sound then slumped into it.

"No sign of her but not knowing where she is or when she's going to come in next is somehow even worse."

"Worse than having her around?" Jill asked.

Meera nodded. "Do you know anything about where she is?"

"Sorry. I haven't been told anything. The DCI is saying that Hannah's off sick, and that's all we're getting." Jill could tell there was more going on than the DCI had told her but didn't know anything concrete. And the feeling of being torn between supporting Meera, her wife, and loyalty to Lesley, her boss, was making her uneasy.

This was why she'd avoided applying for Hannah's job. Managing family was too complicated.

Meera looked down into her lap. Her fingernails had been bitten.

"I'm sorry you're so stressed," Jill said. "It'll get easier, I promise."

Meera looked up at her. "What makes you say that? Is there any evidence it'll get easier?"

Jill shrugged. "Maybe taking a bit of time off will help Hannah find some balance."

Meera clenched her jaw. "I know she's your colleague, and you can't say anything bad about her. But she's a bloody nightmare to work for."

Jill pursed her lips. Hannah wasn't exactly easy for her, either. She'd told Meera as much at home. But here, in her office, right next to Hannah's...

"I know it's not been easy for you, Meera, but she's not here right now. You've got the DCI running this case, which should be easier. You've worked for the DCI before."

"I have." Meera held her head up. "And you're right, it's going to be easier. I just need to keep my head down."

Jill tensed. They'd had this conversation plenty of times. Jill was ambitious. She'd risen through the ranks quickly. But Meera just wanted a quiet life. She was happy to remain a DC for her entire career, to focus on their family.

Maybe that was a good thing. After all, it meant Jill could advance without feeling guilty that Suzy wasn't being looked after.

Suzy was at nursery right now, and Meera would be finishing early to pick her up. She'd negotiated part-time hours when Jill had returned from maternity leave. But Jill sometimes felt guilty. She felt like she didn't do being a mum *or* being a DI well enough. She knew all parents felt like that sometimes – well, all mums, at least – but it didn't make it any easier.

"I'm sorry," she said, standing up. "But I need to go and speak to my team. We've had a potential new case come in."

Meera cocked her head. "Sounds interesting. A body?"

"Nothing like that," Jill told her. She rounded the desk and took her wife's hand. "It's potential evidence from a prison inmate who knows about a historic case."

"Which historic case?"

"Frank Kelvin. You heard of him?"

"By reputation, yes. I was on the murder investigation for his brother. Arthur." She pulled a face.

Jill considered. "Have you ever come into contact with Vera Kelvin?"

"No, thank God. I've heard she's a monster."

Jill had dealt with monsters before. She could handle a difficult witness. Plenty of them were, after all.

"OK," she said. "You get back to the MCIT. They'll be wondering where you are, and you've got this big case."

Meera nodded, her eyes downcast again. "Yeah. You're right, I suppose. And it's nice having Tina back."

"Good." Jill smiled. "See, there's something to be positive about. Now, let me go speak to my team and work out what we're going to do about this prison evidence."

CHAPTER FIFTEEN

Lesley arrived back at the crime scene to find Gail on her phone. She waited, trying to work out who the crime scene manager was speaking to.

"So you sure you can't get here?" Gail said. There was a pause while she listened to whoever was on the other end. Gail sighed. "Fair enough. Well, we'll take plenty of photos, and the body will be brought to the morgue at Poole Hospital. I've got Lesley here now. Do you want to speak to her?"

She held out the phone without waiting for an answer.

"Who is it?" Lesley whispered.

"Bamford," Gail said. "He can't come out."

Lesley nodded and took the phone.

"Gareth," she said, "Gail tells me you won't be able to attend our crime scene."

"Sorry, Lesley," he replied, "we're just stacked out here."

"This is a murder case."

"You think I don't know that? I'm covering the whole county, doing multiple PMs each day. It's not easy finding the time to trudge out all the way to the Fleet and have a look at your body."

Lesley frowned. That had never stopped him before. But she'd be churlish to argue.

"I don't think I'm going to be attending many scenes from now on," he added.

"Really?" Lesley asked.

She'd always found it helpful, standing over a body with Gareth, listening to him work out how that body had found its way there, and letting the cogs click into place in the very spot where the person had breathed their last, or at least been taken after breathing their last.

But she knew that this was the way things were going in pathology. In medicine and policing in general.

"I guess we'll just have to cope," she told him. "So what do you need from us to be able to make an initial assessment?"

"I'm not sure I'll have much time to make an assessment until the post-mortem," he replied, "but send me what photos you've got. Gail's already discussed that with me. And any notes you have."

"OK," Lesley said. "There's a gash on his face, but it isn't what killed him."

"I've heard about that," Bamford replied. "Is there much blood around the body?"

"Hang on a moment," Lesley held the phone away from her ear. "Gail, is there a lot of blood?" She hadn't seen much.

"Hardly any, apart from his teeth," Gail said. "Either his death was bloodless, or he was brought here afterwards."

"And you still haven't moved him?" Lesley asked.

Gail shook her head. "We will now I've spoken to Gareth."

"Good," Lesley replied. "Well, why don't you get on with moving the body and seeing what you can find?" She brought her phone closer to her ear. "Gareth, did you catch all that?"

"I did."

"Good. I presume arrangements have been made for the body to be taken to the morgue?"

"A van will be arriving with you in about half an hour," he replied.

She sighed. "Well, I'll guess we'll have to hurry, then. Your guys will need to be patient, if we're not finished when they arrive." She hated being rushed, but the sooner they got the body to the morgue, the better it would be preserved, and the sooner the post-mortem might take place. "Any idea when you can do the PM?" she asked him.

"Not till tomorrow, at least," he told her. "Like I say, I'm stacked out."

Another sigh. "Well, let me know when you've got some concrete information."

"Of course."

"Thanks." She hung up. "Right, Gail, the van's on its way. Let's get to it."

CHAPTER SIXTEEN

"Good morning, folks," Jill said as she entered the cold cases team room.

DC Katie Young perked up, all but jumping out of her chair. "Morning, guv."

Jill gave her a tight smile. Katie was keen. She worked hard. She was ambitious, anxious to progress.

But sometimes she could be a little bit much.

Stanley was sitting at his desk, typing out an email. He turned as she closed the door behind her. "Morning, guv. I hear we've got a new case."

Jill nodded. "We might. There's an inmate at HMP Exeter who claims to have evidence about the death of a man who disappeared in 1993. A man we'd assumed was alive and in hiding."

"Well, that'll be a cold case, alright," Stanley said.

Jill nodded. 1993 was at least easier than 1973, when their last victim had been killed. Poor Rowena Sharp had drowned in Poole Harbour, and her body had only been dredged up this year. Fortunately, the mud had done a good job of preserving her, and so they were still able to identify her.

"We got Johnny joining us?" Katie asked. "I mean, with Mike on parental leave, Johnny can swap over and cover for him instead of Tina."

Jill shook her head. "I wouldn't count on it. The MCIT have got a big case. Body over at Chesil Beach."

"Oh." Katie's face fell, then she perked up. "Well, we can manage without him."

Stanley gave her a wink. "Of course we can. So what's with this inmate, guv?"

Jill sat down at the desk that had been vacated by Mike last Friday. They'd all gone out to the Ship Inn for his leaving drinks. He'd be off for four months.

"I don't know much yet," she said, placing a hand on the desk. Mike had left a photo of himself with Tina and their two kids, the little one not much more than a wrinkled face in a blanket. Maybe he was expecting Tina to pick it up and put it on her desk in the MCIT. Or maybe he'd assumed she'd move over here.

No chance. The boss liked having Tina in the MCIT.

"So," she said, "his name's Lucas Parsons. He's done some sort of deal over his sentencing, and he's named a bunch of cases where he says he might be able to provide evidence. He claims he knows something about the death of Frank Kelvin, who disappeared in 1993."

Stanley whistled. "Kelvin?"

Jill looked at him. "One of the infamous Kelvin family, no less. Brother of Arthur, son of Vera."

"Shit. Does that mean one of us has got to go and talk to Vera?"

Jill hadn't met Vera Kelvin, but she'd heard of her. The woman had repeatedly told the DCI to *fuck off* during the investigation into the death of her son, Arthur.

"We can cope with Vera Kelvin," she said. "Besides, she might be pleased that we've got news about her son."

"Telling her he's dead, and not sunning it on the Costa del Crime," Stanley said. "I don't think so."

"Do we need to bring in the Organised Crime team?" Katie asked.

"Let's see what we've got first," Jill told her. She looked between the two DCs, working out a plan of action.

"Right," she said. "Katie, I want you here, going into background. Find everything you can on Frank Kelvin. Go back as far as you need to."

She paused. Stanley was looking at her, waiting. Katie looked disgruntled.

"Stanley," she said, "you and I are taking a trip."

CHAPTER SEVENTEEN

Half an hour later, Gail and her team had photographed the body from every angle they could. When they'd done that, they'd moved him away from the wall of the chapel to get a better view, photographing him on his front, his back and each side. Now the poor man was splayed out on the grass, staring blindly up at the sky.

That gash over his right eye was more prominent now it was no longer hidden by the hood that had been drawn up over his head.

The man was well covered but not well wrapped up. He wore a heavy woollen coat over a hoodie, a pair of black jogging bottoms, some cheap trainers and a pair of gloves. The fingertips of the gloves were crusted with blood.

"I reckon the skin of his fingers has been cut off," said Gail.

Lesley wrinkled her nose. "Makes it harder for us to identify him."

"Exactly. Which means this is no random crime of passion."

Lesley felt her shoulders slump. "No."

Gail put her hands on her hips, staring down at the body. "And there's his mouth."

Lesley looked down at the man's face. It was grey and shrivelled.

The cut over his eye was almost unbearable to look at. And then there was his mouth. It had closed as they'd moved him, but his lips were sunken in, like his mouth had been hollowed out.

"His teeth have been removed," said Gail.

Lesley nodded. "That and the missing fingertips means identification's going to be even harder."

"They were pretty thorough," said Gavin. He was moving around the body, taking photographs, zooming in and out, moving gently so as not to disturb the ground.

Lesley stared down at the man. "So I think we can assume that some fairly serious people did this."

"And that he was a fairly serious person himself, too," added Gail.

Lesley grunted. "Not necessarily. Sometimes innocent people get themselves caught up in things."

"Well, if he isn't so innocent," said Gail, "then working out who he is will probably take you directly to whoever killed him. That's my bet, anyway."

Lesley looked up at the crime scene manager. Sometimes she wondered if Gail should become a detective. She'd seen more crime scenes than most, and often sat in on briefings, keeping tabs on a case as it progressed. Lesley had worked with a highly competent CSM in Birmingham, Ady Hanson. But Gail was a cut above.

"Right," said Gav. "I've just had a text to say the mortuary van's on its way. They're going to use the track that leads up here from Abbotsbury, there's a gate and I've spoken to the farmer to get it unlocked. Is there anything else we need before he goes?"

Lesley looked down the hill at the track Gavin was referring to. It was a wide swathe of flattened grass, not really a path. But it was broad enough for a vehicle to gain access. Was that how the man had been brought here?

She turned back to him. "Is it possible to take a photograph of his mouth with the lips open?"

"I can try," said Gav. He got a lolly stick out of his bag and parted the man's lips, pulling the top lip up to reveal the gap beneath where his teeth should have been.

Lesley shuddered. "Poor guy."

"At least he wouldn't have experienced that," Gail said. "Look at the sockets. This was done postmortem. No bleeding."

Lesley squatted to get a closer look. "So do we reckon this was all done here or before he was brought here?"

"Well, he certainly wasn't killed here," Gail said. "Somebody would have spotted him earlier, and this guy looks to me like he's been dead a while. Look at the skin."

Lesley couldn't see much of the man's skin, only his face and the very top of his neck. Gav pulled down the hoodie to show a thick red mark around his neck, darkening at the back.

"He's been garrotted, poor bastard," he muttered.

"He might have deserved it," Gail said.

Lesley eyed her. "Nobody deserves this."

She heard voices behind her; the pathology team, come to take the body away.

She sighed. "We've got all we can for now. Let's just hope the PM reveals more."

CHAPTER EIGHTEEN

JILL YAWNED as they finally left the Dorchester traffic behind.

"Is it always like this, guv?" Stanley asked.

"Is what always like this?"

He shrugged. "Getting round Dorchester."

Jill eyed the DC. "Is this not a journey you've done before?"

Another shrug. "I live on Purbeck. Don't have much call to come this far west."

She laughed. Dorchester was, what, ten miles from Winfrith? Hardly the Wild West. And if he was this freaked out by Dorchester, what would he be like about going to Exeter?

"You don't do a lot of travelling, do you, Stanley?" she asked.

He shook his head.

She slowed as brake lights flashed ahead of them, fighting down the frustration.

"I did do one big trip though, guv. With the boss, the DCI."

"Ah, yes," she said. "Your jaunt to Birmingham. I did hear about that."

He grinned. "It was fun. Those roads, though. Bloody hell, they've got this thing called Spaghetti Junction. Worst thing I've ever driven in my entire life. Don't know how anybody can work up there."

She laughed. Jill had lived around the country, including some time in London. She was pretty sure she'd take Spaghetti Junction in her stride. And she had no idea what Stanley would make of the Hanger Lane Gyratory.

"So what was it like spending a day up there with the DCI? Did you find out much about her old mates in Birmingham?"

He nodded. "I met a few of them. That DI Zoe Finch, the one she's so keen on. And then there was a woman called..." He paused. "Sheila. Sheila Griffin. That was it. She was their organised crime DS, good mate of Zoe's, by the looks of it. We went round to her house, met her kid and her dog." He chuckled. "The dog was cute."

"And I'm assuming you made headway on the case, too."

Another nod. "It was a fruitful day, even if it did mean taking a Sunday out."

Jill realised she didn't know much about Stanley, apart from that he lived in Worth Matravers. She didn't know who he lived with or what kind of family he had.

"So what do you normally do on a Sunday afternoon then, Stanley?" she asked.

He smiled, pursing his lips and nodding. "Metaphor Refantasio. Well, at least, that's the one at the moment."

"Meta what?" she said.

"It's a video game. I play online, with some mates. Well, I say mates. I don't know what any of their real names are, and I've got no idea where they live, but, yeah, we're mates."

"So you live on your own?"

He gave her a look. "I don't mean to be funny, guv, but are you assuming that because I play computer games, I live on my own?"

She felt blood rush to her face. "That wasn't what I meant, Stanley. I'm sorry, I just—"

He laughed. "I live with my mum. She's cool. And she works on a Sunday anyway, Sainsbury's in Wareham."

So Stanley, who she happened to know was twenty-nine years old, was really a glorified teenager living at his mum's house and playing on his computer all weekend. Still, he was a decent copper, who occasionally had some insights.

"Right," Jill said, "so I hope you can cope with the mega metropolis that is Exeter."

"I think I'll be alright. I mean, after Birmingham, nothing's gonna faze me, right?"

She smiled. "This man we're talking to, Lucas Parsons. While I'm sitting in this traffic, could you do some digging into him, find out more about his background?"

"Of course." Stanley pulled his phone from his pocket. "What do you want to know?"

"I want to know what we can expect from him. What's his attitude going to be like, what's his history? Is he a hardened criminal or did he just get unlucky?"

"Sounds pretty hardened to me, if he was mixed up with Frank Kelvin."

She nodded. "You could be right, but let's arm ourselves with as many facts as we can before we get there, okay?"

"No problem." He bent to his phone as the traffic picked up. She just hoped it wouldn't get any worse.

CHAPTER NINETEEN

Lesley plonked her bag down on her desk and rubbed her temples. It was good to be back working on a case again, but the ramifications of Hannah's complaint were niggling at her.

She slumped in the chair and allowed her eyes to close for a few seconds.

Almost twelve hours now since the body had been found, and they were no closer to an ID. Which was no doubt what the killer had intended.

Still, there was that scar. How many people had a wound running from their forehead almost down to the corner of their mouth?

The wound had been inflicted before the man's death, so someone might be able to recognise him from it. It hadn't fully healed or formed a scar yet, which meant it couldn't be all that long pre-mortem.

And what kind of man got himself into a situation that led to a wound like that? It could be coincidence or just bad luck, could even be connected with his death. But Lesley's instincts were telling her this man was connected to organised crime. Innocent bystanders didn't need their fingertips and teeth removing so they wouldn't lead the police to their killers, after all.

"Right."

She stretched her arms above her head and flapped her hands a couple of times.

She'd hoped that might wake her up. It didn't.

Screwing up the muscles of her face and releasing them again, she pushed back from her chair and went to the door. She missed her old glass-walled office, from which she'd been able to see her team at work. She still had plenty of glass; behind her, looking out over the car park. That was nothing new, but at least now it was double-glazed, and there were blinds she could close if she needed privacy.

She closed her office door behind her, locking it for once – Hannah's actions had made her wary – and strode to the MCIT team room. They were all in there, deep in discussion. DS Nathan Strunk, who she still wasn't sure she could trust. DC Meera Vedra, whose opinion of herself was far too low, and who reminded Lesley of Tina in the early days. Tina herself, of course, yawning and scraping something off her sleeve.

And Johnny. Don't forget Johnny.

The hum of voices quieted as she entered and strode to the front of the room, the view out over the car park and fields behind her. It would be a while yet before that view darkened, even though it was past the time she should have sent the team home.

A quick recap, and then they could all get home to their families.

"Right," she said. "I know it's gone six, and you'll all be itching to get home. So I won't keep you. But we do need to confer on where we are so far."

A chorus of murmurs, nods and hums. Johnny looked up at the clock.

Nothing changes.

"So," Lesley continued. "our priority is an ID. Are we making any progress?"

"I've been running through mispers and HOLMES, boss," Meera said. "No sign of a match for that wound yet."

"What kind of trawl are you doing? Visual or metadata?"

"Both, boss."

Of course. Lesley sighed.

"Have you run through everything?"

Meera glanced at Nathan.

"Our next step," he said, "is to speak to neighbouring forces. Hampshire or Devon might recognise him."

"Or the Organised Crime team," chipped in Johnny. "I mean, it's obvious, isn't it? They don't want us knowing who he is 'cos he's one of them."

"Not necessarily," said Nathan. "There could be some other explanation. Like—"

"I don't see how there can be," interrupted Johnny. "They don't want us knowing who he is because as soon as we do, we'll know exactly who killed him." He clenched his jaw. "I bet it's the Kelvins."

"As I was saying," continued Nathan, giving the DC a look, "Johnny's hypothesis is valid. In fact, it's probably the most likely option. But it's not the only option. So—"

"Sorry, Sarge." Johnny's neck had turned red. "You're right. I didn't mean to..."

Nathan bit down a smirk, then gave Johnny a nod. "You're probably right. But I don't think we should jump to conclusions."

"No."

Lesley watched all this with amusement. Johnny had been catapulted into the team at virtually no notice, and Nathan would be expected to supervise him. She hoped that would become easier.

She drew in a breath. Nathan's previous role had been in PSD. How much did he know about Johnny's past? Could he have investigated him?

She shook her head. There had never been a PSD investigation.

She and Dennis had discovered that Johnny was being blackmailed, and she'd immediately arranged for his secondment to the Met. Not even Carpenter had known why.

It was fine. *Stop worrying.*

"Of course, you do know the best way to solve this argument, don't you?" said Tina, looking between the two men.

Nathan raised an eyebrow. "And that is?"

"Find out the ID, of course."

"Well, we know that," said Johnny. "I mean—"

Tina put up her hand. "They'll be running his DNA, I presume. Maybe we'll find a match."

"Only if we already have it on file," Lesley said.

Which would only be the case if the man had previously been a suspect in a major investigation. And if that was the case, one of them should have recognised him.

"But what if he's a Kelvin?" Tina said. "I don't mean someone with the Kelvin name, they're all accounted for. But someone with Kelvin blood. They're the kind of family that—"

"You're right," said Johnny. Tina gave him a frown, which he didn't register. "There's God knows how many offshoots." He turned to Lesley, grinning. "How about we make a family tree?"

Lesley rolled her eyes. "This isn't *Who Do You Think You Are,* Johnny."

"But he's right," Meera said. "If we can pull together a diagram of the extended family, then we can work our way through them. Even if he's not the victim, some of them may be worth talking to." She shrugged. "Who knows, someone may be able to ID him."

Lesley resisted a snort. "I don't mean to be funny, DC Vedra, but have you had many dealings with the Kelvin family?"

Meera flushed. "Personally?"

Lesley nodded.

The flush deepened. "Not much. But I have done some research."

"They don't give each other up," said Nathan. "Not even the ones who hate each other."

Lesley gave another nod. "Because they hate us more. But pulling together a list of Kelvin associates and family members might be useful. It could be putting the cart before the donkey; but in the absence of anything else..."

"Except DNA," Johnny said.

Lesley looked at him. "True, except DNA. But that'll take time."

"We can ask for it to be expedited," Nathan said.

"I'm surprised you haven't already."

Tina gave a small smile. "I did. I hope that's OK."

Lesley wasn't surprised. "Of course. There are budget considerations, so ideally you should have approved it with a senior officer, but yes... it's the obvious next step."

"And in Tina's defence," said Nathan, "you and I were both at the scene for most of the day. And mobile signal was poor."

Lesley very much doubted that either her or Nathan's phone records would show evidence of Tina trying to get through. But she liked that he was defending his team.

"True," she said. "So what else do we have? Any witnesses? CCTV?"

Nathan shook his head. "Apart from the chapel itself, the abbey is the nearest place with people around, and its only cameras are inside the shop. And it's almost a mile away."

Lesley nodded. No surprise there.

"What about the Fleet, and the beach?" she asked. "If the killer gained access that way, they might have been picked up by cameras in the car parks. If there are any."

"I think there are," said Meera. "We can speak to the council."

"Good. What about the chapel?"

Johnny shook his head. "It's locked up, barely visited. Not exactly Corfe Castle."

Nathan snorted. Johnny chuckled. Lesley felt the tension in the room loosen.

In the last twenty-four hours, this team had lost its leader, even if only temporarily, gained one new member, and welcomed another back from leave.

And now they had a murder to solve. With a victim they might not identify for some days yet. Would it be too much for them?

"OK," Lesley said, "here's what happens next. "Meera, you and Johnny work on this list of Kelvin associates and family members. Let's find someone with this wound."

Meera nodded. "I'd like to suggest we speak to the sarge." She glanced at Nathan. "The old sarge."

Lesley frowned. "Dennis?"

A nod.

"He did spend years investigating them, boss," Johnny said.

And sometimes got too close for comfort. But he had a point.

"That's fine. Meera, Johnny, you make arrangements to visit Dennis tomorrow."

The two DCs nodded, exchanging grins. Lesley wasn't sure if putting them together would turn out to be a good idea or a very bad one.

"And Nathan," she said, "I want you working with external partners. Put pressure on to get those DNA results. Find out when the PM takes place. And keep in touch with Gail and her team."

"Boss." The DS nodded.

"What about me, boss?" asked Tina, whose eyelids were drooping.

"Continue with the trawl. Pick up from where Meera left off. HOLMES, mispers, neighbouring forces. Widen it to include social media. See if anyone in digital forensics can point you in the direction of any tools that can help. Nothing public, though. Security of data."

"Of course." Tina was making notes on her pad.

Lesley gave her a sympathetic look. Tina would be functioning on reduced sleep, with hormones raging through her body. Not to mention feeling torn between her new baby and the job she loved.

She straightened up. “Thanks, everybody. It’s time I sent you all home.”

CHAPTER TWENTY

JACKIE HADN'T LEFT the house for two days.

She knew it wasn't fair on Yiannis: a Greek man was far more likely to be noticed at Kolltveit's tiny grocery store than a blonde Englishwoman.

But the news report had freaked her out.

Yiannis was still keeping an eye on the BBC's Dorset pages, local Facebook pages, too. But then, Yiannis had always been a news geek.

Jackie couldn't see the point. If there was nothing you could do to change the shit that was going on in the world, why go to the effort of knowing about it?

Once every five years, she paid attention. Briefly, just enough to confirm her decision to vote the same way she always had. Yiannis couldn't even vote in UK elections, for God's sake.

But she knew why he was monitoring the news now. And despite her outward show of not caring, she was grateful to him. He was monitoring the local news because he wanted to protect her.

When she'd gone on the run, Yiannis had mounted a campaign to find her. He'd been convinced she was out there somewhere, alone.

When the police had dredged up a body from Poole Harbour, he'd refused to believe it was her. Jackie might have been behaving erratically, he'd told the detectives, but she wasn't suicidal.

He'd been right. And she'd rewarded him for his loyalty by not contacting him for over a year.

But she'd had good reason. She'd been terrified.

Still was.

"Jackie! Jackie, love!"

Jackie rolled over on the bed. She'd been lying on top of the covers, fully clothed, staring at the ceiling. Tracing a crack that ran up from the window, wondering if it was related to the damp patch in the corner.

She blinked. Yiannis's voice sounded urgent.

"What?" Her voice was thick and heavy, like someone with a head cold. When was the last time she'd spoken?

"Jackie, I think you should see this." He was standing in the bedroom doorway, hand halfway through his hair.

She propped herself up on her elbows. It was dark outside. It got dark way too early, here in Norway.

"Just come." He turned away and hurried back into the flat's main room.

Jackie's skin was tingling now, her breathing shallow.

What was it?

Had they come for her?

She glanced at the window. The curtains were open – damn, she should have closed them – but there had been no lights outside, no vehicle sound.

But people like them... they could be stealthy.

"Jackie, please."

She pulled in a tight breath and pushed herself up from the bed. In the main room, Yiannis was at the table, hunched over his laptop. As ever.

"What is it?" She stood behind him, frowning over his shoulder.

"They've put out a description." Yiannis pointed at the screen. "The man they found near Chesil Beach."

The photo onscreen was the same as the last time: the area behind Chesil Beach, the lagoon, distant police vehicles, crime scene tape.

No victim.

"I can't..." she began.

He reached behind him, fumbled for her hand. Jackie took his hand, a lump growing in her throat.

She sat down next to him, not letting go.

"There." He pointed. "He's got..."

"Let me read it." Somehow that didn't seem as bad as hearing it.

She scanned the article, searching for the description he'd referred to.

There.

Police have released a description of the victim in the hope a member of the public will be able to identify him. He's a white male, aged between thirty and forty, with curly brown hair. Detectives have given a brief description of a facial wound, which they describe as distinctive.

She looked up at Yiannis. "Distinctive?"

He nodded.

"But that could be anything," she said. "I mean, lots of people have—"

"Read that bit." He had his finger on the screen, further down.

Jackie leaned in.

The wound on the victim's face is believed to have occurred prior to the events leading to his death but would have been fresh. Senior Investigating Officer DCI Lesley Clarke was reluctant to provide more details but did say that the wound covered his eye.

Jackie felt her stomach hollow out. Yiannis slid his arm around her, taking her weight.

"His eye," she said. She was staring at the screen, but her vision had blurred.

He nodded. "When you told me what you saw that day..."

She looked into his eyes. "Is it him?"

"I don't know, love. But you might—"

She shook her head. *No*. "I can't." She gripped his hand. "We're safe here. They haven't found us." She gestured at the screen. "Someone else will recognise him. That wound. I won't be the only one who's seen it."

Yiannis's eyes were searching her face. "True."

"There's a 'but' in that sentence, isn't there?" She could hear her voice, high pitched and tense.

His chest rose and fell. He didn't move his gaze from her face. "There is. And you know what it is."

"But they'll—"

"The police can protect you."

She grunted. "I'd rather stay here."

Yiannis sighed. "And that's your choice."

"It's still there. That 'but'."

He lowered his gaze for a moment. "I know how scared you are, Jack. I am, too."

"But you think that if I come forward, then I'll be safer."

A shrug. "Can we stay like this for the rest of our lives?"

He was right. But...

"I escaped them, Yiannis. Why would I let them find me again?"

"We don't have to go back. You can call the number they've given." He pulled a hand through his hair. He'd stopped shaving. Why hadn't she noticed that?

"They'll trace the call," she said.

He shook his head. "I can go to Bergen. It's a larger town, more anonymous. Buy a burner phone."

She stroked his chin. "I love you, Yiannis."

He smiled back at her. "You don't have to decide just yet."

She glanced at the screen again. "After all, someone else might come forward who recognises him."

He was stroking her fingers, the ones resting on his chin. His hand stopped moving.

"It's not as simple as that, though, is it?" he said. "Someone else might know who he is. But..."

He was right. She waited for him to say it.

"But no one else witnessed his murder."

CHAPTER TWENTY-ONE

Lesley was at the County Gates Gyratory when her phone rang: Jill. She'd been trying to get hold of the DI all afternoon and kept missing her.

"Jill," she said, cursing as she found herself in the wrong lane as usual. "Everything OK?"

"Er, yes. Any reason to think it shouldn't be?"

Lesley realised she was getting jumpy. Hannah's complaint had started to make her paranoid about the other new members of her two teams, especially Jill, the other DI.

"Sorry, Jill," she said. "No reason. Have you got an update for me?"

"I just wanted to let you know that Stanley and I are headed for Exeter prison. We've called ahead and arranged an interview with Lucas Parsons."

Lesley nodded. "The guy claiming to have information about Frank Kelvin."

"That's the one."

There was a moment's silence before Jill spoke again.

"Boss," she said. "I really called because I wanted your advice."

Lesley eyed the phone on its cradle, resisting a laugh. The last time anyone had wanted her advice had been DI Zoe Finch, back in West Midlands over four years ago. And she'd only sought it reluctantly, at least at first.

She composed herself. "Happy to help," she said. "What do you need?"

"Frank Kelvin. Well, the Kelvins in general, really. Stanley only knows them by reputation. It wasn't all that long after he joined the team that Arthur died."

And I kept him away from them, mostly, Lesley thought. She'd needed experienced officers talking to Kelvin family members after the death of their lynchpin. Herself and Dennis.

"You want some background," she said.

"Not that. Not really. Stanley's filled me in on all that."

Lesley was heading for St Paul's roundabout now, preparing to take the right turn towards Southbourne. "So what is it you need?"

"Well," Jill said, "I'm assuming that Parsons was an associate of the Kelvins. Or an employee. You've had dealings with both. How do you suggest I play this?"

Lesley heard Stanley's voice in the background, pointing out a turnoff. She smiled. She had no doubt Jill had a perfectly good idea of how to approach the interview with Parsons. But she'd have heard about Hannah. And she'd be wanting to build trust with her DCI. Show some respect.

Why the hell can't they all be like this?

She took the left turn onto Christchurch Road. The home straight now. "How would you consider handling it, Jill? Give me your ideas, and I can course correct for you if necessary."

Jill cleared her throat. "OK. So I'm assuming that he's at least exaggerating, if not fabricating information. Parsons pled guilty to supply of a class A drug three weeks ago, and he'll be trying to curry favour. Hoping for favourable treatment."

Lesley nodded. All of that was fair.

"So," Jill continued, "I'm thinking the best approach is wariness.

Keep our cards close to our chest, ask open questions, be careful not to lead him and see where he goes. But then probe. Challenge what he says, pick at the holes."

"Subtly," Lesley said. "You don't want to scare him off."

"No. But we don't want to let him lead us a merry dance, either."

Lesley noted the word 'us'. She wondered if she'd ever heard Hannah use that word. "What do you see Stanley's role as?" she asked.

"We've been discussing that. The plan is that Stanley will simply mirror his words back at him, get him to reiterate his statements."

"And you'll be leading him to open up more."

"Exactly."

Lesley was on the coast road now. She slowed for the first of many speed humps and glanced towards the sea. She took a deep breath.

"Sounds like you've got it all under control, Jill. Are you close to the prison? It's getting late."

"Ten minutes away, boss. And we'll both be heading home straight afterwards."

"Good. Come and debrief me in the morning."

"I was hoping you might join me with my team for that."

Another smile. "Of course. Unless there's anything that needs an urgent response. You can call me if that's the case."

"Of course."

Lesley took a left turn towards her and Elsa's house. She was looking forward to a quiet evening, perhaps a stroll along the beach.

Was she getting dull, in her old age? She'd even started cooking, for fuck's sake.

"Boss?"

Lesley blinked a couple of times. "Sorry, Jill. It sounds like you and Stanley have this under control. Bring me some useful information and you'll make me a happy woman."

"Will do, boss."

CHAPTER TWENTY-TWO

KATIE GLANCED at Johnny as they turned the corner into former Detective Sergeant Dennis Frampton's road. It was a neat road of well-tended semis just outside Bere Regis, exactly what she'd been expecting.

Johnny's expression was intent, not giving anything away. Was he looking forward to visiting his old boss, or was he apprehensive? What kind of history did the two of them share?

He pulled up opposite Frampton's house and looked at her.

"You sure you're OK doing this? I mean, you're not even supposed to be on this case..."

She smiled at him. "It's partly a social call, right? I've always wanted to meet DS Frampton. I haven't got anything else to do while Stanley and the DI are in Exeter."

Which was true. Katie was still paying off credit card debt – something she'd managed to keep from her colleagues – and a weekday evening meant beans on toast in front of the knackered TV in her bedroom. A bedroom in a house she shared with a group of medical students, something else she'd kept from her colleagues.

"I'm happy to step in," she said.

The boss had asked Johnny to come here with Meera. Katie wasn't even a part of the MCIT. But she was available, and Meera needed to get home to her daughter.

And besides, until nine this morning, Johnny had been part of the Cold Cases team, too. If he could float, why couldn't she?

"What's he like?" she asked, unbuckling her seatbelt. "Will he be helpful?"

Johnny chuckled. She'd noticed that he tended to be either chuckling or staring into space with a haunted look in his eyes.

"Oh, don't worry," he said. "He'll help. Dennis misses the old job. He loves poking around in our work. After all, you'd never have found Peter Didson without him."

"We would have eventually," she corrected him. And maybe if they'd taken more time, Didson – a suspect in the Cold Cases team's last case – would be alive now.

Johnny shrugged and opened the driver's door. "Come on. I want to get home before the kids' bedtime."

She felt a little stab of envy. It seemed all of the rest of her team had family. Katie didn't even have parents or siblings, not to speak of.

The former DS was at the door before they reached it. He smiled at them, holding it open. She'd been expecting a walking stick – it had been an injury that had forced his retirement – but he seemed sprightly.

"Johnny, Katie," he said. "It is Katie, isn't it?"

She nodded.

"Lovely to see you both. Come on in, Pam's got the kettle on."

They followed him inside and into an old-fashioned living room in the house. The DS sat in a velour-upholstered wing-backed chair and Johnny made himself comfortable on a floral sofa. Side tables held various nicknacks: china ornaments, photos of what she assumed must be a son and his grandchildren. The largest photo was of Dennis himself in full dress uniform, holding what looked like some kind of award.

"Oh, hello." A well-built woman with blonde hair and bright pink lipstick appeared in the doorway. She looked at least ten years younger than her husband, but that could have been the hair and lipstick. "Johnny, good to see you."

Johnny stood up and exchanged kisses with the woman, one on each cheek. He sat back down and she turned her gaze on Katie.

"I don't believe we've met." The smile stayed in place.

Katie stood up and held out her hand. "DC Katie Young. Thank you for accommodating us at such short notice."

The woman grabbed Katie's hand with both of her own, holding it without shaking. "And I'm Pam. The long-suffering police wife." She glanced at her husband with a raised eyebrow. He shook his head in response.

"Anyway," she said. "I'll not get in your way. But I'm assuming you'd both like drinks, yes?"

Johnny opened his mouth to speak. Pam released Katie's hand and put a restraining hand on Johnny's shoulder.

"Builder's tea, two sugars," she said.

"Just one please," Johnny replied, patting his stomach. Katie had no idea what he was on about: Johnny was lean, not a man who needed to cut down.

But then, maybe he hadn't always been lean.

"And how about you?" Pam asked Katie. "Tea, coffee?"

"Tea, milk and no sugar," Katie replied. "Thank you."

Pam retreated through the door, the sarge watching her without comment. Katie wondered if this was the dynamic of their marriage: him sitting in a chair, her doing the chores.

"Right then," said Dennis. "What is it you're needing me for? And tell Lesley she's overdue a visit, won't you?"

Johnny's neck reddened. "I..."

Dennis laughed. "It's OK. I'll tell her. But I hope you're not scared of her."

Johnny cleared his throat. "Of course not."

"Her bark's worse than her bite. She's done a lot for you."

Johnny's neck reddened further, the flush moving up to his cheeks. Katie wondered what she was missing.

"Yeah," Johnny muttered. "Anyway, we wanted to ask you about a case. A victim we're having trouble identifying."

Dennis raised an eyebrow just as the door opened; Pam, carrying a tray of mugs.

"Don't mind me," she said. "I didn't do a pot, what with Johnny liking his so strong you could strip paint with it."

Johnny smiled, the blush fading. "Thanks, Pam."

She shrugged, placing a mug on a side table next to Katie. "My pleasure." She gave Katie a wink then straightened up and turned to Johnny. "And tell Alice I'm looking forward to our trip to Blue Pool."

Johnny frowned. "Sorry?"

"I never see my own grandchildren, so your little ones are going to have to stand in. Alice and I have arranged a day out, next Tuesday."

"Oh." Johnny sipped at his tea. "That's nice."

"It will be." Pam gave Johnny a smile and left the room. Katie slumped back in her chair, feeling like an outsider.

Stop it. DS Frampton isn't even part of the team anymore.

"That victim Johnny was talking about," she said. "We found him – well, a photographer found him – on Chapel Hill, above Chesil Beach."

Dennis nodded. "Near the Fleet. I saw it on the news. I see Sadie Dawes is still keeping you on your toes."

Johnny waved his already empty mug. "They removed his teeth and fingertips, Sarge. They want to make it as difficult—"

Dennis raised a hand to stop him. "I'm not your sarge anymore, remember? You've got DS Strunk now." He wrinkled his nose. "But there's a wound, am I correct? Over his eye? Was that there before his death? Will it help you identify him?"

Katie resisted an urge to put her finger to her face and trace the line of their victim's wound across her own skin. She'd seen the photographs, and it had made her stomach turn. How the man had managed to keep his eye...

"The wound looks like he got it before his death," said Johnny. "It's not fresh, but the scar tissue's still raw."

Dennis nodded. "And you were wondering if I'd ever come across anyone with a wound like that."

"It's a long shot, but—"

"How long d'you think it is since I retired, lad?" Dennis was looking at Johnny, his head cocked to one side.

Johnny stopped waving the mug. "I've only just rejoined the team, so I mean..."

Dennis shook his head. "You were here, Johnny. You came right here, to my house, to visit while I was recovering from the injury."

Katie had been new to the team when that had happened. The body of a PSD officer found in Tyneham, and a man who was working with corrupt officers kidnapping the DCI's daughter and keeping her captive in an enclosure at Monkey World. Dennis had fallen while attempting to rescue her.

"You're right," admitted Johnny. "I did." He put the mug down and started counting off on his fingers. "That was... that was over two years ago."

"Exactly. And you're telling me this poor feller's scar hasn't healed yet. It's too fresh."

Johnny slumped back. Katie looked from him to the former DS.

"Not necessarily," she said.

Dennis turned to her, one eyebrow raised. His brows were thick and bushy, with a few stray hairs.

She nodded. "Pathology still haven't established when he died. They're not sending anyone to the scene, so we have to wait for the PM to establish how long he's been dead."

Dennis shook his head. "Budget cuts," he grunted. Johnny snorted.

Katie shrugged. They all had to work with the available resources. It was just the way things were.

"What if he's been dead a while?" she said. "Two years, even? The wound could date back to when you were still in the job."

Dennis's eyes twinkled. "You've got a point there. Well done."

She bristled at the sense of being patronised but said nothing.

"What about it, then?" said Johnny. "Forget that you retired two years ago. Did you ever come across anyone with a wound like that?" He got out his phone, scrolled to the crime scene photos, and handed it to Dennis.

"And there might have been more than one person with that kind of wound," Katie said. "Maybe it's a marker, a brand. Step out of line and we'll maim you, that kind of thing."

"You're working on the assumption that this is organised crime," Dennis said.

Both Katie and Johnny nodded. Johnny threw Katie a disgruntled look.

Ignore him. She was only doing her job. Well, the MCIT's job. And he wasn't her boss.

Dennis sighed. "So given that they removed the fingernails and teeth, they know his identity would lead you to them."

"Yeah," Johnny said.

Dennis handed the phone back. "And they also know that you won't have his DNA on file. Otherwise they wouldn't have gone to that effort."

Katie closed her eyes. He was right. Why hadn't they thought of that?

Dennis picked up his mug and slurped loudly. He leaned over towards the plate of digestives Pam had left on the table beside him, picked one up and dunked it into his tea before biting off over half the biscuit.

Katie watched him, Johnny, too. She was itching to leave, to get back to the car and report in.

But it was late. They'd all have gone home.

"So," said Dennis, after swallowing the rest of the biscuit, "I can't help you with an ID. I'm afraid I've never seen this chap in my life.

But what I do think is likely, is that he's not a part of any organised crime gang, but that he became associated with them. Perhaps by legitimate means, like being their accountant or lawyer." He shuddered. "No, not lawyer."

"And he pissed them off, somehow..." Johnny began, then hesitated at a cough from Dennis. "Sorry, he, er... he made them angry. And they took their revenge."

"Must have made them pretty angry," Dennis said.

"But the wound," Katie said. "Surely someone like an accountant or lawyer... people would notice? They'd ask questions."

"Which gives us a lead," said Johnny. "Professional bloke, got himself a nasty wound, then disappeared."

Katie let out a long breath. She wasn't much looking forward to meeting whoever had killed their victim, when they did track them down.

CHAPTER TWENTY-THREE

Lucas Parsons was a ratty little man, short and wiry with tattoos of eagles clustered around his neck, and more tattoos of cobras encircling his forearms. He had scruffy grey-blond hair, with bald patches that had Jill wondering if he was in the habit of tearing it out with his bare hands.

If she'd been expecting a man who wasn't the stereotype of a prison inmate, she'd have been disappointed.

He sat opposite them at the metal table in the prison interview room, scratching at his skin and occasionally giving a loud and meaty sniff. Jill wondered where he'd had those tattoos done. Probably right here, or somewhere very much like it. Hence the scratching.

He screwed his face up in response to the question she'd asked him after running through the introductions. To his apparent surprise, she hadn't asked him to tell them what he knew about Frank Kelvin.

He gave one of those sniffs and shuffled on his chair. Jill glanced sideways to see that Stanley had a fist balled in his lap. Was this getting to him?

"I'm sure you heard me the first time, but would you like me to repeat the question?" she asked.

A shrug. "May as well."

So that was how he was playing it. She sighed, thinking of Meera and Suzi at home.

This had better not be for nothing.

"Tell me, Lucas, what is it that's prompted you to come forward with this information now, when you could have done so years ago?"

He looked at her. "Who says I knew anything about it years ago?"

Fair point. "You've got me there. Presumably, given you've been here at HMP Exeter for over three months, you've known this information for a little while."

"Uh-uh." A sniff, followed by him dragging his sleeve under his nose. Jill fought to hide her disgust.

"No?" she said.

"Nope." He grinned. His teeth were as bad as the rest of him, yellowing and gappy.

"OK, then," she said. "I've read the file. You're claiming to have information about the murder of Frank Kelvin, and about the whereabouts of his body."

"That I do."

She allowed herself another sigh. "So if you've discovered this information while you've been incarcerated here at HMP Exeter, who was it you got it from?"

He frowned, and then sniffed. "Look, lady, do you want to know where Frank Kelvin's body is or not?"

"I want to know if I can trust what you tell me. I want to hear your story about how you came by this information, so I can make my own judgement."

He shifted in his seat, looking behind him at the prison guard standing quietly outside the door, eyes up, mouth tight.

Parsons wasn't going to get any help there.

"Listen, I don't see why it matters where or how I got the information. Do you want to know where he is, or don't you?"

Jill licked her lips. She leaned towards Stanley, beckoning for him to bring his face close to hers.

"What is it, guv?" he asked. "D'you want me to ask him something?"

She brought her hand up to cover her lips and leaned in closer. "You carry on as you are. I just want him wondering what we're talking about."

Stanley smiled. "Right. So what *are* we talking about?"

"Anything you want. What are you planning on having for your tea, when we're done here?"

The smile broadened. "Chicken curry, guv. I made one at the weekend, put portions in the freezer. Batch cooking."

She nodded, impressed. She hadn't pegged Stanley as the kind of man who went in for meal planning.

"Look," spluttered Parsons. "I don't know what you're whispering about, but it was two weeks ago, right? There was a bloke getting released on parole, crowing about how he'd been a co-conspirator in a murder twenty-odd years ago and no one had even found the body, let alone arrested him."

"Don't look up," Jill muttered to Stanley. "Don't give him your attention. Not yet."

"Right." Stanley frowned, then closed his eyes, as if it would make it easier to ignore Parsons.

"Why aren't you listening to me?" Parsons' voice was growing more high-pitched. From the corner of her eye, Jill noticed the prison guard outside turn towards them.

Resist, she told herself. Parsons was angling for a sentencing deal, or so the authorities here had reported. But she suspected that what he really wanted was attention.

"I'm not telling you his name, you know? I'm not stupid. Bloke kills someone and gets away with it for decades. Bloke like that's dangerous. No way I'm telling you who he is."

Stanley's eyes opened, just long enough for him to exchange a glance with Jill. Did Parsons think they wouldn't have access to the release records?

Jill straightened up. She turned to look at Parsons. Stanley followed suit but didn't mirror her smile.

"I'm not telling you!" the prisoner shouted.

"That's a shame." Jill pushed back her chair and stood up. "We thought you had useful information."

"I do!" Parsons leapt up from his chair, then crashed back down again as he noticed the guard.

Jill eyed Stanley. *Ignore him. Don't look round.*

"He's in the freezer."

Jill stopped moving, her hand on the back of her chair. Stanley had frozen halfway through standing up.

Freezer? What freezer?

Parsons laughed. "It's brilliant. Bloody genius, wish I'd thought of it myself."

Neither Jill nor Stanley spoke.

"Don't you want to know which freezer?"

Jill turned to face Parsons, keeping her features impassive.

"Which freezer, Lucas?"

Another grin. "His own freezer, for fuck's sake. Frank Kelvin's been in the freezer at his mum's house all these years."

CHAPTER TWENTY-FOUR

Lesley knocked on Carpenter's door, then pulled in two short breaths and looked down to check she didn't have any stains on her jacket while she waited. She'd grabbed a yoghurt from the mini fridge she'd installed in her office – much to the annoyance of the building manager and the electrician who'd had to be summoned to safety test it – and had managed to get a blob of it on her lapel as she'd opened it.

"Come in!"

She cleared her throat, pushed her shoulders back and opened the door, hoping Carpenter would be alone this time. She wanted to get home.

"Ah," he said, raising an eyebrow as she entered. "My favourite DCI. Sit down."

Lesley pulled over one of the hard-backed chairs reserved for visitors who had to face him across the desk, visitors who weren't afforded the luxury of the easy chairs by the window, with their view of what was now a building site but would eventually become landscaped gardens, budget and public opinion willing.

"Sir," she said as she placed the chair opposite his vast designer one, the only one like it in the building. "I thought you might appreciate a briefing on my team's two cases."

The eyebrow pushed up further. "You're a busy woman."

"My teams certainly are busy, yes."

"You don't think they need you?"

She resisted a widening of the eyes. "They do, Sir. Two cases kicking off on the same day, one of them potentially delicate. They need leadership."

He grunted and leaned back. "Well, think yourself fortunate. At least, I would, if I were you. Two murder cases, coming in together like this." He smiled. "It's almost as if you arranged it."

Carpenter was too experienced to genuinely suspect a thing like that. He was just trying to rattle her. And it was working.

"Which case would you like me to start with, Sir?" *Stick to business*. Safer.

"The body found at the chapel. Do you have an ID yet?"

Her heart sank. "Not yet. The team are working through records in the hopes of finding someone with injuries like his. But it's—"

"But it's unlikely, since the evidence points to his injuries being inflicted not long before death."

"Not immediately before death, though," she said. "There is an outside chance—"

"An outside chance. What about DNA? Witnesses? CCTV? Are you making any progress at all, Lesley?"

She frowned. Carpenter had been abrasive when she'd first moved to Dorset. It had taken her years to reach the point where she could trust him. But it had been a while since he'd been as hostile as this.

But then, she hadn't had a formal complaint raised against her by a direct report before.

She swallowed. "We've requested top priority analysis of the DNA," she said. "My team have examined the area around where our victim was found, but it's too remote for CCTV... and for witnesses, I'm afraid."

He cocked his head. "So you're nowhere."

"It feels like that right now, Sir. But we're working through the avenues available to us. Even when that doesn't bear fruit, it's still progress."

He grunted. "And this inmate who claims to have information on the death of Frank Kelvin. Is he legitimate?"

"DI Scott and a member of her team are at HMP Exeter right now, interviewing him." Lesley glanced at the clock to her side then directed her gaze back at the super. "I'm confident we'll know if this is worth following up very soon."

She hated this. Having to pick out her words, guard her body language. This was like being with Carpenter four years ago, or like working with David bloody Randle back in Birmingham.

Another grunt. "And if it turns out that Frank Kelvin was indeed murdered here in the UK, rather than fleeing the country as we believed at the time, then what will be your Cold Cases team's next course of action?"

"Well," she said, knowing that what she was about to describe would be quite different in this case than in others, "we will obviously revisit any information we received at the time that led us to believe he was still alive. Check for any missing person's report."

Carpenter nodded.

"But I'm aware," she continued, "that the priority is to inform next of kin. We will need to pay a visit to Frank Kelvin's mother."

"To Vera Kelvin."

"To Vera Kelvin," she confirmed.

Carpenter relaxed into his chair. "God help the poor bugger who lands that job."

Lesley allowed herself a smile. "I couldn't agree more."

He wrinkled his nose. "Do you think it'll be a surprise to her?"

"To Mrs Kelvin?"

A nod.

Lesley had already considered this. "I honestly don't know, Sir."

"Which is why you need to look into the information held at the time. The existence or not of a missing person's report."

"It is. But it was a long time ago. We can't afford to wait before we speak to next of kin. We can't afford—"

"We can't afford for her to hear on the prison grapevine, via her grandson."

Lesley nodded. There was always the possibility that news would reach Vera via Kyle Kelvin, currently incarcerated at the other end of the country for the murder of his uncle, Arthur Kelvin. Frank's brother.

She frowned. Was Kyle Frank's son, or was there another brother?

Dennis would know.

"So I'm assuming," Carpenter said, "that if the visit to Exeter proves fruitful, Vera Kelvin will get a visit this evening."

She nodded. "DI Scott and myself will—"

"No." The super leaned forward, the flat of his palm on the desk. "No. Not you."

"I think with a delicate situation like this, Sir, not to mention the history, it's approp—"

"No." He balled his fist on the desk. "You're bloody lucky you're still here, Lesley. Strictly speaking, you should be suspended pending a formal investigation into DI Patterson's allegations."

She nodded. She could try to defend herself, but that might make things worse.

"I wouldn't be surprised if PSD's hand is forced very soon," he continued. "I'm keeping you here because your teams have two particularly tricky cases, and because despite everything, I know you have the capability to solve them."

"Thank you, Sir."

"Don't thank me. I'm being a bloody idiot, most likely, and if my high-ups or PSD overrule me, well... there's nothing I can do." He eyed her. "But these things can take time. So you need to prove yourself. Make progress on both these cases. Don't piss anyone off, and for God's sake don't put yourself in the way of any member of the public who might be minded to make a complaint about you."

She folded her hands together in her lap. "No, Sir."

"Indeed. Now bugger off and do your job, before I have no choice but to send you home."

CHAPTER TWENTY-FIVE

"Shit," muttered Jill as she slid back into the car.

"You alright, guv?" Stanley asked as he buckled his seatbelt.

She sighed, then rubbed the bridge of her nose. A headache was brewing. "I'm fine, thanks, Stan. Sorry, you probably don't like being called that."

He chuckled. "Oh, I'm used to that. And worse."

She screwed up her face, then pulled her mouth wide and shifted her jaw from side to side. Anything to relieve the tension; her skin felt two sizes too tight.

"What did you make of that, then, Stan?" she asked.

Stanley eyed her for a moment, then looked forward through the windscreen. Their view was of the high fence surrounding the prison and its grey walls beyond.

"He seemed legit," the DC said at last.

"He did." Jill started the car, then turned in her seat to reverse out of the space. "And you know what that means."

"The freezer."

She nodded. "Frank Kelvin's fucking mum's freezer." She tightened her grip on the wheel. "Vera Kelvin's freezer."

"You think he's telling the truth?"

"I think he would have lied to us if we hadn't made him feel like he was being ignored. So yes, I think he's telling the truth."

Jill really wished she was wrong. Her maternity leave had coincided with Arthur Kelvin's death and the arrest of his nephew, Kyle. She'd hoped she might never have to cross paths with that family again.

Bloody idiot, she told herself. *You took the job running the Cold Cases team. What did you expect?*

"You know what I was hoping, Stan?" she said as they made their way to the A30 towards Dorset.

"No. Sorry."

She waggled her jaw again. "When he said he knew where Frank Kelvin was, I was hoping this would be simple. I was hoping we'd be able to unearth the body and take things from there. Forensics, pathology, all that."

"But with a body that old..."

"Forensics and pathology aren't that much use," she confirmed. "It's all about the people. Witnesses, family, friends. Relationships. Finding motives and trying to square that with what little physical evidence we can glean."

Truth was, this was what had attracted her to the job. Piecing together the web of relationships, betrayals and lies that had led to a person's death. Puzzling it out. Proper detective work.

She hadn't factored in the idea that a body might be hidden on the property of Dorset's most notorious crime family.

"I'm going to have to speak to the DCI," she said. "Vera Kelvin isn't the kind of woman whose door we can just knock on in the hope she'll let us in."

"But she's next of kin, guv. If we suspect her son was murdered, we have a duty to—"

She turned to him. "This is Vera Kelvin, Stan. How much contact have you had with her?"

He pointed ahead. "You need to take the slip road."

Jill frowned at the road sign. He was right; they were at the turnoff for the A35. How had that appeared so fast?

"Thanks," she grunted. "But the question still stands."

He cleared his throat. "Not much, to be honest, guv. It was always other officers who went to the house. And the DCI was the one who faced off against her after Arthur died."

Faced off. That was an interesting choice of words. "Vera was hostile?"

"From what I heard. Seemed to hold Dorset Police responsible for her son's death, despite—"

"Despite the fact that it was her own bloody grandson who killed him," he replied.

Over a woman, of all things. Amanda Frobisher, Arthur's wife and Kyle's lover, whose so-called suicide had been staged not long after Arthur's death. The police had never managed to find conclusive evidence that she'd been murdered, but no one who'd dealt with the Kelvin family believed she'd taken her own life.

Jill pulled in a deep breath. "What can you tell me about the Kelvins and their activities during the time I was away?" she asked.

"Err... sorry, but when were you away?"

"I went on maternity leave a month before Suzi was born, and I came back when this unit was established just over a year ago."

He nodded. "Right. So, there was the Harry Nevin case, just after you went off. The lawyer in charge of the firm—"

"The firm where the DCI's wife used to be a partner. What's the Kelvin connection?"

"The firm represented him. Still represents the family, as far as I know. Nevin was killed by his girlfriend, as it turned out, but we thought it might be—"

"But like you say, Nevin's death wasn't connected to his work with the Kelvins. Anything else?"

Stanley closed his eyes for a moment. "Sorry. There was the Fogarty and Lawson case. The couple who were found just outside Lyme Regis in 2022."

"That was something to do with an AFO, wasn't it?"

He nodded. "Christian Davison, from the firearms team. It was a gun registered to him that was used to kill them."

She narrowed her eyes. "But they died years earlier, didn't they?"

"Ten years earlier. Davison was a firearms officer back then, too. He was bent, worked for the Kelvins. It was Darren Kelvin, the other nephew, who was the link."

Jill glanced in the rear-view mirror. They were on the A35 now, and the afternoon rush hour was beginning to kick in.

"But he didn't shoot them?" she said. She'd researched the case, what with it being a cold one.

"No. That was..." Stanley bit his bottom lip, thinking. "A bloke called Leonard. Steven Leonard, I think. He took Davison's gun and used it to shoot the two lawyers."

"And he was on the Kelvin payroll."

"He was."

She nodded, putting her foot on the brake as red lights appeared up ahead. "Anything else of interest?"

"Obviously there was Arthur Kelvin's death and discovery at Blue Pool."

"For which his nephew Kyle was convicted."

Stanley took a swig from the water bottle he'd pulled from his messenger bag. "He was. Nasty bastards, the Kelvins."

Jill raised an eyebrow. "And the nastiest bastard of all was Gerard. Vera's late husband."

"I never came across him," said Stanley.

"Nor me," said Jill as the traffic slowed to a standstill. Bloody A35. "He died before I joined the force."

"Me too. Suspicious?"

She shook her head. "Natural causes, believe it or not. Leukaemia."

"Nothing suspicious about that. Have you researched him?"

Jill felt her stomach clench. "I have. Although it's not easy."

"Why not?"

"He had so many coppers in his pocket back in the day, there's barely anything on record about him. Believe it or not, the best source of information is from press reports."

"He didn't have them in his pocket, too?"

"Oh, I'm sure he did," Jill said. "But you can read between the lines. Nothing's online, though. I spent a very dull few days in Bournemouth library with a microfiche reader."

The DC frowned. "What's one of those?"

Jill resisted a laugh. "They compress old documents into tiny, tiny text, and you can only read them on this machine that's like a cross between a computer monitor and a magnifying glass."

"Sounds like hard work. So when Gerard died, Arthur took over the family business?"

The traffic started moving again. Thank God. At this rate, they wouldn't make it back to the office before everyone else had left. And Jill wanted to catch DCI Clarke.

"He did," she said. "But not without a fair bit of help from his mother, from what I've been able to glean."

"And how does Frank fit into all of this?"

Jill glanced at Stanley. "That's the thing. From what I've been able to discover, Frank disappeared within weeks of Gerard's diagnosis."

Stanley frowned. "The diagnosis made him a threat to Arthur, his younger brother."

"Younger?" She gripped the steering wheel, resisting the urge to speed up too quickly. "But does that mean Arthur killed him, is the question."

"Or had him killed, based on Arthur's MO."

Jill sucked her teeth. "And the other question is, if Frank's been stored in Vera's freezer for all these years, was she involved, too? And what kind of woman kills her own son?"

"The grandmother of a bloke like Kyle Kelvin, who killed his own uncle."

Jill felt a shiver run across her skin. "Yeah."

"But that's not a question you want to ask her directly."

"No," she confirmed. "It bloody well is not."

CHAPTER TWENTY-SIX

LESLEY FELT energised as she pulled into the drive of her Edwardian house in Southbourne. Scaffolding had appeared at its side since she'd left that morning, or had she just not noticed it before?

Elsa was in the living room at the front, reading legal documents. She looked up. "Hey, sweetie."

Lesley bent to kiss her. "Is that scaffolding I saw outside?"

"For the work on the roof. They put it up today. The builders start tomorrow."

Lesley grimaced. Their bedroom was at the back of the house, under the section of the attic where they'd found the leak.

"How long's that going to take?"

Elsa stood and stretched out her shoulders. She closed her file and tucked it under her arm, careful not to let Lesley see her work papers. Sensible, no matter how much they trusted each other.

"Till the end of next week," she said. "Assuming they don't find anything untoward."

Lesley pulled a face. Old houses were beautiful, but *untoward* was their stock in trade.

"Did you see the message from Sharon?" Elsa asked.

"No." Lesley pulled her phone out. "Is she OK?"

"She's fine." Elsa smiled. "Shared a photo of herself with her new boyfriend on the family WhatsApp group. And she said she wanted a chat."

"Oh. OK." Lesley pushed down her rising concern – *it's just a chat* – and left the room, pulling up her daughter's contact details as she did so.

"Mum," Sharon said when she picked up. It looked like she was on a bus. "I'm on my way into town," she lowered her voice, "and I don't want to be antisocial."

"You want me to call back later?"

Sharon shook her head. She'd cut her hair short and had blue highlights. Or were they lowlights, in blonde hair?

Lesley knew she should compliment the new hair... but she also knew Sharon had a sixth sense for a lie.

"No," Sharon said. "I'll be straight into 'spoons when I get in, and that's too noisy. Hang on."

Lesley watched as her daughter shifted sideways, inserted earbuds into her ears, then gave her the thumbs-up.

She was expected to speak. But what about?

"Er..." she said. "What d'you want me to talk about?"

Sharon shrugged. "Anything," she mouthed.

Lesley smiled. Her daughter just wanted to hear her voice.

"OK," she said. "I'll tell you about my day."

Sharon rolled her eyes.

"No?" Lesley said. "How about the building work. Elsa found a leak in the roof after we spotted a damp patch."

She paused, waiting for another eye-roll. Instead, Sharon gave her another thumbs-up.

Really?

"OK," she said. "This is very dull. There's a hole in the roof. They put scaffolding up today, and they're going to start the work to fix it tomorrow. So then there won't be a hole." She shrugged. "That's about it really."

"Hey, Sharon."

Lesley turned to see Elsa enter the room, waving towards her phone screen. She dipped her head to one side so her wife and daughter could get a better view of each other.

Elsa blew a kiss. Sharon mimed catching it and sending it back. Elsa pretended to catch it.

This was their thing, lately. Lesley did all the talking while Elsa and Sharon mucked about, blowing each other kisses.

The background behind Sharon shifted. She was moving, getting off the bus. She moved her lips closer to the screen.

"Anything else, Mum?"

Lesley cocked her head, pretending to think.

"I know you don't want to hear about work, but..."

"Oh God..." Sharon was off the bus now. It moved off behind her.

"...today we had a new murder case come in, potentially two of them. And one of my team raised a formal complaint about me."

"Really?" said Sharon. "That's outrageous."

"Don't tell me," added Elsa. "Hannah Patterson."

Lesley turned to her. "Yep."

Elsa shook her head. "That woman. What has she accused you of?"

"Bullying and intimidation," Lesley said.

"Say that again," said Sharon.

Lesley turned to face her phone. "Bullying and intimidation. Of staff, and of members of the public. She's being thorough, you can give her that."

"Ouch." Sharon was walking now. "I hope you give her what for."

"It's not like that," Lesley replied. She thought of Zara Weathers and her pinched expression.

"I'm sorry, love." Elsa's hand was on her shoulder. Lesley reached up to stroke it.

"Anyway," Sharon said. "I'm at the pub now, but I've got news."

"News?" Lesley said. This had been the real purpose of the call, she was sure. She resisted asking Sharon if she was OK, and she waited.

"Nick's coming to Exeter. He's doing a master's."

Lesley frowned. "Nick. Who's Nick?"

Sharon widened her eyes in exasperation. "Nick Finch, of course. Your mate Zoe's his mum."

"Ah." Lesley wondered what Zoe would make of that. Nick was in his final year at Stirling, which was far enough from Zoe in Cumbria. Exeter was even further.

"Bye, Mum! Enjoy your scaffolding." The screen went blank.

Lesley turned to Elsa. "Why does it always feel like such an anti-climax when I talk to her?"

Elsa put an arm around her back. "I think it's normal, sweetie. Now tell me what that bitch Hannah Patterson has done."

CHAPTER TWENTY-SEVEN

"THAT WASN'T FUN."

Jill put her bag down on the kitchen table, then noticed Meera wincing.

She picked it up and put it on the floor, under the table where she hoped it couldn't be seen. "Sorry," she said. "But I've had a sod of a day."

Meera sidled up to her and placed a hand on her back. She hesitated, and Jill nodded. Meera started rubbing her back.

Jill closed her eyes. A back rub from Meera always made her feel better. But today the tension was refusing to dissipate.

"You've got knots the size of satsumas," Meera said. "You really have had a tough day."

Jill leaned into Meera's hand, trying to force the contact to work. "Stanley and I had to go to HMP Exeter, interview an inmate."

The rubbing stopped for a moment, then started again. Jill shifted her shoulders up and down. The knots were easing.

"What was that about?" Meera asked.

Jill didn't open her eyes. "I'm sorry. I can't tell you."

The rubbing intensified. "Why not?"

"I need to speak to the boss first. I need to... We don't even know if we have a case yet." She pulled away from her wife's hand and turned to face her. "I'm sorry. It's a sensitive one. I can't even share all the details with my team."

"Stanley went with you."

"Really? Professional jealousy. Of Stanley?" Jill held her hands up. "Sorry. That was out of order. It's just that sometimes—"

"Yeah, I know. You're a DI, and I'm a DC. You can't tell me stuff." Meera sighed, then patted Jill's arm. "It's OK."

It doesn't feel it. Jill looked around. "Where's Suzi?"

"It's almost eight pm," Meera replied. "She's in bed."

"Of course. Sorry. Did I miss anything good?"

"She talked to me about her day at nursery. She's getting more articulate."

Jill felt a pang. "She's wonderful."

Meera smiled. "She is. Now, d'you want some of the risotto I saved for you?"

"That would be perfect. Thank you."

Meera opened the fridge and grabbed a container, which she put in the microwave. Jill sat down and slid off her shoes. Her feet were swollen from so much time in the car.

"So how are you finding having a new member of your team?" she asked.

Meera turned to glance at her. "Johnny Chiles?"

Jill nodded. "Johnny Chiles."

"He was supposed to be in your team, wasn't he? Cover for Mike's parental leave?"

Jill rubbed her feet. "Things were quiet with us this morning. You lot had a new murder case. I hear the victim's in a bit of a state."

Meera nodded, her back to Jill. "Teeth and fingertips removed. Nothing confidential there."

"Sounds like you have your work cut out."

A shrug. "DNA's being fast-tracked. It won't take long."

Jill stood up and squeezed past her wife to grab a bottle of beer from the fridge. She stood close to Meera, who was emptying the hot risotto into a bowl.

"You won't find a match," she said.

"No?" Meera looked up at her. Jill was at least three inches taller.

"They wouldn't have gone to all that trouble if you could just get a DNA match. I'm betting he's not known to the police."

Meera held out the bowl. "Maybe they're just trying to slow us down."

Jill took the bowl and placed it on the table, her beer beside it. "Maybe." She turned back to the cupboards, grabbed a plate, and put it over her bowl. "Give me a minute."

She slid out of the room and crept upstairs to their daughter's room. A couple of minutes later she was back at the kitchen table, where Meera sat swigging from her own beer.

"She's cute when she's asleep," Jill said.

Meera raised an eyebrow. "She's certainly quieter."

"You're finding it hard?"

Meera put down her bottle, perhaps a little too hard. "Absolutely not."

"Because it's OK, if you are. When I was on parental leave, I—"

"Jill." Meera put a hand on the table. "I am not struggling. She's cute when she's asleep, and she's cute when she's awake. I love being the one who picks her up from pre-school, who spends time with her in the afternoon. If bloody DS Strunk could just remember I'm on short hours and not act all surprised every time I get up to leave, it would be perfect." She took an impatient swig.

"He giving you trouble?" Jill asked.

"No." Meera sighed. "It's just... I don't think he has kids. He doesn't get it." She looked up. "Do you know anything about his home life?"

Jill shook her head. "I don't think anyone does."

"What about Johnny Chiles? What d'you know about him? The DCI must have told you something, putting him in your team."

Jill looked at her wife. "All I know is he was in the MCIT till three years ago, then had a stint in London. Development opportunity, I assume. Or maybe he intended for it to be permanent. His dad's in Dorset and he's not been very well, so..."

Meera screwed up her nose. "So he left to advance his career, then came back for family. No mystery."

Jill smiled. Meera liked to see secrets where there weren't any. It had led to some awkwardness when they'd first been dating.

"No mystery at all," she said, picking up her clean plate. "Now let's go watch some TV and forget about work for an hour or two."

CHAPTER TWENTY-EIGHT

Jackie turned her head to see Yiannis beside her, snoring lightly. She turned back to stare at the ceiling.

They both found this stressful. Trying not to be noticed, not to stand out. Resisting the urge to make contact with family and friends. Her sister, Gloria, lived in Portsmouth. What would she be thinking? Would she have watched the news reports in the summer, when they'd found that woman's body and everyone thought it was Jackie?

And what about Yiannis? Were his family in Greece worrying about him? Looking for him? Assuming he was dead?

She blinked back a tear.

Being on the run like this... it was keeping her alive.

Alive.

But was this really living, in any meaningful form?

It wasn't. They never went anywhere, other than to buy food. They'd broken off all contact with friends and family. One of their neighbours in this building, an English speaker, had tried to be friendly when they first arrived. They'd been monosyllabic in return, almost rude, at first. Then they'd been reduced to hiding from him.

It was no kind of life. And she certainly didn't want to do it forever.

She glanced at Yiannis. Maybe he was right. Maybe she should go to the police. Tell them what she knew.

They'd found the man now. He was dead.

If she told them what she'd seen, and when she'd seen it...

That would give them evidence. The people who had killed him would go to prison. Then she'd be safe.

Wouldn't she?

Maybe they had enough evidence already. Maybe the man's killers had left DNA on his body.

She didn't know how that worked, but she knew it could happen.

But they'd been watching the news. And there had been no reports of arrests.

She let out a long, juddering breath. She was scared. Lonely. Miserable. How much of this could their relationship tolerate?

She put a hand on Yiannis's back. He didn't stir. She started rubbing. Still nothing.

She started to shake him, her movements impatient.

She wanted to talk to him. Needed to. Right now.

He groaned. He raised an arm, half-consciously pushing her away. His back twitched.

"Yiannis," she said.

Another groan.

"Yiannis."

He turned to her, eyes still closed.

"I need to talk to you," she said. "I'm sorry, but I need to talk to you."

CHAPTER TWENTY-NINE

MEERA WAS JUST SITTING down when the door to the team room opened and the DCI walked in, looking like someone had given her a box of chocolates, then forced her to sit and watch while they ate them all in front of her.

She drew herself in, keeping her movements small so as not to draw attention to herself. Johnny was at his desk in the far corner of the room, and the boss had given him plenty of attention so far.

"Meera," the boss said. "Johnny. Glad you're here. How did it go with Dennis?"

"Err..." Meera looked at Johnny. She stood up. "I know this is awkward, boss, but I had to go home. I'm on a reduced hours contract, what with the family responsibilities."

The DCI raised an eyebrow. "How come I didn't know?"

"It's something I agreed with DI Patterson."

"Ah." The boss eyed her for a moment longer than felt comfortable. Meera held her gaze. Tina and Mike were sharing their maternity leave. Johnny was privileged; he had a civilian wife to take the slack. She wasn't doing anything wrong.

The DCI nodded. "Good for you. So Johnny, you went on your own I assume?"

He shook his head. "I took Katie Young."

A frown. "But she's in the Cold Cases team."

"She was clocking off when I bumped into her, and she didn't have anything to do. The rest of her team were out—"

"I know where they were. OK, so how did you and Katie get on?"

Johnny nodded. "Dennis had a couple of insights."

"Like...?"

"Firstly, he reckons we won't have the victim's DNA on file. Otherwise, they wouldn't have gone to so much trouble with the teeth and fingerprints."

She nodded. "Makes sense. Anything more?"

Johnny nodded. "He reckoned that the victim would be someone connected with their killer."

"We're already assuming that."

Another nod. "Someone respectable, like. Someone without a record."

"So someone employed in a professional capacity. Like a—"

"Like a lawyer or an accountant, boss. Only, not a lawyer." He looked down. "We know who all the lawyers are."

She laughed. "Yes, Johnny. We bloody well do. So an accountant, someone like that. Makes sense. When you're looking at the papers, keep an eye out for people like that."

"Will do, boss."

"Good. Meera, have you got any further with identifying any sources of CCTV? What about witnesses? Still nothing?"

Meera swallowed. "That's what I was about to go and do, boss."

The DCI frowned. "Sorry?"

"I've been trawling for potential sources of footage, checking social media. I've left calls with local traffic enforcement." She shrugged. "But I'm getting nowhere. So I thought it might help to get out there. Drive the roads, walk the paths. See if there's anything I can find."

"But DS Strunk has already done that."

Meera licked her lips. "I spoke to him, boss. He admits he hasn't had the time to be as thorough as he'd like."

The door opened, and DS Strunk entered. He paused a moment then composed himself.

"Boss," he said. "Meera's about to head out to the area around where our body was found. We figured that eyes on the ground might—"

"On her own?" the DCI interrupted.

Meera felt her face grow hot. "There's no risk," she said. "It's not like—"

"No," the boss said.

Meera felt her hands clench in her pockets. She was thinking of the time she'd been sent to Tyneham after the body of a PSD officer had been found there. She'd lost a suspect and almost blown the case.

She was sure the DCI was thinking of the same thing.

"This is a recce," she said. "Trawling for ideas, as much as anything."

"No," the boss repeated. She took a step towards Meera, her expression softening. "This isn't personal, Meera. And it isn't because of what happened in Tyneham."

Meera rubbed her forehead. Would her cock-up that day ever leave her?

"Johnny," the boss said.

Johnny was already halfway between his desk and Meera's. Ready for whatever the boss had to throw at him, it seemed. Meera wondered what his history was with the DCI. How long had they worked together before he mysteriously buggered off to the Met?

"Yes, boss," he muttered.

The DCI turned to him, looking him up and down in a way that made Meera think that maybe he wasn't a threat.

The DCI frowned at him. "Go with Meera," she said. "Two pairs of eyes are better than one. I trust you're getting nowhere with identifying potential eyewitnesses?"

"No."

She pursed her lips. "Well, you never know, getting over there might unstick things. Knock on some doors, see if there's anyone we haven't spoken to."

"Johnny's spoken to the Heritage people managing the chapel," the DS said. "When people use drones for photography, they need permission. Which means contact details."

The boss nodded. "When was the latest time that happened?"

DS Strunk's face darkened. "Over a month ago. But we have a copy of the local electoral register. If there are people from the village going up to the chapel on foot for photography, we can—"

"We can match them up," the boss said. "Good. Which means knocking on doors. Meera, Johnny, you up for a bit of shoe leather work?"

"Meera already suggested the same thing, boss," the DS said.

The DCI smiled at Meera, but a frown creased the skin of her forehead. "Good. And if both of you get out there, it'll speed things up."

Meera picked up her bag and slung it across her body. She looked at Johnny. "Who's driving?"

He chuckled. "You can. I'm out of practice on country lanes."

CHAPTER THIRTY

"Oh," said Tina as she entered the team room, two coffee mugs in hand.

DS Strunk, sitting at his desk with his back to her, turned to face her. "Tina. That for me?"

"Er... one of them's for Meera. Where is everyone?"

"Meera and Johnny have gone over to Chesil Beach and Abbotsbury. See if they can make any more progress on CCTV or potential witnesses."

Tina put both mugs down on her desk. "I thought you'd already done that."

"The boss thought two more pairs of eyes might help."

Tina nodded, wondering how the DS might feel about that. "D'you want this coffee, then?"

"Is it black?"

"White, no sugar."

He pulled a face. "Better than nothing. Thanks." He walked over to her desk and grabbed the mug that had been destined for Meera.

Tina sat down at her desk and checked her inbox. "Excellent," she said.

The DS was still standing beside her. "A lead?" He leaned in to see the screen.

"Potentially." Tina opened the email she'd received from PC Taylor on the missing persons team. "It's from Mispers. I asked them for details of recent reports matching our victim's description, as you know."

The DS pulled a chair over from Meera's desk, the closest one. "They've got a match?"

"Not one. Three." Tina scanned the screen. "Three men, all reported missing in the last two years."

"You asked them for that far back?"

She shrugged. "I know we don't have an estimate from pathology yet, but what they have given us indicates he could have been dead a while."

He grunted. "Give me the names, then."

Tina took a breath. "Right. So we've got an Andy Draycott first, reported missing in January this year. He'd been diagnosed with depression by his GP, his employer contacted the police after two weeks' unexplained absence."

"Two weeks? Who waits that long before getting worried?"

Tina clicked on a link: the report of Andy Draycott's disappearance. "Looks like he'd had quite a lot of absence, Sarge. The assumption at the time was that he was a suicide who hadn't yet been found."

"Which is unusual."

"It is." Most people who committed suicide did so in a way that all but guaranteed they'd be found relatively quickly. "And it's only ten months ago."

"We think our victim's from before then."

"Pathology aren't sure yet, Sarge. But yeah, most probably."

"OK. You say he was reported missing by his employer. What was his profession?"

She wrinkled her nose, working through the email. "Bookkeeper, Sarge."

"Dennis Frampton has a theory that our victim might have worked for their killer in a professional capacity."

"Why?"

"Connected to them, but no one with a record. He reckons we won't get a DNA match."

"That makes sense. OK, I'll follow it up. Want to hear about the next one?"

"Please."

Tina returned to the email. "Two more. Zack Catterall, known to the police for various petty crimes. And Mark Ashforth, a taxi driver reported missing by his wife."

"What are the timescales for those?"

"Both reported missing summer 2024. Mark by his wife, like I said. Zack by his dad."

"And Zack's known to us."

She sighed. "Yeah. He's been getting into trouble since he was twelve. He was twenty-six when he went missing."

"What sort of trouble?"

"Shoplifting, to start with. A bit of antisocial behaviour, progressing to burglary and low-level dealing around the time he would have left school."

"The kind of person who might have connections to more serious criminals," the DS said.

"Which would explain why they don't want us identifying him. Not quickly, anyway."

But they had his DNA on file.

And his prints, not that they were much use.

The DS tapped his fingertips on Tina's desk. "Let's follow up on that one."

Tina nodded but couldn't push back a frown. "I'm not sure, Sarge."

"No?"

"He's too small. Too... too petty. Why would anyone care if we identified a bloke like Zack Catterall?"

"Sometimes organised criminals keep people like him out of trouble. If he's a runner for them, we won't have picked him up for anything significant."

Tina sighed. "You're probably right." Zack Catterall had been just the sort of kid who'd be a target for organised crime. Broken home, drug use, low-level criminal activity. "What do you suggest?"

"He was reported missing by his dad?"

"Yes." Tina had Zack's record open on her screen. "The two of them lived together in a council flat in Turlin Moor, Poole. His mum... looks like she left the area around the time he started getting into trouble."

"Nice."

Tina shrugged. It was never a good idea to judge people, no matter how different their lives were to your own. Still, she couldn't imagine leaving her own kids.

"Right," said the DS. "I can keep in touch with Meera and Johnny by phone. Let's pay a visit to the elder Mr Catterall."

"What about Andy Draycott?"

"Why don't you give his employers a call while we're driving, see what they can tell you about him?"

She nodded. "Fair enough."

Tina closed down Zack Catterall's record and glanced at the email from PC Taylor. She'd make the call about Andy Draycott, but it looked like Zack was their best bet. Mark Ashforth, the taxi driver, felt like a dead end.

She closed down her computer and pulled out her phone as she rose from her desk. The wallpaper was a photo of Mike, Louis and Daisy.

Tina smiled, placing her fingers on each of their faces in turn.

Thank God I've got a loving family.

"Coming?" The DS was at the door.

Tina plunged the phone into her pocket. "Coming."

CHAPTER THIRTY-ONE

Lesley looked up at the sound of a knock on her office door. It would be Jill, reporting back from her prison visit.

She bent her head once to each side to relieve the tension in her neck and scratched her chin. "Come in."

The door opened. It wasn't Jill.

Standing in the open doorway, the thinnest of smiles on her lips, was Zara Weathers. The PSD woman.

Lesley forced herself not to react. Instead, she pushed a blank expression onto her face and waited for the woman to speak.

"DCI Clarke," Weathers said at last.

"DCI Weathers. How can I help you?"

The DCI smiled. "I'd be grateful if you would come with me, please."

"Do you mind if I send my DI a message? She'll be expecting to speak to me about a live case."

A frown. "I won't keep you long."

"It's a sensitive case, involves... you don't need to know what it involves. It won't take a moment."

Fucking hell. In the time they'd taken to have this conversation, she could have messaged Jill.

"Very well," Weathers said at last. "Leave your phone in your desk when you're done and make sure you log out of your computer. We don't want any security breaches." She turned in the doorway. "I'll be right outside."

Lesley narrowed her eyes. What did the woman think she was, a flight risk? She pushed down her irritation and fired off a message to Jill.

If you're looking for me when you get in, I am in the building, just in a meeting. I'll call you when I'm available.

She sent the message, logged out of her computer, feeling like a teenager being reminded of how to behave by their mum, and tossed her phone into the top drawer of the desk.

Fuck it. She'd done nothing wrong. She could handle this.

Weathers was outside her office, standing upright against the wall with hardly any points of her body in contact with it. Her lips were moving, very faintly, but no sound came out.

Jesus bloody Christ. Was she meditating?

Lesley cleared her throat and Weathers opened her eyes.

"Ah, DCI Clarke. That was quick."

Lesley grunted. She knew she had to co-operate, but surely she didn't have to make small talk?

"Lead the way," she said.

The woman raised an eyebrow and turned to walk away. Lesley followed her to the lift, where they ascended to the top floor.

Lesley hadn't been up here. She knew it would eventually be a management suite for the high-ups, but the building work wasn't yet finished.

Outside the lift was a blank space; almost the entire top floor of the building had no partitions or walls.

"Blimey," she said. "Are you sure we're in the right place?"

Weathers eyed her. "I requested privacy. I have to admit, I wasn't expecting this level of isolation."

"Be careful what you wish for." Lesley remained standing by the lift doors, wondering if Weathers would change her mind and return inside. Instead, she strode through the empty space, then turned left twice so that they were next to the space where the lifts were, facing two doors in the one wall that had been erected.

"This is me," she said, gesturing towards the right-hand door. "At least, for a temporary period."

Lesley followed the woman's outstretched arm and opened the door. Beyond was a small office containing a table in the centre, four chairs, and a smaller table to one side with a briefcase and a pile of files sitting on top of it.

"Take a seat," DCI Weathers said. She followed Lesley inside then closed the door.

Lesley wondered if Carpenter knew about this space. She walked to the seat closest to the smaller table, allowing herself a quick scan of those files. Nothing of interest.

"Ever the detective," Weathers said, sitting down opposite her. "Now, as you know, you're entitled to representation. If you'd like to fetch someone, we can wait."

Lesley eyed her. It was 4:30 on a Tuesday afternoon, and Weathers had already dragged her all the way up here.

If one of her team had been in this situation, Lesley would absolutely have advised them to wait for the rep. But the longer this dragged on, the more likely it was that she would be put on suspension.

And besides, she'd done nothing wrong.

"It's fine," she said. "Let's just get this over with."

Weathers raised an eyebrow and nodded. She placed a laptop on the table next to her and started typing on it.

"Is this being recorded?" Lesley asked.

A nod. Weathers turned the laptop towards her and indicated the recording icon at the top. "You'll be provided with a copy," she said.

Lesley pursed her lips. Clearly, PSD had different procedures from CID.

"OK," she said. If she objected, that would just slow things down. "What do you want to know?"

Weathers turned the laptop back towards herself and clicked the trackpad. "DI Patterson's complaint includes some serious allegations."

Lesley swallowed. "I know." *None of them true.*

"She cites some specific incidents, but overall the picture appears to be one of bullying and intimidation."

According to Hannah. "Can you provide me with an example of those specific incidents?"

Weathers looked up. "I'm supposed to be asking the questions here."

"I can't defend myself if I don't know what I'm accused of."

"Fair point. Very well. She cites an incident before she joined the Dorset force, when the two of you were working on a case in Lyme Regis."

Lesley considered challenging the relevance. But she didn't want to come across as defensive. Instead, she nodded.

"She claims that you undermined her at every opportunity and made it clear you didn't want her on the case."

"Well, I didn't."

The woman's head shot up. "Pardon?"

"The bodies of Kenneth Fogarty and Catherine Lawson were found below the cliffs east of Lyme Regis. In Dorset. The victims had lived and worked in Bournemouth. Also in Dorset. At the time, DI Patterson was a CID detective in Devon. I couldn't see any benefit to having a second force involved. Quite the opposite, in fact."

"You're not denying that you told DI Patterson you didn't want her involved with the case?"

"No." Lesley licked her lips. "Look, DCI Weathers, with all respect, I thought that Hannah had raised a complaint against me as her manager. In May 2022, I was not her senior officer. I was not even employed by the same force as her."

Weathers looked at her for longer than felt comfortable. "No."

Lesley clenched a fist under the table. "Has DI Patterson raised any specific complaints relating to her time in the MCIT? The time during which I've been her commanding officer?"

"She has."

Lesley felt her shoulders dip. "Go on."

Weathers cocked her head. "DCI Clarke, how did you feel about DI Patterson joining your team?"

Lesley looked at the woman, waiting for her to continue. She didn't.

"Is that it?" she asked. "How did I *feel?*"

"Would I be right in deducing, as DI Patterson did, that you weren't happy?"

Deducing? What was this, a Sherlock Holmes story?

"It was an adjustment," Lesley said. "My previous second-in-command, DS Frampton, was forced to retire after an injury. Direct leadership of the MCIT was taken from me when—"

"Until last year, you managed one DS and a small team of DCs. Only the one team. Is that right?"

"It was hardly my decision how the structure of the unit would be organised."

"DCI Clarke, would it be fair to say that for you, DI Patterson personified the changes to your team, and your role? That you were unhappy at these changes, and that you took that frustration out on her?"

Is that it? Is that all you've got?

"No," Lesley said. "It would not be fair to say that."

"What kind of boss are you, DCI Clarke?"

Lesley felt her mouth fall open. She quickly closed it again. "A good boss, I'd say. And I imagine those officers I've managed over the years would agree."

She thought of the people she'd supervised, people she'd supported as they'd grown in their roles and risen through the ranks. Zoe Finch. Dennis. Tina. And now, she hoped, Jill Scott.

"You're very loyal to those team members who you think highly of, aren't you?"

Lesley blinked. "If someone's a good copper, I support them, yes."

"Sufficiently loyal to have accepted DC Johnny Chiles back into your team after his frankly less than stellar stint in the Met."

Lesley clenched the fist tighter. "That wasn't my decision. Superintendent Carpenter, he—"

"Why did DC Chiles move to London in such a hurry?"

How is this relevant?

"DC Chiles and DI Patterson have never even worked together, DCI Weathers. I don't see how—"

"Would DS Frampton be able to answer my question?"

"I'm sorry, but if you're suggesting that DS Frampton would be able to tell you more about my relationship with DI Patterson, then—"

"You're right."

Lesley frowned. "I'm sorry?"

"You're right. I'm off-topic. And your DS Frampton never did work with DI Patterson. Nor did DC Chiles."

Lesley didn't know whether to feel relief or tension. "No. Once again, I'd like to know if DI Patterson has made any specific allegations about my behaviour as her manager. I've received the harassment and discrimination training. I know on what grounds she would be able to make a legitimate complaint."

"So you're saying DI Patterson's complaint isn't legitimate."

Lesley clenched her teeth. She just hoped Jill wasn't waiting for her, while she put up with this nonsense.

"That's not for me to say, DCI Weathers. All I can do is answer the allegations that have been made. And I can only do that if I'm provided with specific details of those allegations."

Weathers eyed her. "I will be speaking to DI Patterson about her complaint tomorrow morning. I'm sure I'll have more questions for you after that."

Lesley leaned back in her chair. Was that all they had? Alleged bullying and intimidation, with no specifics to back it up? How the hell had it got this far?

Did Carpenter know how thin this was? Was that why he hadn't suspended her?

But the questions about Johnny, and about Dennis...

Did Carpenter know about those?

DCI Weathers closed her laptop with a snap. "I expect you to continue to make yourself available for questioning," she said.

"Of course," Lesley replied.

"Good. You're free to leave, assuming you're able to find your way out."

CHAPTER THIRTY-TWO

"How ARE YOU FINDING IT, you being here and Mike being at home?"

Tina felt her cheek twitch as she heard DS Strunk's question. She turned away from him to look out of the car window, wondering if Mike had ever been asked the same thing when she'd been the one on leave.

She lifted a finger; she was on hold to Reece & Co, where Andy Draycott had worked. The line had just picked up.

"Reece & Co, Kayla speaking, can I help you?"

"Hello, Kayla. My name's DC Tina Abbott, from Dorset Police. I wonder if you could put me through to your HR manager, please."

"Oh, we don't have one of those."

"You don't?"

"There's only six of us here. Would be a bit of a waste for one of them not to do client work."

"Ah. Right." Tina glanced at the sarge with a shrug. He nodded; he could probably hear Kayla's voice, being right next to her in the driver's seat.

"In that case, can I speak to the person in charge, please?"

"That would be me. You thought I was a receptionist, didn't you?"

"I didn't think anything. I—"

"It's OK. I get it all the time. Woman managing an office full of blokes." Her tone shifted. "Hang on, you're police. Is this about Andy?"

"Andy Draycott. Yes. I gather someone from your firm reported him missing last—"

"That was me. Poor bastard didn't have any family to notice he'd gone. But when he hadn't turned up for work for a few days and there was no answer on his phone, I started to worry."

"You reported his disappearance to the police."

"I did. Didn't really need to though, given how it turned out."

Tina frowned. "I'm sorry?"

A sigh came down the line. "They found him. Coastguards. He'd chucked himself off the cliffs at Old Harry." A pause. "I still feel awful about not giving him more help. If we'd known, then maybe..."

Tina turned to the sarge. "Suicide," she mouthed. He nodded.

"When was Andy found?" she asked the woman.

"About a month after he went missing. He drowned, lungs full of water. I'm sorry, I'd rather not talk about it, if you don't mind." Kayla's voice was wavering.

"No. No, of course you don't have to. I'm sorry to bring it back up for you."

"Why were you calling? You don't think it was suspicious, do you?"

"Sorry? What was suspicious?"

"Andy's death. Only, the coroner seemed pretty certain. Well, according to Danesh, who went along. Danesh and Andy were mates, to an extent."

Not very good mates, if he hadn't even realised his friend was suicidal. But Tina had seen plenty of people keep their dark moods from the people around them.

"I'm sorry to have bothered you," she said. "Thank you for your help."

"Is that all?"

"Yes. Once again, I'm really sorry."

She hung up. "How was that not on the system?" she asked.

The sarge glanced at her. "The first missing bloke was found dead?"

She nodded. "Drowned. Old Harry Rocks." She thought of Ameena Khan, the lawyer murdered there, an employee of Nevin, Cross and Short. She shuddered. "So it's not him."

"No."

They continued in silence for a few moments, DS Strunk's two-year-old Toyota eating up the A35 en route to Poole. Tina had got to know him quite well while she'd been on leave. There had been two cases in her home town of Lyme Regis, two cases that her mum had somehow found herself in the middle of. Tina's brother-in-law Dougie had been involved, too, and she'd managed to worm her way in, despite being on leave.

DS Strunk seemed alright. Sure, he'd worked with DI Collingwood, the PSD officer who'd killed DCI Mackie and was now in prison on murder and corruption charges. Sure, there was the slimmest of chances he was still a PSD officer, working undercover. But she didn't believe that. It wouldn't be the best cover, for a start, not with everyone knowing he'd come straight from PSD.

She did believe that she needed to be herself with him. And she hadn't forgotten what he'd asked her, before speaking to Kayla.

She turned in her seat. "Sarge, do you mind if I ask you a question?"

He wrinkled his nose. "Sure."

She took a breath. "When Mike was at work and I was at home with our new baby, would you have asked him that question? About how he was finding it being away from his kids?"

The DS's lips parted. "Touché."

Tina let out a relieved breath. "I get asked a version of that question a lot. It does get old."

He smiled. "Sorry, Tina. If it helps, I wasn't working with your husband, which is why I didn't ask him that question. But you're right, I probably wouldn't have. And I can see how it would get on your nerves."

She smiled. "Thanks. I'm not sure my old sarge would have reacted quite like that."

Tina widened her eyes as she heard her own words. Should she have said that? She didn't mean to be disloyal to DS Frampton.

But then, she'd seen the way the old DS had looked at her when she'd got pregnant before marrying Mike. And she knew he secretly disapproved of the DCI's wife, although that could just as well be because she was a lawyer, as because she was a woman.

"What was he like, DS Frampton?" DS Strunk asked. "To work for, I mean?"

Tina frowned. Why the hell had she mentioned him? She didn't want to get drawn into comparisons.

"He was fine," she said. "Good."

He glanced at her. "I'm sorry," he said. "I'm prying, aren't I?" He smiled. "Curse of the copper."

Tina smiled thinly. She couldn't work out whether DS Strunk was just nosy, or if there was something else going on. He hadn't been like that in Lyme Regis.

"It's OK," she said. "I guess it's the kind of thing anyone would want to know when they join a new team. What your predecessor was like. What it is you'll be expected to live up to."

"You think I should live up to Dennis Frampton?"

"No. Er, no. That's not what I meant."

She didn't know what else to say. Probably best to say nothing.

He gave her another smile. "Let's change the subject, eh? How's your mum and her swimming mates?"

Bloody hell. How was shifting from asking about her kids, to asking about her last DS, to asking about her mum supposed to be changing the subject?

"She's fine," she said.

How far to Turlin Moor?

CHAPTER THIRTY-THREE

Jill let out a long breath as she reached the top of the two flights of stairs that led to the boss's office. She was late, and she needed to speak to her team, but she had to debrief the boss first.

It was her turn to pick Suzi up later; she was supposed to do it once a week. But she had a feeling she'd be calling the after-school club and asking them to keep her daughter until the end of the session.

She hated herself for it. But she'd make it up to the girl; she had a plan to make pancakes.

Her breath was back now. *Bloody fitness kick.* She walked to the DCI's office and knocked.

"Come in."

The DCI looked up from her computer as Jill entered. There was a tension in her face that dropped as she realised who it was.

That's something, at least. She was letting her daughter down, but at least her boss was pleased to see her.

Jill gave the boss a tight smile and sat in one of the chairs that faced her desk. Her office in the new building was smaller than in the old one; you'd never get the whole team in here.

"How did it go?" the DCI asked. "Did he give you anything useful?"

Another deep breath. "He did. At least, I think he did."

"He knows how Frank Kelvin died?"

Jill shook her head. "He knows – or he claims to know – where the body is. That's all."

The boss had a pen in her hand. She kept clicking it open and closed. Jill glanced at it, wondering if she could ask her to stop.

"How did he get this information?"

"Another inmate. Someone who's been released."

"You've got names?"

Jill looked glum. "Not yet. Working on it, though."

The DCI grunted. "Any information from the prison yet?"

"They keep promising the release record for the relevant dates, but we're still waiting. There's only so many times you can push. Stanley reckons that with it being Exeter, there's a good chance Sutton's informant isn't too far away."

"Bugger." The clicking accelerated. "That means Devon getting involved." The boss's right eye twitched and she slammed the pen down on the table.

Jill flinched. "If needs be I can follow that up, if it helps. I've got—"

"No. That's my job. Maybe Carpenter's." She wrinkled her nose. "Shit. Well, let's just hope it doesn't come to that."

"D'you want to know—"

"Of course I bloody do. So where has Frank Kelvin been festering all these years?"

Jill pursed her lips. The boss wasn't normally like this with her. With Hannah sometimes, yes.

With Hannah off sick, was Jill going to be the DCI's punching bag?

Suck it up, Jill. You're a DI now.

She took a breath. "It's not good."

The boss leaned back on her chair, her gaze not leaving Jill's face.

"It never is. Come on, you don't have to wrap it in cotton wool. Where is he?"

"A freezer."

"That's no surprise, he'd be decomposing goop by now if he wasn't in a freezer." The boss cocked her head. "Where is this freezer? One of the Kelvins' businesses, I assume? Easy enough to stash a locked freezer away in a warehouse somewhere."

Jill shook her head. "It's in a house. An outbuilding of a house, according to our witness."

The boss's eyes narrowed. "A house?" She looked at Jill for a moment before her eyes widened. "Oh, shit. Whose fucking house?"

"Vera Kelvin's house," Jill said. "According to Lucas Parsons, if we believe him, Frank Kelvin's remains have been hidden in a chest freezer on Vera Kelvin's property since 1993."

The boss sighed. "We need to talk to whoever gave him this information. An employee of the Kelvins, I assume. They've got enough."

"And a fair few of them are serving time."

The DCI looked at her. "But we can't."

Jill grunted. She was right; it would get back to the Kelvins, if they questioned one of their grunts about this.

Mind you, the grunt in question must know there'd be consequences for him telling Lucas Parsons what he knew.

"Hang on," the boss said. "Vera. She moved. After Arthur died. She moved from Sandbanks to Lulworth."

Jill nodded. "Maybe Frank moved with her."

"Deliberately?" The boss placed her fists on the desk, leaning forward. "I mean, does Vera Kelvin know she's been shunting her son's remains around? Or is it one of those bastards she's related to? Or someone she employs?"

Jill shrugged. "No idea, sorry. I guess the only way to find out is to ask the woman herself."

The boss dragged a hand through her short blonde hair. "Fuck. I was really hoping you wouldn't say that."

CHAPTER THIRTY-FOUR

JOHNNY PULLED up at the side of the road just outside Abbotsbury, not far from where the body had been found. Meera had been observing him during the journey, driving this strangely old-fashioned car around. It was a Vauxhall Insignia, fifteen years old, in a shade of dull brown Meera didn't think they used for cars anymore. On the back seat was a neat pile of guidebooks and atlases, and in the storage bin in the passenger door she'd found a packet of barley sugars.

"No car seats?" she asked as they got out of the car. "I thought you had two little ones."

He glanced back towards the car. "Oh, that's not mine. Alice has our car, she needs it for ferrying the kids around. This one's my dad's." His face darkened. "He doesn't use it anymore."

"Oh." Meera hadn't heard anything about Johnny's dad. Was he local? Was he still alive? "I'm sorry."

Johnny gave her a shrug. "Don't be. His health's improved since me and Alice came back. He likes spending time with the kids."

They were walking along a tree-lined lane, heading towards the

Fleet. Other than one at the pub they'd passed a mile or so back, Meera hadn't spotted any cameras.

"So you've got family locally," she said. "I understand why you came back now."

He gave her a wary look. "I'd rather not talk about it, if you don't mind."

"Oh." Meera felt her cheeks redden. "No. Yes. Of course. Sorry."

He gave her a playful slap on the arm, his expression shifting from wariness to mockery. "You need to lighten up. I don't bite, you know?" He stopped walking. "In fact, what *have* you heard about me? What are people saying?"

"Oh." *Stop blushing.* "Nothing, really." She licked her lips. "I mean, it's not really been long enough..."

Meera turned away from him and started walking, wishing she'd never asked about the car. *None of your business.*

This village was eerily quiet, no walkers out, no sign of life. Just the pretty cottages and the sound of birdsong.

They passed along the main road leading through the village and found a sign for an abbey. Johnny turned off the road, making his way through a car park.

"Where are you going?" Meera asked.

"Looking for signs of someone who might be able to help us. And that abbey might have CCTV."

"We can't even see that chapel from here."

"To get up there, you'd have to drive this way. At least, it's one of the two routes you'd have to drive."

"Which means they might have gone the other way."

He turned to her. "Why so negative?"

Meera shrugged. "Sorry."

Johnny grunted. He strode on ahead, following a path past some cottages and stopping at what looked like some sort of rural visitor attraction: the ruined abbey, a café, a few shops. There was no one around.

"There." He went towards a board holding pinned up leaflets and posters, all behind a pane of glass.

"Tell me what I'm looking at," Meera asked.

"Community groups. That's where we find the people we need." He pointed. "See?"

Meera followed Johnny's outstretched finger. He was pointing to a poster advertising a photography club.

"Maybe Anika Hythe's a member," she said, referring to the photographer who'd found the body.

"Maybe she is. But one or more of them might have gone up there before she did. Maybe the night before. Maybe they saw something."

She nodded. "Maybe." He had a point.

Johnny took some photos of the posters, not just the photography club flier but some others.

"And there's a phone number," Meera said.

"Yup." Johnny had his phone to his ear. He waggled his eyebrows; someone had answered.

"Hello," he said. "My name's DC Johnny Chiles, from Dorset Police. I was hoping I might be able to... yes? Can you give me the precise address? Brilliant. Thanks."

He lowered the phone. "We're going to visit the secretary of the photography club," he said.

"They saw something?"

A shrug. "Not as far as I know. But they might know someone who did."

CHAPTER THIRTY-FIVE

Tony Catterall lived in a narrow terraced house on the edge of Turlin Moor. Behind his house was a tall fence and behind that, a holiday park. The houses were arranged in low blocks, mostly unkempt with cracked windows and weeds in all but a few of the front gardens, if the grassy areas flanking the buildings could be described as gardens. Tina had been here before as a uniformed PC, plenty of times.

DS Strunk parked a few houses up after circling twice to find a space.

As they got out of the car, Tina wrinkled her nose. "Familiar sweet smell, Sarge."

He sniffed and nodded. "Let's just hope they're not growing it."

Tina wouldn't have been at all surprised if Zack Catterall's dad was growing marijuana; she'd seen his son's police record, after all. Now she was wishing she'd checked the dad's.

Could this turn out to be harder than they'd expected?

"Sarge," she said, putting a hand on his elbow. "Should we check out the dad on the system, before we go in there?"

DS Strunk shook his head. "We'll be fine. Just take it slow and follow my lead."

Follow my lead. Until a year ago, Strunk had been in PSD. Tina was pretty sure she had more experience of this kind of thing than he did.

But he was her boss. And it wasn't like she'd never knocked on the door of a drug dealer before.

The DS rapped on the door. Tina stood behind him. It was four years since she'd had the protection of a uniform and all the gear that came with it. Now wasn't the time to start missing it.

The door opened and a man stared at them, blinking, one hand raised to shield his eyes from the light. He wore a Dolphins T-shirt with a large stain on the chest and a tear in the shoulder.

"Fuck," he said. "Pigs. What do you want?"

The DS held up his ID. Tina followed suit.

"I'm DS Strunk, this is DC Abbott. We're here to talk about your son, Zack. I'm assuming you're Tony Catterall?"

"That's me." The man lowered his hand and screwed up his face. Clearly, he'd been sitting in a dark room; it wasn't even sunny. "What now?"

"I think it's probably best if we go inside."

Catterall coughed once, then made a deep hawking noise in his throat and spat onto his own front step. He drew the back of his hand across his mouth, then looked at it.

Tina grimaced. *You're getting soft.*

"You got a warrant?" Catterall asked.

"This isn't really the kind of situation that requires a warrant." The DS sounded puzzled. "You reported your son missing last year, is that right?"

"What? Oh, that. Yeah, don't worry about that."

"Only..." The sarge hesitated. "It's just that..."

Tina stepped forward. "Mr Catterall. We've found the body of a young man, who we believe might be your son. We wanted to speak to you to—"

"Can't be," Catterall said.

Tina ignored the harsh gaze the DS was giving her. "I'm sorry?" she said.

"Can't be." Catterall coughed. He looked past the two detectives. "Can it, you daft fucker?"

Tina turned. A young man was approaching the short, litter-strewn path to the house. A young man with bleached blonde hair and the kind of sunken features that were a dead giveaway for drug use.

A young man fitting the description of Zack Catterall.

Zack stopped walking when he saw the group gathered on his doorstep. He looked at his dad, then at DS Strunk, then Tina, then back at his dad.

"What did you tell them?"

"Nothing, lad. Don't be—"

But it was too late. Zack Catterall was already halfway down the street. And there was no way of catching up with him.

No point, either.

Shit.

Tina turned back to Catterall senior. "Why didn't you tell the police he'd come home?"

A shrug. "No point. You lot don't give a fuck about boys like my Zack. But he's not your bloody body."

CHAPTER THIRTY-SIX

PAUL MERRIMAN peered into his computer screen in his cramped study while Meera and Johnny looked on. The room was packed full of photography equipment: tripods, lenses, pilot cases holding more of the stuff, Meera assumed.

"I'm not sure how happy our members'll be," he said. "Me giving out their details like this."

Meera opened her mouth to remind him this was a murder investigation, but Johnny beat her to it.

"I'll make sure to tell my bosses how cooperative you've been," he said. "It's always a relief to find someone who's willing to give us a hand."

Not all that willing, Meera thought.

Paul looked up at Johnny, who was pacing the room now, perusing the framed photographs on the walls. Paul went back to his screen. He was writing names and addresses on a sheet of paper; a selection of names and addresses.

"Looks like you're fundraising," Johnny said, picking up a leaflet.

Paul grunted. "Rasing money for a new drone. When English

Heritage let us use it." He looked up, towards the window. The chapel was just visible behind houses, if you craned your neck.

He closed the lid of his laptop and placed a hand on the sheet of paper. Meera stepped towards him, hand outstretched.

He looked at her. He didn't move his hand.

Bloody hell.

Johnny stepped between them and slapped a twenty-pound note on top of the paper, right next to the man's thumb.

"For your fundraiser," he said with a grin. "It's not much, but..."

Paul swiped the note up and pocketed it. Meera frowned, wondering where that money would end up. Had she just witnessed Johnny bribing a witness? Or simply giving a donation?

Or both?

She felt her toes clench. This made her uneasy.

"Glad to be of help." Johnny was still grinning. He took the sheet of paper from Paul, who was holding it up for him. "I don't suppose you've added phone numbers?"

A nod. "Where we've got them, yes. And some email addresses."

Johnny clapped a hand on the man's shoulder. "Good man. We owe you one."

Paul glanced over at Meera as if only just remembering she was there. She felt an inexplicable urge to wave. She suppressed it.

"Cheers." Johnny removed the hand and strode to the door. He looked back at Merriman. "You might have just helped us solve our case."

Meera rolled her eyes and followed Johnny outside. As she climbed into the passenger seat, he smoothed the sheet of A4 out on the steering wheel.

"It's not brilliant," he said. "But it's something."

She raised an eyebrow. "So you *don't* think that bloke just blew the case open for us."

"God, no. But it'll keep the boss happy." He looked at the house. Paul Merriman stood in the doorway, looking out at them.

Meera wrinkled her nose. "We need to get back."

"We do." Johnny handed the paper to her and started the car. The names meant nothing to her, but hopefully one of these people would have seen something.

Merriman was waving as they drove away. Meera gave a small wave in return then plunged her hand into her lap.

Johnny shuddered. "God," he said. "What a wanker."

CHAPTER THIRTY-SEVEN

VISITING Vera Kelvin wasn't something Lesley had any intention of plunging into without significant planning and consideration.

Yes, the woman deserved to know about her son.

And yes, there was potentially a freezer on her property that needed examining. With any normal member of the public, Lesley and Jill would be straight there. Breaking the news. Conducting a search of the premises. In fact, for any normal member of the public, Jill would have simply done the job herself.

But Vera Kelvin wasn't any normal member of the public.

The first time they'd met had been when Lesley was investigating the death of Vera's son, Arthur, the man who'd taken over the family business years earlier when his father, Gerard, had died.

Gerard had died of natural causes. A rarity, for a man like him in a family like theirs.

Arthur had not died from natural causes. And neither, it seemed, had his brother Frank.

So before Lesley knocked on Vera's door, she needed to knock on Superintendent Carpenter's door, which she was currently doing.

But the super, it seemed, had gone home for the day.

Lesley sighed and turned back for the stairs down to her own office. Time to go home to her own family. Sharon would be home at the weekend, and Lesley needed to clear out the boxes she'd been storing in her daughter's room.

Over a year since the house move, and still there were unpacked boxes. To be fair, these hadn't moved in with her. They'd been sent down from Birmingham by her ex-husband, Terry.

She hadn't needed whatever was in those boxes for five years. Maybe the best course of action would be to chuck them away without looking at them. Too many memories.

As she arrived at her office door, she heard voices behind her. She turned to see Meera and Johnny emerging from the lift.

Johnny Chiles. Will I ever get used to you being back? Will I ever be comfortable with it?

She forced a smile. "You're back."

Meera looked away from Johnny. "Oh, boss. Sorry, I didn't know you were there."

"And would you have done anything different if you had known?"

Meera blushed. "No, boss."

"I should think not. Did you have any joy over at Chesil Beach?"

Johnny pulled a sheet of paper from the inside pocket of his jacket. Was he wearing the same blue suit he'd worn before going to London?

"We found the photography club, boss," he said. "Got contact details for some of the regulars, people who go up to the chapel a lot."

"One or more of them might have seen something," Meera added.

Lesley nodded. "Good work. Make sure you let DS Strunk know, and you can start following up in the morning. Meanwhile, you've both got young children. Get yourselves home."

"Yes, boss," they chorused.

Lesley turned into her office and gathered her things. Once again, she hadn't eaten, but there was a cereal bar in the glove locker of her car; health food, as far as she was concerned.

She checked her watch as she left the building. *Damn.* Clearing out Sharon's room would have to wait. She dialled Elsa's number.

"Hey, sweetie," her wife said. "How's your day been?"

"Pretty shit, if you must know. But you don't need me grumbling about Hannah fucking Patterson."

"That bad?"

Lesley grimaced. "I'll fill you in later. Look, I need to call in on Dennis on my way home. We've got a new case I hope he can shed some light on."

"I'm still in the office. To be honest, I'm quite relieved you called. Makes me feel less guilty about working late."

Lesley laughed. There were upsides to being married to a solicitor. "I'm just glad you've got enough work to keep you busy."

She stopped walking, her car just ahead. That had come out all wrong.

"Sorry, Els," she said. "I didn't mean—"

"It's OK. Things were tough when I started out on my own, now they're not. That's not your fault."

And it wasn't. Elsa had found herself a small but suitably professional office in Christchurch, not far from the quay. She'd started picking up clients in Hampshire. Clients who knew nothing about her previous job with Nevin, Cross and Short, where she'd represented Arthur Kelvin.

And importantly, clients who'd been arrested by Hampshire and Isle of Wight Police. Which meant fewer opportunities for Lesley and Elsa to find themselves on opposite sides of an interview room.

"You keep on working, love," Lesley said. "I'll let you know when I'm leaving Dennis's. Maybe we can go for a drink in Southbourne."

"Pushing the boat out?"

Lesley was at her car now. She felt her limbs go heavy with the thought of what she needed to discuss with her wife.

"Something like that," she said.

CHAPTER THIRTY-EIGHT

TINA TURNED to face DS Strunk as he pulled into the car park at Dorset Police HQ. They'd passed the boss's car on the way in, and all but two of the offices were in darkness. The building was closed for the evening.

She didn't care. With Zack Catterall ruled out, there was a family out there with a dead husband, son or brother. They needed to know.

"I think we should track down the third guy's family," she said to the sarge's back as he climbed out of the car.

He stopped moving but didn't speak.

She got out of the car and faced him across the roof.

"Mark Ashforth," she said. "That was his name. His wife reported him missing." She shook her head. "Maybe she'll be able to identify him."

DS Strunk looked at her, his jaw slack. "You do remember what they did to him, don't you?"

Tina nodded. The victim had had his teeth and fingertips removed, and it was a miracle the wound running from his forehead to the side of his lip hadn't taken his eye out.

"The PM's due in the morning," he said. "Pathology will clean him up afterwards, make him look presentable. Maybe we show him to her then. Unless the DNA's come back already."

"You don't think it's him."

The DS locked his car and started walking towards Tina's, which was all alone at the far end of the car park.

"What are you doing?" she asked.

He turned to her. "Walking you to your car."

She resisted a laugh. "We're in possibly the most secure car park in Dorset. And it's not 1953."

He smiled. "This isn't a security measure, Tina. I know you can handle yourself. Far better than me, I imagine."

Not wrong there. He'd started walking again. Tina picked up her own pace to catch up.

"So, why?" she asked. "I'm perfectly capable of walking to my own car."

He gave her a sidelong glance. "I'm making sure you don't go back into the office."

"You're..." She frowned. "You don't trust me."

His nostrils flared. "I know what you're like, Tina. You're keen. You're a bloody good detective. Hell, I'm surprised you're not my boss by now."

Tina suppressed a smile. "You're telling me to go home."

They were at her car now. DS Strunk put a hand on the bonnet. "I am. I just got a message from the DCI, saying we need to regroup in the morning. We need more information before we speak to your taxi driver's wife, Tina. At the very least, we need to plan what we'll say to her. Right now, there's nothing concrete."

"You weren't worried about that when we were looking at Zack Catterall."

"We had a starting point with Catterall. A record. Potential involvement with organised criminals."

She sighed. He was right. "And Zack Catterall and Mark Ashforth are very different people."

"They are."

Tina pulled out her key fob and unlocked her car. If she headed home now, she might just see Louis before bed. Not Daisy – at least, hopefully not Daisy – but maybe Louis.

And she could talk to Mike about the case.

"Night, Sarge," she said.

He smiled. She wondered if he had a partner or a family to go back to.

"Night, Tina," he replied. "See you in the morning."

She winked. "Bright and early."

CHAPTER THIRTY-NINE

LESLEY ALLOWED herself to relax into the armchair opposite Dennis's. They were in a different space this evening. Not the front room, where they normally chatted, but a conservatory tacked onto the back of the dining room of his modest semi.

"This is nice," she said, looking ahead of them through the windows. "You've been gardening." She caught herself. "Or Pam has."

Dennis chuckled, then pushed his specs up his nose. He wore a threadbare navy sweater over faded jeans. Lesley had never seen Dennis in jeans, nor had she ever expected to.

"It's all Pam," he said. "She's always been the gardener. I've got a black thumb." He held up the thumb of his right hand. "See?"

Dennis's thumb was the same colour as the rest of his hand, but the point was made. Lesley took a bite of the Victoria Sponge Pam had offered her on arrival, followed by a long sip of her coffee. It wasn't instant, which was something.

"Well, it looks very nice," she said. "Not that I'd know. All we've got is a square of paving and an expanse of grass, which suits me just fine."

Dennis shook his head. Lesley stuffed the last of her cake into her mouth – it really was delicious – and heard her stomach growl.

Dennis raised an eyebrow. "Want some more? You never manage to eat when you've got a new case."

"How do you know I'm here about a new case?"

He raised his eyebrows. "It's not our usual day. You sent Johnny and Katie to talk to me about it. And you've got that air to you. Ten thousand things going through your brain at once."

Lesley felt movement behind her and turned to see Pam placing a tray on the dining table, the other side of the open patio doors. Dennis's wife was as well turned-out as usual: mustard-yellow shirt over brown trousers that accentuated her slim legs. Lesley knew that Pam was only a few years younger than Dennis but would never have guessed it from looking at them.

Pam looked up from the tray. "I made you a sandwich, Lesley. I hope tuna's OK. And there's more cake, of course."

"Tuna's perfect. Thank you." Lesley had never been even the slightest bit of a fussy eater. Decades of policing had taught her to eat what she could, when she could. And she knew how good Pam's sandwiches were.

Pam and Dennis shared a conspiratorial look. He gave her a broad smile, and she retreated towards the inside of the house.

"You don't deserve her," Lesley said as she walked to the tray to fetch her sandwich. "Want some more cake?"

He laughed. "Offering me cake in my own home." He patted his stomach. "Need to watch my weight now the job isn't keeping me active."

Dennis, formerly DS Dennis Frampton, had retired two years earlier after sustaining an injury while attempting to rescue Lesley's daughter. Lesley was still surprised at how well he'd taken to it.

"I thought you'd taken up golf," she said.

"Have you seen the pace at which golf is played? And I don't imagine taking up running would be the best idea at my time of life."

Lesley finished the first half of the tuna sandwich. It was

bloody good. "It doesn't have to be running," she said. "You're within spitting distance of some of the best walking country in Dorset."

He nodded. "Ah, yes. Yes, I've tried rambling."

"You didn't like it?"

"Oh, I loved it. But I couldn't keep up with Pam." He leaned towards her and lowered his voice. "Can't have her thinking I'm a slow coach, so I used the injury as an excuse."

She glanced down at his leg. "I thought that was all healed."

"Doesn't mean it can't be useful from time to time. Now, tell me about this case."

Lesley had been about to start eating her second slice of sponge cake. She put the plate down on the table between them. "Actually, it's two cases."

"Two teams, two cases. But it'll be one of them that's got you knocking on my door at no notice."

Lesley frowned. "Oh, shit. I hope I didn't inter—"

He held up a hand. "Nothing to interrupt. I lead a very dull existence these days. And, please..."

Lesley sighed. *The swearing*. She thought they'd got past this. "Apologies, Dennis. But it's both cases this time. Kind of."

"How so?"

"Well, I'm SIO on the MCIT case because Hannah Patterson's gone off sick with 'stress'." She did air quotes with her fingers. "She's causing trouble again."

"What kind of trouble?"

Lesley shook her head. "I can't talk about it. Believe me, I'd love to. But I can't. Anyway, the upshot is I'm leading her team for now."

"What's the case? Is it the Chesil Beach body? Do you have an ID for your victim yet?"

"Not yet. His teeth and fingertips have been removed."

Dennis sucked his teeth. "Indeed. Poor chap."

She nodded, having just put a mouthful of cake in her mouth. Lesley had attempted to speak through Pam's cake before, and it hadn't ended well. It had been two months before she'd been offered food again.

"He's got a wound, too," she said. "Inflicted to his face before he died. We're waiting for Pathology to tell us how long before."

Dennis nodded; Johnny and Katie would have told him. "Because if he was walking around like that for a while before his death, someone might recognise it."

"Exactly."

"And you suspect organised crime involvement, hence the desire to make it hard to identify him."

"Hard, but not impossible," she said. "We're fast-tracking DNA analysis."

Dennis nodded. "So what is it I can help with?"

Lesley swallowed a bite of cake. *So good.* "It's not the MCIT case. It's the Cold Cases one."

"I haven't seen anything about that."

"You won't have." Lesley glanced towards the dining room and lowered her voice. "An inmate of HMP Exeter claims to have knowledge about Frank Kelvin's death."

Dennis flinched, then frowned. "But Frank left the country," he said. He screwed up his lips, thinking back. "There was a brief period when he went off the radar, and we thought someone had killed him, but then the family told us they'd had contact with him from Spain."

Lesley nodded. "I don't suppose you know which family member made that report?"

Dennis frowned. "I was in Uniform still in 1993. Not all that far off moving into CID, but not there yet. And I was way too far down the pecking order to have had sight of a case like that." A shadow crossed his face. "Yes, way too far down the pecking order."

Lesley had expected this. But she knew how the police rumour mill worked. "Did you hear anything about it at the time?"

He pursed his lips. "There was talk, of course. The assumption was that a rival had killed him. As far as I remember, CID searched for his body, but there weren't any leads, so..." He shrugged.

"And then his family reported him safe and well in Spain."

"They did. Not that I was party to any of that, of course. But it got around." He looked up. "And then old Gerard died. Less than six months later, as I remember."

Lesley nodded. "Thirteen weeks after Frank supposedly turned up in Spain."

"Of natural causes."

"Throat cancer."

Dennis shook his head. "I think there was a sweepstake on how Gerard Kelvin would eventually meet his end. Natural causes wasn't even on it."

"Do you think Gerard's death was suspicious?"

"Good gracious, no. Just one of those things." A smile played at Dennis's lips. "You should have seen the funeral. Pomp and circumstance doesn't even come close to describing it. Three-quarters of Dorset CID was there, in the hope of spotting some targets who'd gone to ground. And a good chunk of *them* were bent." He sniffed.

"Corruption was common?"

Dennis looked up. "Oh, not like it had been twenty years earlier. But yes. There was plenty of it about." He shivered.

"Would you be able to put me in touch with anyone who was on the investigation into Frank's disappearance? Anyone who was watching the Kelvins at the time?"

He eyed her. "Why?"

Lesley licked her lips. "The information we've had about the whereabouts of Frank Kelvin's body. It's... Well, let's just say I want to get as much background information as I can before beginning any physical investigation."

"What's the information?"

"It's probably wrong," she said. "It's certainly ridiculous. Our informant, he—"

"What's the information?"

Lesley took a breath. It was getting dark in Dennis's garden.

Pam's garden. She wondered if Elsa was still working or if she was in a bar, waiting for her.

Sorry, sweetie.

"This is absolutely confidential," she said.

He gave her a look. "Really?"

She closed her eyes. *Idiot.* This was Dennis. The man she'd despised when she'd first arrived in Dorset, then come to trust.

She took a breath. "Our informant says that Frank's remains have been stored in a freezer."

She paused. This really was ridiculous. But Jill believed it, and Lesley trusted Jill.

"In a freezer," she repeated, "on the property of Vera Kelvin."

Dennis gave out a spluttering laugh, then clapped his hand to his mouth.

"Really?" he said.

"Really."

"My word." He looked away from her, towards the darkening windows. "My word."

"Is that your reaction? *My word*?"

"What else is there to say? If this is true... My goodness, Lesley, if this is true, then it's the biggest case in the history of Dorset CID."

"I'm sure you're exaggerating."

"I'm sure I'm not." He leaned towards her. "I won't repeat a word of this to anyone. But I know who you need to speak to."

"You do?"

"You do. And you probably won't like it."

Lesley sighed. "It'll be Carpenter. Or someone from PSD."

Dennis shook his head. "No one you've met. Although you do know his son. Quite well, in fact."

"Who?"

"Eric Chiles. Retired DI Eric Chiles."

"Johnny's dad?" she said.

A nod. "Johnny thinks his dad was an ordinary sergeant. But he was a Vice officer. Undercover, until he was forced to retire in 2004."

"Forced to retire?" This sounded ominous.

"I don't know the details. And nor will Johnny. But I can tell you that Eric Chiles was leading a long-term investigation into the Kelvin family and the corrupt officers who were on their payroll. If you want to know more about Frank Kelvin, he's your man."

CHAPTER FORTY

JOHNNY FLUNG his keys into the bowl on the hall table, missed, cursed under his breath, bent over to pick them up and threw again.

"Bugger." He picked the keys up and placed them in the bowl. One of those days.

He dropped his bag on the floor and was just straightening up when a small body hit his legs.

"Daddy!"

Johnny smiled. He rubbed his forehead – *ignore the bloody headache* – and picked his son up.

"Hey, buddy. What are you doing still up?"

The boy, Brandon, giggled. "Ganda's here."

"Ah."

Johnny slung his son up and over his shoulder, prompting yet more giggles, and pushed open the door to the living room. Eric was inside, watching *The One Show*.

Brandon wriggled out of Johnny's grasp and slid onto the floor. He ran to his grandad and crawled up into his lap.

"Hey-ho, sonny Jim. I thought your mum had put you to bed?"

The boy said nothing, just hesitated and shook his head. He looked up warily at Johnny, who held out a hand.

"Come on," he said. "Let's get you up to your room."

Brandon stuck his lower lip out further than Johnny thought it was possible for a lower lip to go.

"If you think I'm falling for that act..."

Eric tickled Brandon on his tummy. The boy, just four years old and already settling into a Dorset school despite his London accent, squirmed.

"Now," Johnny said, injecting gentle firmness into his voice.

Jesus, if half the arseholes I arrested when I was in the Met could see me now...

"There you are. Why didn't you call?"

Johnny turned to see his wife Alice standing in the doorway, a nappy bag in hand. He glanced at her and wrinkled his nose.

"Don't worry about that. I wasn't expecting you to be late on your first day."

He sighed. Alice was a hairdresser. Sure, she worked late hours sometimes, but she'd gone part-time when they'd moved to London. And she hadn't found a job here yet.

He hoped that would change soon. She hated being stuck at home all day. Especially with Eric in the habit of turning up unannounced.

He turned to his dad. "How did you get here, Dad? I've got your car."

Eric grinned. "Veronica from two doors down. I think she's got a crush on me. She was going out to Dorchester and said she'd give me a lift."

"But Dorchester's in the opposite direction."

Eric shrugged. "That's what I said, but she was having none of it. Either she's still driving the wrong way and wondering where the hell Dorchester is, or she's got a soft spot for me."

Johnny laughed. "Oh, Dad."

"You still haven't answered my question." Alice was glaring at him now.

He swallowed. "Al, love. I'm so sorry. We've got a new case, a meaty one. Body at—"

"St Catherine's Chapel above Chesil Beach," said Alice. "We know. There's been nothing else on the local news. I thought that Sadie Dawes would have moved onto bigger things by now."

Johnny shrugged. He'd only crossed paths with Sadie Dawes the once, but he'd heard plenty about her from Dennis. Someone to avoid.

"I should have called, I know," he said. "I'm sorry. But you know what CID is li—"

"Oh I have no problem with you being late," she replied. "You think I'm not used to it? I just prefer if you keep me in the loop."

He nodded. "I will, next time." A pause. "Which will probably be tomorrow."

Her mouth cracked into a smile and she went to hit him with the nappy bag, then pulled back. "You'll never change." She looked over at their son, who was lying on his stomach as close to the TV as it was possible to get, chin propped on his hands.

"If he wasn't trying to wangle a late night he'd be complaining that it's not CBeebies," she said. "But at least you're here at the perfect time to put him back to bed." She left the room, humming under her breath.

Eric, still in his armchair, was chuckling. "Oh, you got yourself in trouble there, boy."

"It's not like that."

"No? Yes, it bloody well is, son. Pardon my French in front of the little 'un. Long hours, getting obsessed with the job. Been there, got the T-shirt, as they say."

"You were a desk sergeant, Dad." Johnny walked over to Brandon and hauled him up, ignoring the boy's complaints. "You worked regular shifts."

A shadow crossed Eric's face. "It wasn't always that simple. Your mother didn't always understand." He frowned. "Besides, have you not heard of overtime?"

Johnny shrugged. "So is she giving you a lift home again?"

Eric frowned. "Sorry?"

Johnny shifted Brandon on his shoulder. The boy's eyelids were growing heavy. "Veronica. From two doors down."

"Ah." Eric smiled. "Her. No, I wouldn't impose. You'll take me home though, won't you, son?"

Johnny sighed. He'd so been looking forward to grabbing a bottle of beer from the fridge and sitting down in front of Sky Sports. Maybe a movie if that was what Alice preferred.

It looked like his evening wasn't going to be so simple.

CHAPTER FORTY-ONE

"Els." Lesley hurried over to where her wife was sitting at the back of their favourite Southbourne café-bar. "I'm sorry."

Elsa stood up and kissed her. "What for?"

Lesley gestured at Elsa's glass of wine. "For being late. How long have you been here?"

"Five minutes." Elsa eyed the glass. "Do I drink that fast? Bugger, have I got a problem?"

Lesley grabbed her hand and kissed it. "You don't have a problem. You're just a thirsty woman at the end of a long day. I think you're just about perfect."

Elsa's eyes widened. "Perfect, me? What did I do to deserve such praise?"

Lesley shrugged. "Have you got all night?"

"Well, I have actually, but I have to admit I'm starving. So I'm happy to forgo having my ego massaged, if we can order."

"Of course." Lesley sat down opposite her and picked up a menu.

They perused the menu in silence for a few moments, Lesley wondering why she bothered. They came here so often she knew the menu by heart, and she always ordered the same thing.

"Tapas for me," she said. "Want to join me? We can share."

Elsa frowned. "I don't do sharing food, and you know it. Don't you remember what happened the first time we went for Chinese?"

Lesley blushed. She'd found it impossible to believe there were people who didn't just dive into everything when eating with others in a Chinese restaurant. It had been a bloody good job their relationship was already well established at that point.

They ordered, and Lesley's wine arrived within minutes. As she sipped, she forced herself to relax. *Best get it over with.*

"Elsa," she said.

Elsa looked at her across the rim of her glass. "That sounds ominous. What have you done?" She narrowed her eyes. "Is this why you were being so nice to me?"

Lesley shook her head. "No. I meant all those things, honestly. But there is something I need to talk to you about."

"Uh-oh." Elsa put her glass down. She spotted the look on Lesley's face, and her own features shifted to mirror it. "What? What's happened?" She put a hand over her wife's. "Are you sick?"

"No. It's nothing like that. It's... it's work."

Lesley watched Elsa's face change from concern to irritation. "Work."

Lesley nodded.

Elsa licked her lips. "By which I don't imagine you're talking about someone you arrested today who might be about to become my next client."

She shook her head.

A sigh. "You're talking about the Kelvins, aren't you? Bloody Arthur Kelvin and his fucking arsehole wankers of a family."

Lesley looked at her wife. She didn't talk like that, not normally. This was getting to her. Maybe even scaring her.

Lesley reached out. Elsa pulled back. Lesley managed to graze a fingertip.

"You don't need to be worried," she said. "It's not something new. It's not something that will affect you."

"So why the hell are you asking me about it?"

"I'm sorry. It's... it's delicate. We don't know yet if the information we have is correct. But..." She lowered her voice. "Have you heard of someone called Frank Kelvin?"

Elsa shook her head. "No. Is he a nephew, or a grandson, or something? Taking over the family firm now the sainted Arthur is dead." She grunted. "I thought that was Vera's job."

"Not a nephew, or a grandson. A brother."

"A what?"

"Frank Kelvin is – was – Arthur Kelvin's brother. He disappeared in 1993. We thought he'd gone to Spain. Vera Kelvin told the police he'd gone to Spain. But we now think he was killed."

"So why would Vera say he'd gone to Spain?"

"That's what I need to find out."

"So how have you suddenly found out?" Elsa asked. "Has he washed up somewhere? Has he... oh." Her eyes widened. "He's the body at St Catherine's Chapel."

"He's not. That's a separate case."

"So you've got two bodies?"

Lesley shook her head. "It's not... I can't..." She leaned forward. "Look, you know what it's like. I can't share the details with you. With anyone."

"But you've just told me Frank Kelvin was murdered."

Lesley glanced around the bar. "We shouldn't be having this conversation here."

"But we are."

Lesley looked at her wife. Her body language had closed off; her arms were wrapped around her waist, and she was breathing heavily.

"I'm sorry, Els. Please don't."

"You know this triggers me. You know how hard it was for me to get away from that man. That family. The only way I keep myself from being scared is to not think about it."

Lesley slumped back in her seat, just as the waitress arrived with their food. They watched in silence as she put the plates down and walked away.

"I'm sorry, love," Lesley said. She reached a hand across the table.

Elsa didn't move her own hands from her body. Lesley watched her for a moment. *Bloody idiot.* She should have known the effect bringing up this subject would have.

Elsa picked up her knife and fork. "Look," she said. "You clearly have something you want to ask me about. So can you just ask me, and then we can try to enjoy our meal?"

Lesley swallowed. "I'm sorry. I should have—"

"Please. Stop fucking apologising and ask me."

"OK," Lesley said. She thought through what she knew about Frank Kelvin's death. About Vera Kelvin. How could she make this simple?

"One question," she said. "And then I'll never ask you about it again."

"Good."

"In 1993, was your old firm representing the Kelvins?"

Elsa frowned. "*That's it?* You can ask Aurelia Cross that."

"I'm not sure she'd give me an honest answer."

"She'd have to. She's not obliged to tell you the details, but she has to confirm whether or not a given client is, or was, on the firm's client list."

Lesley nodded. "And were they? The Kelvins, in 1993?"

Elsa sighed. "Of course they were."

"Of course?"

"I think if the Kelvins had previously worked with another law firm, we'd know about it. You'd have investigated the deaths of the partners, I imagine."

"You really are still scared, aren't you?"

Elsa's body softened. She dropped her knife and fork. "Yes."

Lesley moved her chair round so it was next to Elsa's. She put an arm around Elsa's shoulders.

"I'm sorry."

"Don't."

"I know you're angry with me, but—"

Elsa shook her head. She wiped her cheek. "Not that. Don't be nice to me." She looked towards the bar. The waitress who'd brought their food was watching; she quickly looked away. "If you're nice to me, I'll cry."

"Right." Lesley withdrew her arm. She moved her chair back to its original spot.

Elsa picked up her fork again. She started to eat. "Go on," she said. "Eat your tapas." She gave Lesley a thin smile. "But don't expect me to share any of my pasta with you."

CHAPTER FORTY-TWO

"Are you sure about this?"

Jackie looked up at Yiannis. He was standing next to her in the baggage reclaim hall at Gatwick, his gaze shifting from the conveyor belt to her and back again.

"No," she replied. "But I've got no choice, have I?"

He frowned. "I think you have."

She shook her head. "Whoever that man is, what if he's got a family? A partner, kids, parents? They need to know."

"But your own safety... you've spent over a year protecting yourself. As soon as you come forward, they'll find you."

The carousel started to move, and the crowd pushed forward. Jackie and Yiannis stayed put.

"I've been thinking about that," she said. "That detective I spoke to in Cumbria."

"Zoe Finch?"

"No. The other one, DCI Clarke. She said they could protect me."

He frowned. "And you believe her?"

She turned to him, ignoring the impatient travellers pushing past them. "I can't live the rest of my life like this, Yiannis. Hiding away, not working. Not having any friends."

"If you give evidence, they'll kill you."

"We don't know that. The police will know more." She put a hand on his arm. "This is about what's right, love. I just wouldn't feel comfortable if I didn't come forward."

He took a long, shaky breath. "I just want you to be safe."

She gave him a smile. Her limbs felt heavy, and her brain was like mush. She had no idea if she was being reckless. But she knew she couldn't do nothing.

"You don't have to come with me," she said. "No point in you putting yourself at risk. You could go to London, disappear. Go back to Norway."

He shook his head. "If they come for me, it'll be to get at you. People like that can find me wherever I am. And if I'm not with you, I won't know you're OK."

Jackie squeezed his hand. "I do love you, you know."

His expression softened. "And I love you."

She reached up and stroked his cheek. It was rough with two days' stubble.

"It'll be alright," she said. "I'll speak to DCI Clarke, tell her what I saw. The police will find us somewhere safe to stay."

He sighed. "You've been watching too many movies."

The conveyor belt was empty now except for four items: a battered cardboard box that looked like it had spent the whole day there, an anonymous black rucksack, and their two suitcases. Both were new, bought in Edinburgh six months ago. Cheap and nondescript, unlike the set of matching lime green designer luggage Jackie had owned in her old life.

Yiannis stepped forward and grabbed the two bags. He wheeled them back to her and she took one.

She offered him another smile, which he ignored.

"Come on," he said, his voice dull. "Let's find out if we can get a train to Bournemouth."

CHAPTER FORTY-THREE

Lesley rolled her shoulders as she waited for the lights to change on Poole Road. Every day she sat in this jam, and every day she told herself she was going to find a better route to work.

But the satnav always said this was quickest. And the satnav, as far as Lesley was concerned, was God.

She reached out for her phone in its holder and hit the speed dial button for her old colleague DI Zoe Finch. This wasn't a topic she wanted to discuss with anyone from Dorset Police. And definitely not with Elsa, after last night.

"Lesley!" Zoe's Brummie accent rang out from the speaker, making Lesley instantly feel at home. "To what do I owe this honour?"

Lesley scoffed. "Do I call you that infrequently?"

"It's been a while. But to be fair, it's been a while since I last called you. So we're kind of quits, I'd say."

Lesley smiled. "Where are you right now?"

"I'm in my car, just turned off the A595 towards the Hub."

"That's not enough. I want the view."

"Oh, that. Hills, fells, the usual Cumbria views. I can just about glimpse the sea in my rear-view mirror. And it's just starting to rain. What about you?"

"I'm in one of Bournemouth's most irritating regular traffic jams."

"Let me guess. County Gates Gyratory?"

Lesley laughed. "I just left that behind. Remarkably clear this morning."

"But now you're paying for it. Let me guess, you're crawling towards Homebase and John Lewis and then you've got that weird right turn where you feel as if you're going the wrong way."

The laugh intensified. "How the hell do you know that?"

"I've paid a few visits to your neck of the woods, remember. The road system left its mark, it's just so illogical."

Lesley moved forward two car lengths, then stopped. "Sometimes all this traffic makes me feel like I'm back in Brum."

"Uh-uh. Have you forgotten the Aston Expressway when you're going in the wrong direction? Or Five Ways in rush hour?"

"It's always rush hour in Birmingham," Lesley said.

"It bloody is. Although sometimes I'd kill for a dual carriageway or a set of temporary lights that were there because of a construction project and not just Cumberland Council filling in some potholes."

"You miss civilisation?"

"Oh, I do. I bloody do. Can you imagine what it's like having only two curry houses to choose from?"

Lesley laughed out loud. "We haven't got that many of those in Southbourne. It's all café-bars and tapas. Moseley-on-Sea."

"Sounds pretty good to me. Anyway, you didn't call to discuss curry houses and traffic jams. You need to bend my ear about something too sensitive to discuss with Dennis."

The traffic ahead started to move. Lesley reached the second roundabout and turned right, just as Zoe had described.

"The Cumbria air has made you a very perceptive woman, Zoe Finch," she said.

"Something like that. Look, I'm in the car park at the Hub and I can see Fiona's in her office. You'll have to make this quick."

"Right. OK. Well, this is something I have discussed with Dennis, as it happens. Something Dennis told me."

"He's more use to you now he's retired than he was when he was your DS."

Zoe had a point. A conversation Dennis had overheard at his golf club had helped them solve their last cold case.

"He has his uses," Lesley said. "But this is about Johnny Chiles."

"The one who transferred to the Met."

The traffic slowed again. Lesley dragged a hand through her hair; she was going to be late.

"He's back," she said. "He wasn't happy in London, and his dad's ill, so he requested a transfer back to Dorset."

"That's good, isn't it? More resource."

Lesley glanced at the phone. She'd never told Zoe why Johnny had moved to the Met. The only other person who knew the full story was Dennis.

The fewer people who know, the better.

"It is," she said. "But it's not actually about Johnny. It's his dad, Eric."

"His dad."

"He's a retired sergeant. Well, that's what Johnny thinks. It's what I thought until yesterday."

"He's not a retired sergeant?"

Lesley licked her lips. "He was actually a DI, in what was then the Vice team. He took a desk sergeant job so he could observe the activities of crime gangs and, more specifically, the dodgy coppers they had on their payroll."

"So he was PSD?"

"They didn't have PSD in those days. But yes, effectively he was PSD."

"When was this?"

"He retired in 2004. He took the desk sergeant job in the early eighties."

A whistle came down the line. "That's a long time to keep a secret like that."

Lesley nodded. She'd reached the top of the hill where she turned left onto Herbert Avenue. At last, she was close to leaving Poole behind.

"It is," she said. "Anyway, we've got a new case. Bloke called Frank Kelvin, brother of Arthur. We thought he'd emigrated in 1993, but we've got a witness saying he was murdered. And Dennis thinks that Eric Chiles might know something about it."

"Is this Eric still alive? Is he compos mentis enough to talk to you?"

"He is. The only illness he has is physical." Lesley realised she hadn't even registered what was wrong with Eric. "But the question is, do I tell Johnny?"

Silence.

"Zoe?"

"Sorry. Just getting out of the car. The super's beckoning. You say Johnny's back, but is he in the Cold Cases team, or MCIT?"

"MCIT."

"Well, you don't need to tell him."

Lesley frowned. "Surely he deserves—"

"This is family stuff," Zoe said. "Yes, it's a bloody long time to keep a secret like that, but that's what Eric chose to do. And what would Johnny gain from knowing the truth?"

"But he might hear from another source."

"What other source? Who knows?"

"Just me and Dennis, as far as I know. Superintendent Carpenter, maybe."

"So he's not going to hear from them. If he learns about this from anyone, it should be his dad."

"But his dad lied to him." Lesley thought about the lies she'd told her team about Johnny. The reasons for his transfer. The lies she'd told Carpenter.

"That's their business," Zoe said. "Look, I know a bit about what it's like for a family to have secrets. To lie to each other."

"Your mum," Lesley said. Zoe's mum had been an alcoholic.

"Yeah. And... well, and other stuff. But the only person someone should hear it from, if someone they love has been lying to them, is that someone. If Eric wants to tell Johnny, that's his business. Not yours."

Lesley sighed. "You're right."

"Sorry if it wasn't what you wanted to hear. Look, I've got to go. Good luck with the case."

The line went dead as Lesley joined the A3049 and finally picked up speed. Normally, this was the point where her mood lightened.

Today, not so much.

CHAPTER FORTY-FOUR

"Who's a gorgeous girl?"

Tina tickled Daisy under the chin and the baby giggled. She shouted something unintelligible and slapped Tina's cheek with her chubby fingers.

"Ouch. You're getting strong."

"She is." Mike appeared at her shoulder and reached out to take Daisy from her. "Come on, stinky. You need your nappy changed."

The baby shrieked and reached out for Tina. Mike held her to him, making shushing noises. Daisy reached over his shoulder as he walked away, crying now.

Tina swallowed the lump in her throat. She sank into one of the two chairs they'd squeezed into their tiny kitchen and put her head in her hands.

Christ, this was hard. Harder than it had been with Louis.

She frowned. *Give yourself a break, idiot.* It was only her second day. On her second day back at work after having Louis, she'd cried all the way to Winfrith.

Not that it was all that far, from their house in Sandford. She checked her watch: half past seven. Time to get moving.

"Mummy."

Tina looked up to see Louis standing in the doorway, clutching Mr Bear by the toy's one good ear, as usual. Behind him was the box with his train set. He'd dragged it from the living room, which currently looked like an explosion in a branch of Toys R Us.

"Hey, Louis." She reached out and he walked towards her, his expression wary.

"Mummy play trains with Lou-lou."

She felt her stomach dip. "I'm sorry, sweetheart." She sank onto the floor and knelt beside him, a hand on his shoulder. She desperately wanted to hug him, but knew he'd only cry more when that hug ended.

He frowned at her. "Mummy go to police."

She nodded.

"Solve mudders."

Tina suppressed a laugh. "Not just murders, sweetheart. Mummy does other things at work, too."

But yes. Mainly solving 'mudders'. Where had he got that from?

"Is he on about solving murders again?" Mike was in the doorway. No sign of Daisy. He spotted Tina's questioning look. "She's in her cot. I wanted to wish my wife a proper goodbye, without being covered in dribble."

Tina smiled. She stood up, grabbing hold of Louis's hand and walked over to Mike. She put a hand on his chest. He winked at her.

She felt her stomach flutter. Mike was still as gorgeous as when she'd started working with him five years ago. Light brown skin with barely a blemish, dark brown eyes she could lose herself in. His hair wasn't the close crop he'd had back then; he seemed to be growing a modern Mohican, which she was in two minds about. But even after two kids, he still made her heart race.

"I hope your day goes smoothly," he said, after kissing her gently on the lips. Louis was tugging at her hand, muttering something about trains.

"Why don't you take them on the Swanage Railway?" she said, keeping her voice low.

His eyes widened. "Tina Abbott, you are a bloody genius." He held her head in both hands and kissed her forehead.

"I know." She gave him a wink. "But don't swear in front of him, yeah? He copies things."

Mike winced. "Sh... I mean yes, you're right. At least you'll get your quota, with the sarge and his swear box gone."

"You'd be surprised. I think he tamed the DCI."

Mike laughed. "Never."

She smiled. "Anyway, I promise not to be too late tonight." She looked into his eyes. "We can put the kids to bed, get an early night."

He cocked his head, frowning. "One day back at work, and you're knackered already."

She shook her head, and recognition appeared on his face.

"Oh," he said. He looked down at Louis, then picked the boy up. "Steam train today?"

"Yeah!" Louis clapped his hands in excitement. He mimed pulling on a cord. "Woo, woo!"

"Woo, woo!" repeated Mike and Tina in unison.

Tina pulled back and slid around them towards the front door. She was going to be late.

Mike grabbed her hand as she passed. "A steam train and... and an early night, all on the same day. I really am the luckiest man alive."

She shook her head. "Replace the steam train with solving mudders. *I'm* the luckiest woman alive."

CHAPTER FORTY-FIVE

LESLEY WAS SURPRISED to find only Nathan, Meera and Johnny in the MCIT team room when she arrived.

She scanned the room. "No Tina?"

Nathan shrugged. "I'm sure she'll be here soon."

Lesley glanced at Johnny. If anyone was late, she'd have expected it to be him. "OK. Briefing in here at eight thirty, OK?"

"No problem, boss," Nathan replied.

Lesley stuck her head around the door of Jill's office. No sign of the DI yet. That wasn't such a bad thing; she had things to look into before she spoke to Jill.

She fired up her computer and opened the intelligence database, inputting a search for *Kelvin.*

Bloody hell. The entries went on for eight pages. She narrowed it down to *Frank Kelvin.*

Only three entries. Two from 1993, relating to his disappearance: the initial investigation and the report of him being alive and well in Spain. Allegedly.

Why had they taken the word of Vera Kelvin? Had she produced some sort of evidence? Photoshop would have been around in 1993 to fake a photograph of Frank in Spain, but it would have been crude.

She opened up the record. There was a document attached: a letter from police in Malaga saying that Frank Kelvin had presented himself at a station and shown his passport.

She frowned. Passport technology wasn't as sophisticated in 1993, but it wasn't the Dark Ages. And the Kelvins would have known plenty of forgers.

Vera, why didn't you want us looking for your son?

Was this related to Gerard's death? To Arthur's inheritance of the family business? Had Vera had one son killed in furtherance of the other's interests? Or had Arthur stage-managed the whole thing?

Arthur bloody Kelvin. There was just no shaking the man off. As Elsa, all too sadly, knew.

Lesley felt bad for talking about the Kelvins at dinner. She wouldn't do it again. Not until all of them were dead and buried. Not until she could present her wife with good news.

She opened the third record. It dated back to 1982, when Frank was sixteen. A shoplifting arrest, followed by a slap on the wrist and no charges.

Really? Frank Kelvin, son of Vera and Gerard and brother of Arthur? The worst thing he'd done was shoplifting?

Was that why they'd killed him? Was Frank the only honest one? Had he threatened to expose them? Was he preparing to inherit Gerard's empire and shut the whole thing down?

Arthur and Frank would have inherited jointly. How much trouble would Frank have been able to cause his brother?

She sighed. There was nothing useful here. And she didn't even know if Lucas Parsons had been telling the truth.

The only way to know that was with a raid on Vera Kelvin's house, and they'd never get a warrant for that without intelligence that was completely watertight. Which it most definitely wasn't.

Aurelia Cross. She would speak to the family's lawyer. Find out what she could about Gerard's will.

But before that, she needed to bring Jill up to speed. And before that – more's the pity – she needed to speak to Carpenter.

CHAPTER FORTY-SIX

"OK." Lesley stood at the front of the MCIT team room, the whole team – including Tina – looking at her. She'd dropped in on Jill en route and promised to be with her in half an hour.

Being SIO on a case with no ID, at the same time as overseeing what could turn out to be the most sensitive and explosive case she'd handled since finding DCI Mackie's killer, she needed to find a better way to make this work.

Dennis, sometimes I miss you.

"Sorry I was a bit late, boss," Tina said. "I heard you—"

Lesley shook her head. "You weren't late, Tina. Not with the time you finished last night."

Tina nodded. Nathan gave her a look that Lesley couldn't read.

"Good," Lesley said. "Now, our guy at Chesil Beach. Are we any further on in getting an ID?"

Heads shook around the room.

"Tina and I have been narrowing down our mispers list," said Nathan. "We had been working on the assumption it was a Zack Catterall from Turlin Moor. History of minor crimes, reported missing by his dad."

"So likely to be associated with the kind of people who remove your teeth and fingertips," Lesley said.

Nathan nodded. "Unfortunately, Zack turned up while we were talking to his dad."

"Not so unfortunately for him, mind," added Tina.

Nathan glanced at her. "He ran as soon as he saw us. Clearly his little stint of being AWOL hasn't impacted on his criminal tendencies."

"But he's alive," said Lesley. "So he's not our man."

"No," Nathan confirmed.

"Who else have you got?"

"Mike Ashforth," said Tina. "Taxi driver, reported missing by his wife over a year ago."

"June last year," added Nathan. Tina looked at him with a puzzled expression.

"OK," said Lesley. "We need to check the case file, go and see the wife. Does anyone know if there are any distinguishing features on the body?"

"Only that facial wound," said Meera. "And we don't know if that happened before or after he went missing."

Lesley nodded. "Only one way to find out. Tina, can you follow that up?"

Tina pulled a face. "I was hoping to attend the PM. It's been a while."

Lesley eyed the DC. Tina's strength was in dealing with members of the public. A potential widow was right in her wheelhouse.

But Tina had the potential for promotion. And sticking to her wheelhouse wouldn't get her there.

"OK," she said. "You go to the PM. Nathan, can you speak to Mrs...?"

"Mrs Ashforth," he said. "No problem." He made notes in his pad.

"So that's the PM and the best we've got on an ID," Lesley said. "What about potential witnesses? CCTV? Meera, Johnny?"

"We drove around the area yesterday evening," Johnny said. "Only CCTV is in the car park."

"We've already checked that," said Nathan. "There's nothing suspicious."

Lesley nodded. "You said you'd spoken to someone at the photography club?"

Johnny grinned. "We did." He pulled out his phone. "Found a flier in the village, on a notice board." He looked around the room. "Pretty good lateral thinking, I thought."

No one commented. Tina shifted from foot to foot and Meera sniffed.

This is not the same MCIT you left in 2022, Lesley thought. No Dennis. And Mike, when he wasn't on parental leave, in the other team.

Johnny coughed. "Yeah. Like I say, we got the flier. Chatted to the guy running the club. He was... Well, he helped us out."

"He gave us names and contact details for their members," Meera said.

"Yeah," agreed Johnny. "Meera and I are going to work through them, soon as—"

"I already spoke to a couple of them," Meera said.

Johnny looked at her. "You did?"

"Yeah. Sorry. It was on my mind last night, so I did a bit of online research. Found a Facebook group. Some of our names were active on there, so..."

"Good work, Meera," Lesley said. She gave Johnny a look. "We may not be the Met, but some of us move fast."

"It was his first day," said Nathan, frowning.

Lesley gave the DS a look. Yes, she was winding Johnny up. But she didn't like Nathan undermining her.

He's not undermining you. He's just showing the newest member of the team we don't play favourites.

Dennis would have done the same. *No, he wouldn't.* He would have taken Johnny's side over Meera's, every time.

Maybe Nathan was an improvement. He'd have to work hard to convince her of that.

"OK," she said to Meera. "So what did you get?"

"Two separate people saw suspicious activity in the area where the body was found."

"When?"

"Monday morning, early."

"Time?"

Meera consulted her notes. "The first witness said five am. The second said five thirty. They were there for the dawn; even earlier than the woman who found the body."

"Were they up there at the same time?"

"Not that I can tell. The first witness said he left the chapel around five fifteen. The second arrived at five thirty, which was when he saw someone moving around in the spot where our body was found."

There was a hush in the team room. *A lead, at last.*

"The second witness," Meera continued, "wanted to investigate but was worried for his safety."

"They couldn't just wait?" Lesley asked.

"It's pretty exposed," Nathan said. "They did the sensible thing."

"And there's fencing all around the chapel," added Johnny. "Makes it harder to get close without being seen. Reminded me a bit of some of the buildings we investigated at Brownsea Island."

Lesley couldn't remember Johnny doing much on Brownsea other than empty his guts from seasickness. It was the last case they'd worked together before...

Before she'd been forced to wangle a transfer away from Dorset for him.

Should she have put up a fight about Johnny coming back? Dug her heels in with Carpenter?

No. That would have meant telling Carpenter the truth.

Meera was looking at her.

"You want me to follow up?"

"Please. Go and speak to your witnesses. Find out what they remember. And why they didn't report what they'd seen at the time." It had been another photographer who'd actually reported their victim's body, under an hour later.

"I'll go, too," said Johnny.

Meera flinched then nodded. "Thanks."

He shrugged.

"OK," Lesley said. "I need to update the super." She checked her watch: over half an hour. "And get a briefing from the Cold Cases team on their case."

"Oh, they've got a new case?" asked Johnny.

Lesley narrowed her eyes. He had good reason to ask; if that case had come in first, he'd still be with Jill.

Thank God he isn't.

"Nothing much," she said. "Probably a wild goose chase."

"Oh."

She eyed him. Zoe was right; he didn't need to know.

Didn't he?

No. If he had to find out about Eric's past, it wouldn't be from her.

Nathan's phone rang. He pointed at it, raising his eyebrows at Lesley. She nodded and the briefing started to break up; people grabbing their coats, picking up their phones, finding their car keys.

"Er..." Nathan held his phone out, looking at Lesley.

"Yes, Nathan?"

The rest of the team stopped what they were doing and looked at him. His face had paled.

"There's someone here to see you, boss," he said. "A walk-in."

She frowned. "A walk-in?"

"Someone's winding you up, Sarge," said Johnny. "This is HQ. We don't get walk-ins."

Nathan flashed him a *I know that* look. "Like I say, a walk-in." He turned his gaze to Lesley. "Wants to speak to you, boss."

"Who is it?" she asked.

He shrugged. "Apparently this person will only give their name to you."

"OK." She went over the possibilities in her mind and came up blank. "Did they say what they wanted to talk to me about?"

He nodded. "They did." His eyes were bright. Whatever this was, it was big.

"What is it, Sarge?" Tina asked.

Nathan glanced at her then looked back at Lesley. "Our body over at Chesil Beach, boss. They say they know what happened to him."

CHAPTER FORTY-SEVEN

LESLEY SURVEYED THE TEAM. They were all staring at her. Waiting.

"Right," she said. "Change of plan. Johnny, you're following up with both photographers. Meera, you come with me."

She wanted to have someone with her in case she was pulled away while interviewing this new witness. And in an unknown situation like this, two heads were better than one.

"But it was me who—" Meera began.

Lesley eyed her. "Seriously, Meera? That's what you'd rather do?"

Realisation landed on Meera's face. "No, boss. I'm coming with you."

"Lucky bastard," Johnny called after her as they hurried out of the room. Meera raised a hand in response.

Just a hand, at least. Not the finger. Lesley would have to keep an eye on those two.

They made for the stairs, ignoring the lift; no time to wait.

"What's the plan, boss?" Meera asked as they clattered down the stairs.

"I'm not... oh, shit." Lesley stopped walking.

Meera frowned. "What? What's up?"

"Jill. I promised her I'd... hang on a minute." Lesley took a moment to send a message to DI Scott.

Urgent interview with walk-in witness. So sorry. Don't wait for me.

She deleted the last sentence and typed again.

Be with you in thirty minutes for background briefing. Pls wait.

A message came back within seconds: *No problem.* Lesley felt her shoulders relax. Making Jill wait wasn't ideal, but at least the DI wasn't running off and pursuing Frank Kelvin's potential killers without consulting her.

She smiled, wondering what Zoe Finch would do in the same situation. *Best not to think about it.*

The reception area was busy, just one civilian at the front desk. Lesley approached her.

"I've been told I have a walk-in. Where are they?"

"Sergeant Jenner thought it best to use a meeting room, Ma'am." She pointed.

"Right." Lesley headed for the meeting room, Meera right behind.

At the door, she stopped. She took one deep breath in, followed by a long one out. She closed her eyes for a moment and shook out her arms.

"Are you OK, boss?" Meera asked.

"Just capturing my focus." If she'd had a Twix or a cereal bar – ugh – in her pocket, she'd have shoved it in her mouth. No breakfast, as usual.

"Right." She pushed open the door. Inside, Luke Jenner was sitting opposite a man with dark hair and a scruffy beard that she wasn't sure was supposed to be a beard.

Lesley narrowed her eyes. "Have we met?" she asked. He seemed familiar, but she couldn't place him.

The man stood up. He pushed back his hair and held out his hand. "I'm—"

"Yiannis," said Meera. "Yiannis Kallas."

"You've been in hiding," Lesley said, shaking his hand. His handshake was limp. His cheeks were puffy and his eyes red-rimmed.

He nodded and sank back into his chair. He'd been alert when they'd entered the room, but now he was like a rag doll.

"You're Jackie Kendall's partner," she said.

He nodded, not making eye contact.

Meera sat down opposite him. "Did you find her? The campaign, you were... are you OK?"

Jackie Kendall had been missing more than a year. When that body had been found in Poole Harbour in the summer, everyone had assumed it was her. But it wasn't. It was Rowena Sharp, killed by her lover fifty years earlier and preserved by the mud.

A sound came from Yiannis that made Lesley flinch. It was a high-pitched wail, a kind of keening.

Shit.

She sat down next to Meera. "What's happened, Yiannis? Is it Jackie? Did you find her?"

And what is it you know about our Chesil Beach victim?

Now wasn't the time to ask.

He looked up, his mouth opening and closing. Tears were flowing freely now.

He shook his head.

"She found me," he said. "I went with her, to Edinburgh and then... to the back of beyond in Norway."

Meera leaned in. "Is that where she is? Did she send you, to tell us why she went into hiding?"

She looked sideways at Lesley, both of them no doubt thinking the same thing.

Was Jackie Kendall's disappearance connected to the death of our Chesil Beach victim?

Yiannis wailed again. PS Jenner had left the room; he returned now with a box of tissues, which he thrust in front of the man.

"You need to tell us," Lesley said. "I know it's hard, but we can't help you if we don't know."

He stared at her. "We came back. Jackie insisted. The TV... she said..." A sniff, the kind of sniff you could cut butter with. "She said she couldn't live with herself if she didn't tell you."

"Tell us what, Yiannis?" Meera's voice was softer than Lesley's, but there was dread in it. "Where is Jackie? Is she hiding somewhere? Is that why you—"

"No," he wailed. "No. Nononononono!"

Lesley and Meera exchanged glances. Lesley swallowed.

"Is Jackie OK?" she asked. She'd spoken to the woman briefly, when she'd been on the run in Cumbria. "Is she safe?"

He shook his head and let out another wail.

"No," he spluttered. "No, she's not safe. I told her not to come. I should have insisted. Oh God, I was such an idiot!"

"Yiannis," Lesley said. "Tell us, please. If Jackie's in danger, if someone's got her, we can help."

"She's not in danger." He stared at her. "She was in danger, but she's not anymore."

He stood up and flung his chair aside. Sergeant Jenner rose, his arms out.

Yiannis punched the wall behind him. "She's not in danger anymore." He turned to face Lesley. "Because she's dead. She's dead, and it's all my fault!"

CHAPTER FORTY-EIGHT

LESLEY'S PHONE BUZZED: a message from Jill.

Sorry boss, but my team are twiddling their thumbs. Any idea how long you'll be?

Damn. It had been half an hour, and they still hadn't got much detail from Yiannis. Nothing coherent, anyway.

On my way, she replied.

She stood up. "Yiannis, if you don't mind staying here, we'll get you a cup of tea and something to eat. You can have a rest. Meera, do you mind keeping an eye on Yiannis, then taking a statement when he's ready?"

"Of course." Meera nodded.

"I want to stay here," Yiannis muttered. "It's safe here."

"We'll keep you safe," Lesley told him. "You don't need to worry about that."

What had the man gone through? What had he seen?

She walked to the door and beckoned for Meera to follow her.

"What d'you need from me?" the DC asked.

Lesley lowered her voice. "We need to find out two things.

Firstly, what happened to Jackie? He hasn't told us how she died, but I'm hoping he knows."

"I'm assuming he witnessed something."

"From his reaction, you'd think so," Lesley replied. "But you can't assume anything. The other thing we need from him is what Jackie knew about our Chesil Beach guy. When I spoke to her in Cumbria, she said something about a house she was selling, but she wouldn't give me the full details."

"A house that belonged to one of the Kelvins' companies."

"Yes. *Shit.*" Lesley balled a fist and punched herself in the thigh. "Those fuckers get bloody everywhere." She glanced at Yiannis, who was slumped over the table. "When he came in, he said he knew something about our victim. I need you to find out what that is."

"But gently."

She nodded. "It looks like that'll be the most effective way. He's a witness, and he's in shock. But we need that information fast. Especially if the same people who killed our guy also killed Jackie. Your photographers could be at risk."

Meera's mouth fell open. "I hadn't thought of that. I'll call Johnny."

"You do that." Lesley gave Meera a thin smile. "Thanks, Meera. I'm glad it's you looking after him."

She ignored Meera's look of surprise and left the room. Two minutes later she was in Jill's office, where Stanley and Katie sat opposite the desk from the DI, looking bored.

The entire Cold Cases team, as things currently stood. Lesley had almost forgotten about them.

"Jill," she said as she slid into the room. Stanley and Katie stood up; she gestured them back down again.

There were no more chairs, and not a lot of space. Lesley walked to the desk and perched on its edge.

"D'you mind?" she asked Jill, who shrugged. Katie pulled her chair back to give Lesley some room.

Lesley pulled in a breath. Her mind was racing. "I don't suppose any of you have got a bottle of water?" she asked. "Or even better, something to eat?"

Stanley bent over and brought a bag out from under his chair. "I've got both, boss," he said. "Well, depending on whether a slightly squished sausage butty floats your boat."

Lesley reached out a hand. "A slightly squished sausage butty sounds absolutely perfect, Stanley." She withdrew the hand. "But only if you can spare it."

He shrugged. "I had one yesterday. And I had a big bowl of Special K for my breakfast." He grinned. "Trying to be healthy, gave up the Coco Pops."

Lesley bit back a laugh. "Stanley, you are a lifesaver." She grabbed the butty and unwrapped it; it smelt of fat and tomato ketchup.

Elsa never needed to know. Neither did Sharon.

She turned to Jill. "I'm sorry about this but trust me, I'm better when I don't have sugar cravings."

Jill smiled. "I've heard."

Lesley nodded as she took the first bite and felt the ketchup burst into her mouth. "Where are you with Lucas Parsons?" she asked.

Jill glanced at Katie, who sat even more upright than she had been.

"We've been looking into the release records around the time he claims to have been told about Frank," she said. "And we added a two-week buffer either side."

"Time works funny when you're in prison," Stanley said, his eyes on the sandwich as Lesley worked her way through it.

Katie gave him a look. "Really?"

He blushed. "I don't know from experience, silly. D'you think they'd..." He waved a hand. "I've interviewed enough people in custody to know that time plays tricks on them."

Lesley nodded; he was right.

"Right," said Katie. "Anyway, we've narrowed it down to two potential informants." She looked at Lesley. "As you know, Parsons wouldn't tell us who it was he got the information from. But both these men were serving sentences for offences related to the Kelvin operations."

"Although the big question," said Stanley, "is when we go and interview Vera Kelvin."

Lesley looked at Jill. "I told you it wasn't as straightforward as that."

"And I understand that." Jill frowned at Stanley. "Where's Mike Legg when you need him, eh?"

Stanley opened his mouth to speak, then thought better of it. This was all good-natured, or at least Lesley hoped it was.

"Look, Jill," she said. "There's more background to this that you don't know yet."

"My team have been filling me in. Stanley's been around the block a few times. And Katie's been researching the Kelvin family's past."

I bet she has. "There's more to it than that," Lesley said. "Sensitive elements, things we have to tread carefully around."

"That's the Kelvins for you," said Stanley.

Lesley rolled her eyes. She couldn't expect them to get it if she didn't tell them.

And she wasn't about to tell them. Not yet.

"Jill," she said. "I need to brief you and I need to brief Superintendent Carpenter. I'm being pulled in all directions as SIO on the Chesil Beach case, so I'm going to need you to do some of the liaison with the super. You OK with that?"

Jill's face brightened, and her back went even straighter than Katie's. "Of course."

"Good. In that case, I'll brief you and the super together. Saves me some time and gives you an opportunity to get to know him. Can your team occupy themselves on background research?"

"The two potential informants," Katie said. "I've got addresses. We could speak to them."

Jesus. "No," Lesley said. "You absolutely don't do that. These are dangerous men with even more dangerous bosses." She looked between the two DCs. "You got that?"

Katie nodded. Stanley grunted, "Yes."

"You heard the boss," Jill said. "Go back to the team room, get as much background info on those two as you can. Kelvin connections, opportunities to visit the house, motive to tell Parsons what they knew. I'll come and find you when I'm done."

"Yes, guv," the DCs chorused, rising from their chairs.

"Thanks for the breakfast, Stanley," Lesley said.

"No problem, boss." He grinned.

Lesley watched them leave. Keen was good, but were they too keen?

CHAPTER FORTY-NINE

"Is THERE anything I need to know about before we go in?" Jill asked as she and Lesley walked to the super's office.

Lesley turned to her. "I could fill you in on a whole heap of things. But I don't want to do it in the corridors, and it would take too long. I hope you don't mind me doing it like this."

Jill shrugged. "Doesn't look like I have much choice."

Lesley looked at her. Jill was a DI. Lesley expected – no, wanted – her to have a mind of her own. But she sure as hell hoped she wasn't getting another Hannah Patterson.

"It's fine," Jill said. "What you said about me doing point with the super..."

"I meant it," Lesley replied as they continued walking. "I'm going to be tied up with the SIO role on the Chesil Beach case, and you could benefit from the experience."

"Thanks. I appreciate it. How's that case going? Got an ID yet?"

They were at Carla's desk now, Carpenter's PA. Lesley raised her eyebrows at her and she picked up her phone.

She turned to Jill. "Not good. We have a witness, a walk-in this morning."

"I heard."

Of course. Winfrith didn't get many visits from members of the public.

"But it also looks like we could now be dealing with two murders," she continued. "Possibly related."

"The walk-in?"

"Yiannis Kallias. Jackie Kendall's partner. He says Jackie's dead."

Jill's hand flew to her mouth. "*Shit.* Oh my God, the poor woman. I thought she'd disappeared."

Lesley shrugged. Carla coughed to get her attention.

"He's waiting for you, Ma'am."

Lesley looked at Jill. "You'll hear more when we're in there. Ready?"

"Ready." Jill pushed back her shoulders and tugged down the sleeves of her jacket. It was part of a pale blue trouser suit that complemented her shoulder-length strawberry blonde hair. Very Jill.

Lesley knocked and entered without waiting. Carpenter was at his desk; he looked up and raised an eyebrow at the sight of Jill.

"I brought Jill," Lesley said, gesturing for Jill to take one of the chairs opposite the desk. "She heads up the Cold Cases team."

Carpenter gave Jill an appraising look. She remained standing, meeting his gaze. "Sir."

He smiled. "DI Scott. I hope you're settling in well. Where was it you were before?"

"CID in Poole," she replied.

"Ah. Good. Let's sit in the corner, make ourselves comfortable." He led them to the small group of armchairs in front of the corner window.

Lesley knew that these seats usually meant that he wanted a more drawn-out discussion and less formality. But sometimes it meant he was trying to sweeten some bad news.

"Before we start on your cases, Lesley," he said. "That other matter we've been discussing, DCI Weathers wants another chat with you. She says she'll come to you, this time, if you give her a call."

Lesley drew in a breath. What questions would there be this time? What fresh bullshit had Hannah come up with?

"Of course, Sir," she said, glancing at Jill. All her team knew was that Hannah was off sick. "But we're here to brief you about the two new cases my teams are investigating. I'll start with the Chesil Beach case, and then Jill can help me fill you in on Frank Kelvin."

"Whatever. Go ahead. Do you know who the body is yet?"

Lesley shook her head. "We don't. But we're getting closer. A witness came to the building this morning, a man whose partner claimed to have information."

"His partner? Why isn't she here?"

Lesley pursed her lips. "That's the problem, Sir. The witness is Yiannis Kallias, and his partner is – was – Jackie Kendall. She's now dead, I'm afraid."

"Jackie Kendall." The super frowned. "That's the woman who went missing last summer." He licked his lips. "Is her death suspicious?"

"Given that she went into hiding because of threats she received after what she witnessed, Sir, I think that's likely."

He shook his head. "Goodness me. Poor woman. Is there a body?"

"Not yet. DC Meera Vedra is interviewing Yiannis right now, though, so I'm hoping—"

Jill made an involuntary sound. Lesley looked at her.

"Sorry." Jill blushed. "Ignore me."

Carpenter looked at her for a moment then turned to Lesley. "Let me know if we have a second murder investigation on our hands. Your team is already stretched, what with one person on parental leave and DI Patterson off with stress."

Lesley grimaced. She hadn't told Jill that much.

Carpenter crossed his legs. "So, the Frank Kelvin case. Anything concrete?"

"Jill's team are working on identifying the released prisoner who provided our witness with the information." She looked at Jill.

"We have two possibles," Jill said. "My team are doing background on them, but we'd like to speak to them in person."

Carpenter nodded. "Of course." Jill smiled.

"I think we'd be putting them at considerable risk if we went to speak to them," Lesley said.

Carpenter turned to her. "That's never stopped you speaking to members of the Kelvin operation before."

"We've never been—"

He waved a hand. "You investigated Arthur Kelvin's murder, barged into the Kelvin house when his wife died. You arrested Kyle Kelvin. What's the hesitation this time?"

Lesley looked back at him. "This involves Vera. If Frank's body is on her property, she'll move it as soon as she gets wind of it."

"And then we'll never find it." He looked from her to Jill then back again. "You're right, Lesley. Hold off on the interviews until we have more information. What else do you need to speak to me about?"

"As I'm currently SIO on the Chesil Beach case," Lesley said, "there will be times when I'll be asking Jill to speak with you directly about the Frank Kelvin case, if we need approval."

Another nod. "Fine."

"But before Jill can do that," Lesley continued, "there are aspects of this case I haven't had the opportunity to brief her about yet, and I'd like to brief you both now."

Carpenter sighed. "Is all this beating about the bush because your DI's in the room? Get on with it, Lesley."

"Yes." She bit back a *sorry*. "So, I went to speak to Dennis Frampton about this last night, to get some background."

"You spoke to a civilian about the possible death of a member of the Kelvin family?"

"With respect, Sir, Dennis isn't exactly a civilian. I wanted to know if he could tell me anything about the Kelvins' operations in 1993."

"And could he?"

"No. He wasn't involved in any relevant cases. But he did give me the name of another retired officer who might be able to help."

"Surely there are serving officers you can call on? Members of the Organised Crime team, for example?"

"It was thirty-three years ago. Anyone with the seniority to have known what the Kelvins were up to back then is retired or dead by now. And investigations into criminal organisations like theirs were run differently then."

"I don't need you to give me a lecture on the history of policing, DCI Clarke. Who is this officer?"

"His name is Eric Chiles, Sir. He's a retired—"

"Chiles was just a desk sergeant." Carpenter barked out a laugh. "I worked under him, for a short while."

"It seems he wasn't, Sir. He was an undercover DI in the Vice team."

"Don't be ridiculous." Carpenter waved a hand.

Sitting beside Lesley, Jill was silent. Wondering how much Johnny knew, maybe.

"This is highly confidential, Sir. I don't believe that even Mr Chiles's family know the truth. But I trust Dennis Frampton. And I believe him when he tells me Eric Chiles was an undercover DI investigating corrupt officers who were working with the Kelvins. And that he can help us with this case."

Carpenter gave her a long look. He wrinkled his nose.

"I think you should leave, Lesley. You and your DI. And you're not to speak of this to anyone."

CHAPTER FIFTY

Meera had left Yiannis with PS Jenner in the most comfortable room they could find. It was the room used for witnesses watching a video line-up: a sofa, a low table, a TV on the opposite wall.

She'd used the time to bring herself up to speed on the Jackie Kendall case. She'd worked on it over the summer; she and the DS had gone to Jackie and Yiannis's house and seen firsthand how Jackie's disappearance had affected Yiannis.

She knew this wasn't going to be an easy interview. But she still knew next to nothing about what had happened to the couple, or where they'd been, for the last four months.

She picked up her phone as it buzzed; a message from PS Jenner.

He's ready.

Good. Meera blew out a long breath and made her way to the witness room. She knocked on the door.

"Come in." Sergeant Jenner's voice.

She entered to the sight of Yiannis on the sofa, hunched over himself but quiet. The sergeant was in an upright chair, watching him.

"You alright if I head off, Meera?" he asked. "I'm not supposed to be doing front desk any more, they've got me working in the evidence store." He glanced at Yiannis. "There's no risk to you."

Meera nodded. "Thanks." She approached Yiannis and sat in a low chair at right angles to him. "Hello, Yiannis. I'm Meera. DC Vedra. You were talking to me and my boss, DCI Clarke, a little while ago."

He dragged the back of his hand across his face. "You came to my house."

She smiled. "I did. Back in June."

He looked up. "Why did I let her do it?"

Meera considered. *Let her do what?* But there was a bigger story to uncover here.

She sank back into the chair, trying to project calm. "D'you mind if I ask you to start at the beginning? I last saw you in June, and after that you left your house empty. I'm assuming you left the area to join Jackie."

He sniffed and looked up at her. "She called me. From a burner phone." A smile. "Jackie was clever like that." He swallowed. "She was in Edinburgh. She'd been moving around for almost a year, spent a lot of time in Cumbria. She even got a job there."

"She spoke to DCI Clarke and DI Patterson while she was there," Meera said. "She said she'd witnessed a man being killed but was reluctant to give details."

He stiffened. "I suppose you want me to tell you."

Meera considered. Which was more urgent: finding out more about their Chesil Beach victim, or learning what had happened to Jackie?

"I will need you to tell me what Jackie saw," she said, "assuming she told you about it. But that can wait. What I'd like to know now is about you and Jackie. Where did you go, in Edinburgh? After Edinburgh? How did you stay safe?"

Slow down. She was asking too many questions.

"Start with the where," she said. "Tell me where the two of you have been living, the last four months."

He nodded. "We started in a flat in Edinburgh. Grotty, but better than where she'd been in Cumbria. A studio, full of damp but it was a long way from Dorset. No one knew we were there."

Meera nodded. "What made you leave?"

"The festival. In August. The landlord put the rent up. I managed to get a bit of bar work, cash in hand, and Jackie was cleaning the cages in a pet shop. But it wasn't enough. The city became too expensive."

"So you moved on."

"Yes." He screwed his eyes shut. "To Kolltveit. A pissy little place at the back-end of nowhere."

"I haven't heard of Kolltveit."

"You won't have. It's in Norway. Only ten houses. Jackie had to walk a mile to the next village to buy food."

"Jackie did that?"

He gestured towards his face. "Not many Greeks in rural Scandinavia. I'm sure you get the same thing when you go abroad."

"I do," Meera said. Even worse, what with being a two-mum family. But he didn't need to know about that. "What made you come back to the UK?"

His head dropped. His body started trembling. *Keep going,* she thought. *Hold it together.*

He looked up, his eyes brimming. "I saw a news report. Your body at Chesil Beach." He shuddered. "I made the mistake of telling Jackie."

Meera nodded, waiting for him to go on. He stared at her for a moment then continued.

"She recognised him," he said. "Your victim." He traced an imaginary line down his face. "That wound. She saw it on him, before he died."

Meera felt her breath catch. Had Jackie witnessed their victim's murder?

Focus on Jackie. On what happened to her.

"So you came back to the UK," she said. "Jackie wanted to give evidence."

He nodded. "We got a flight to Gatwick last night. Caught a train from there. But..."

"That didn't work out?"

"They came to the hotel." He screwed his eyes shut. "We got a Premier Inn, used my credit card." He sniffed. "I never thought they'd trace it."

"Which Premier Inn?" she asked.

He looked at her. "How did they trace my credit card payment, Detective? How do they do that kind of thing? It's not like we were on the run from the government or something."

Meera had no idea; that would be a job for digital forensics. But if she was correct, Jackie was in a Premier Inn somewhere nearby. Probably dead, but maybe alive.

"Which Premier Inn, Yiannis? I'm sorry, but I need to know."

He shook his head. "I don't know. How am I supposed to know? All I can see is Jackie's body, lying there."

"Lying where, Yiannis?"

"On the bed, of course. She needed to sleep. I went out to buy food. Oh..." He let out a wail that made Meera jump. "Why did I do it? Why did I leave her on her own?"

He slid off the sofa and collapsed into a shuddering ball on the floor. Meera bent over and put a hand on his back.

"It's not your fault, Yiannis. It's not your fault."

CHAPTER FIFTY-ONE

"Is he always like that?" Jill asked as she and Lesley left the super's office.

"No. Well, yes." Lesley shook her head. "The super's complicated, he blows hot and cold. But I'm pretty sure we haven't heard the last of this."

"I hope so," Jill replied. "I'll need the go-ahead for my team to interview these two ex-cons we've narrowed it down to. At some point, anyway."

"Keep looking into them," Lesley said. "I want details of any connection with the Kelvins. But don't speak to them yet. If Carpenter knows something we don't, it could backfire."

Jill sighed. "OK. What should my team be doing while we wait?"

"Keep working on background. The system has only three entries for Frank Kelvin. Two when he disappeared, and one when he got caught shoplifting as a teenager. I find it very hard to believe that's all the involvement in crime he had, given his family."

"We need a body, boss. We don't even know if we've got a case."

Lesley stopped walking and turned to face the DI. "We always knew cold cases would be complicated. We discussed that when you—"

"Don't worry. I'm fully prepared for the chain of evidence to be a hot mess and for witnesses to be non-existent or to have forgotten the whole thing. But all we've got is the word of a convicted criminal—"

Lesley held up a hand. "I know it's thin, Jill. But this is Frank Kelvin. Do you really think he strolled off into the sunset thirty-two years ago?"

"No."

"Exactly. And I promise, I'll do my best to progress this. But it's a slow one." She paused. "If it turns out that Vera Kelvin was involved in Frank's death and your team bring her in, it'll be the making of your career."

"Or the death of me."

Lesley put a hand on the DI's arm. "It doesn't work like that."

Her mind turned to Jackie Kendall. Was she giving Jill false reassurance?

"Just keep digging," she said. "Imagine you're Zoe Finch with a pile of financial documents in front of her."

"Who?"

Lesley smiled. "Former colleague," she said. "Cracked open West Midlands Police's biggest case for decades by pulling apart hundreds of sheets of financial irregularities."

"Oh. Canary?"

"You know about that?"

A shrug. "I like to do a little background research of my own, when I get a new boss." Jill gave Lesley a wary smile. "I hope that doesn't freak you out."

Lesley laughed. "It doesn't freak me out in the slightest. Quite the opposite. But I need you to use those skills to—"

"To do background on Frank Kelvin." Jill gave a mock-salute. "Got it."

They were back at the row of doors leading to the team offices now. One door for each team room, and two more doors for the DIs' offices. Nathan was standing outside Hannah's office, looking uneasy.

"Nathan?" Lesley said. She gave Jill a nod as the DI disappeared behind her own door. "Everything OK? I thought you were out speaking to our taxi driver's wife?"

"I spoke to her on the phone, boss. Thought it best to check she'd be in before trekking all the way to Sherborne."

Lesley wasn't familiar with the place. "Far away?"

"Top left-hand corner of the county. Almost as far as Yeovil. Which is in—"

"Which is in Somerset. Yes, I know. So I assume Mrs Ashforth isn't at home?"

"She works in a school, boss. Admin. She said she could get off at lunchtime."

"You didn't consider visiting her at the school?"

He frowned. "I need to discuss the disappearance of her husband with her, possibly his death. The details are... Well, it's not the kind of thing I'd like to discuss at work."

Lesley wrinkled her nose. If something like that happened to Elsa, she was pretty sure she'd rather hear about it here at work, where there were people around.

But that wasn't standard procedure. And Lesley wasn't like most people. And her workplace wasn't full of children, either.

"Fair enough," she said. "So what is it that's got you lurking around in the corridor like this?"

He smiled. "Can we speak in private?"

Lesley glanced up and down the corridor; empty. She threw him a frown then shrugged.

"Let's use DI Patterson's office," she said, suddenly remembering that she was supposed to contact the woman from PSD.

That would have to be next on her list. The case came first.

"What is it you need to discuss?" she asked him when they were both inside. They stood flanking the desk, neither of them wanting to sit in Hannah's chair. There was little in the way of personal effects on the desk, no family photos. Just a framed postcard, featuring a map of Devon.

Bloody hell.

"I've got a suggestion," he said. "Something to take the pressure off."

Lesley frowned. "To take the pressure off who?"

"Off you, boss."

"Ha!"

She couldn't resist the laugh. As if Nathan Strunk understood half of the pressure she was constantly under as a DCI.

She sighed. "Go on, Nathan. What's your suggestion?"

He had a hand curled around the edge of the table, and was digging his nails in. She'd annoyed him. Maybe even humiliated him.

She shook her head. *Oh, grow up.*

"What, then?" she said. "Tell me, so I can continue with my highly pressured day."

"Well." He looked down and then up again, holding her gaze. "DI Patterson would ordinarily be SIO on the Chesil Beach case, but she's off sick, so you've taken over the reins. But now there's what sounds like a pretty complicated cold case for you to oversee... so..."

"I've handled bigger workloads than this in my time, you know," she told him.

"...so I thought it might be appropriate for me to step up as SIO on the Chesil Beach case," he concluded.

Lesley's mouth fell open. "What?"

"It achieves two things. It frees up your time to oversee both cases, and it gives me some valuable experience."

He was looking past her shoulder now, at a spot on the wall.

Lesley opened her mouth to speak, then forced herself to slow down.

"Nathan," she said at last. "It's an interesting suggestion, although not one I can approve without involving the super. And I appreciate the fact that you want more experience."

"Thank you. I won't—"

She held up a hand. "But right now, you have a team of highly experienced and competent DCs to manage." *Well, most of them.* "And I need to see you doing more of that before I grant you management of a murder investigation."

Potentially a double murder investigation, she thought.

"Oh," he said.

"Oh, indeed." She offered him a thin smile. "Look, I assigned you the taxi driver's wife because I figured with your experience in PSD, you'd be able to handle sensitive interviews."

"Yes. I mean, I can."

"Good. And when you get back, I expect you to check in with your team. Some of them will have had a pretty tough morning."

His gaze went back to her face. "Care to be more specific?"

"Meera is currently interviewing Yiannis Kallias, who—"

"Jackie Kendall's partner," he breathed.

Lesley nodded. "He tells us Jackie's dead but wasn't in a fit state to give more details when I was in the room. If he's opened up to Meera, that won't have been an easy conversation."

"No," he said.

"Find Meera. Get her to debrief you. And if Jackie Kendall is dead, we'll have a second murder case on our hands."

He looked at her, not speaking. She could almost read his mind.

"And yes," she said. "That might be something I need your help with."

The tension in his cheek muscles released.

"Thank you, boss," he said.

She eyed him. SIO, on a murder investigation with organised crime links and an unidentified body?

No chance.

But maybe he could prove himself on the investigation into Jackie Kendall's murder.

If, indeed, she had been murdered.

CHAPTER FIFTY-TWO

The last time Tina had attended a post-mortem, she'd been pregnant with Daisy. She was relieved to find that this time, she didn't want to puke into a corner.

She stood a good way back, letting Dr Bamford and his assistant get on with their job. The body of their unknown man lay on the table, his insides already exposed by the distinctive Y-cut.

Tina wondered what Louis would think if he knew that this was what *solving mudders* involved.

"He's in a bad way," Bamford said. "It's not going to be easy to determine the cause of death." He shook his head. "Poor bastard's got at least five injuries that could have killed him."

"But surely you can tell which injuries were inflicted before or after he died?"

The pathologist looked over his shoulder. His mask moved in a way that indicated he might be smiling. Or grimacing.

"It's not as simple as that," he said. "For starters, there may be life-threatening injuries that didn't have time to kill him because another one, a more severe one inflicted later, did the job first. And then for... for finishers, we're not miracle workers."

Tina smiled. "I thought you were."

"Ah. That's an illusion we pathologists like to project. But sometimes, when there's multiple potential causes of death, we just can't tell."

"But you do know that he died from a beating," Tina said.

"That much is certain. But what if you lot manage to work out who our poor guy is, and then you work out who killed him, and there's more than one of them? Will you need to know which injury killed him, so you can identify which suspect inflicted that injury." He extended a hand and his assistant passed him a tool Tina didn't recognise but was very glad he wasn't using on someone still alive.

She shook her head. "Joint enterprise. If there were multiple suspects, they'd all be sentenced as if they delivered the fatal blow."

"Tina Abbott," he said, not looking up. "I heard a rumour that you were a perfectionist. Was that source incorrect?"

She smiled. *Good to know my reputation precedes me.* "I've got two kids. You learn not to stress too much about perfection when you're juggling that with police work."

"Bollocks," he muttered.

"Pardon?"

He looked up. "Don't settle, DC Abbott. I'm going to work out which blow killed this poor fellow, and you're going to work out who it was that inflicted it."

She nodded. She wasn't so sure she agreed with him, but the confidence was reassuring.

But before they worked out who had inflicted the fatal blow, they had to work out who they'd inflicted it on.

CHAPTER FIFTY-THREE

Lesley sat down at her desk and closed her eyes.

Yes, she was busy. Yes, she had to admit she was running to keep up. But appoint Nathan Strunk as SIO?

She didn't even know if she could trust him yet. His last posting had been in PSD, working for DI Robert Collingwood. The man who'd killed DCI Mackie.

It was true that Nathan had been in the MCIT for over a year now. And yes, he'd been instrumental in solving a couple of simple murder cases in the west of the county, not all that far from where he lived in Bridport.

But how did she know he wasn't secretly still PSD? Maybe he was working undercover for DCI Weathers, watching her?

Maybe he wasn't. Probably he wasn't. But she still hadn't seen him exhibit the kind of leadership skills needed by a SIO on a case like this.

She'd see what had happened to Jackie Kendall, then maybe give him responsibility there. That would give him the chance to prove himself.

Right now, she needed to call Weathers back. But she also

needed to check if Meera had taken a witness statement from Yiannis Kallias yet.

She opened up HOLMES. Sure enough, a statement was on the system. *Well done, Meera.*

She scanned it. Meera had narrowed down Jackie's location to three Premier Inns: one in East Cliff, one in West Cliff, and one in the town centre. There was a request for uniformed support to attend the one in East Cliff, which was closest to Bournemouth station. That made sense.

She picked up her phone and dialled Nathan. "You've seen Meera's request for uniformed support?"

"I helped her submit it," he replied.

"Where are you now?"

"In the team room. About to head out to the Ashforth house."

"Leave that for now. You and Meera go to the hotel together. If you find Jackie, tell me."

"Of course, boss. Mrs Ashforth is finishing work early, so she can go home and I can visit her."

Lesley rolled her eyes. "So send another member of the team." *For fuck's sake.* "You'll work it out."

"I will."

"Good." She hung up. *You need to do better than that, Nathan.*

Deep breath. She couldn't put it off any longer. She dialled Zara Weathers' number.

"DCI Weathers speaking."

"DCI Weathers, it's DCI Clarke. I gather you wanted to see me."

"You took your time."

"I'm overseeing two murder cases right now. It—"

"I heard one of them is probably a wild goose chase."

Part of Lesley was hoping she was right. "It's still been distracting me. For which I apologise. But I'm free now."

"In your office?"

"Yes."

"Good. Stay there."

Lesley wrinkled her nose. "You wouldn't prefer me to come to you?" Back to the building site.

"No. I'm on my way out of the building anyway." The line went dead.

Hopefully for good, Lesley thought. She stuck her tongue out at the phone then berated herself for being immature.

She just had to hope Hannah Patterson hadn't dreamt up more lies. Was Hannah planning to come back to work, or would she stay away with her 'stress' indefinitely?

Lesley knew she wasn't the right person to ask that question. But if this went on much longer, she'd need to find someone to fill in as the DI in MCIT. And not Nathan Strunk.

There was a single rap at her door. She smoothed down her hair.

"Come in."

DCI Weathers had replaced yesterday's maroon suit with a brown one, paired with a cream blouse. It still didn't suit her.

"DCI Weathers," Lesley said. "Please, take a seat."

But the woman was already sitting down. Had she perfected the art of reaching a seat fast in order to assert her dominance?

"Lesley," she said. "You'll be pleased to know I've concluded my investigation."

"You have?" *That was quick.*

"I don't hang around. And you'll be pleased to know that, as far as PSD are concerned, you have no case to answer."

"I don't?"

"No. I've sent a report to HR, of course; their standards are less robust than ours. You're not the best people manager, Lesley. But the allegations of bullying and intimidation... well, they don't hold up."

"I thought you were interviewing DI Patterson again."

"I was. And I did." Weathers swallowed. "She's a very damaged woman. Quite a frustrated one, too. You'll have your work cut out when she returns to work."

"She's coming back?" Lesley felt her stomach dip.

Weathers shook her head. "Not imminently. Her GP has signed her off for two weeks. You have a stay of execution."

Lesley smiled. So the woman had a sense of humour. "Thank you," she said.

"Don't thank me. Just doing my job." Weathers stood up. "Let's hope we never meet again."

Lesley watched as she left the room. *Yes, let's.*

CHAPTER FIFTY-FOUR

"Right, folks," said Nathan. He and Meera were in his car, heading for the Premier Inn in East Cliff. Tina was on her phone from Poole Hospital, and Johnny was in his car, en route from the first of the two photographer witnesses to the second.

"Boss," said Johnny down the line. Tina said something indistinguishable. Meera gave him an expectant look. She was holding her phone in her lap, voices coming through the car's speaker system.

"I've got bad news," he said, tapping the brakes as red lights appeared on the back of the lorry ahead. They were on the A35, speeding into Bournemouth.

"Get in the right-hand lane," Meera muttered. "You want the underpass."

Nathan did as he was told. *Jeez, Bournemouth traffic.* The worst he was used to was Dorchester, or maybe West Bay on a bank holiday.

"What's the bad news, Sarge?" Johnny asked.

Meera held up a hand, pointing at the road. *Focus on the driving.* He should have accepted her offer to drive, so he could communicate properly with his team.

His team. Was that what they were, with DI Patterson away? Hannah, as she insisted they all call her.

The DCI certainly didn't think so.

He'd show her.

"The bad news," said Meera, "is unconfirmed as yet, but it's about Jackie Kendall."

"Isn't she missing?" Tina asked.

"Her partner Yiannis came into HQ this morning," Meera continued. "He was the DCI's walk-in. He's given me a statement saying he and Jackie were in a hotel in Bournemouth last night. He went out to buy food and returned to find her dead in the room."

"Dead?" said Tina.

"Who's Jackie Kendall?" asked Johnny.

The satnav told Nathan to take the right turn at the next roundabout. He got into the outside lane.

"Jackie witnessed the murder of our Chesil Beach victim," he said. "Or at least, that's what Yiannis says she told him. She's been in hiding ever since."

"She came back to tell us what she'd seen," added Meera. "After seeing a news report."

A whistle came over the speakers. Johnny, most likely. Nathan was trying not to make assumptions about the man, but it was a challenge.

"Poor Jackie," muttered Tina.

"We're on our way to the hotel now," Meera said. "I phoned ahead. They have a booking in Yiannis's name, and a maid went in there two hours ago. Jackie's in there, apparently."

"They didn't report it?" Tina said.

Nathan squinted at the satnav then looked up. He'd taken a wrong turn somewhere and was heading for the seafront. *Damn.*

"The maid is an illegal immigrant," he said. "She didn't tell anyone what she'd seen until Meera called and the duty manager gathered the staff together. She's since disappeared."

"So we can't take her DNA and prints for exclusion," Tina said.

"Indeed," Nathan confirmed. "We haven't got long." They had to be close by now. "So I wanted to check in with you all. Find out if you've made any progress."

Silence.

He rolled his eyes. "Tina first."

"Thanks, Sarge. OK, so the PM's done, but toxicology still needs to be run. Dr Bamford's pretty confident we have a cause of death, though."

Nathan caught a glimpse of the Premier Inn sign up ahead. *Thank God.* "Which is?"

"There are multiple wounds to his head and torso. The cut on his face, which was between six and twenty-four hours pre-mortem. To be honest, there are multiple injuries that could have killed him, but the one that did was a kick to his abdomen."

"Ouch," said Meera.

"Ouch indeed," repeated Tina.

"Any forensics?" Nathan asked.

"Nothing specific. You're not going to get a boot print from a flesh wound. But the pathologist estimates it was inflicted by a shoe or boot of at least size eleven, with enough force for there definitely to have been a leg behind it."

"Any hair fragments, skin?"

"He's been pretty thoroughly cleaned up," Tina replied. "Any dirt on him appears to be from the area where he was found. It looks like he was washed before he was moved there."

"So the killer knew what he was doing," said Johnny.

"Killers, multiple," corrected Tina. "Too many wounds too close to the time of death for it to have been the work of just one person."

There was a moment's silence. Nathan and Meera had arrived at the hotel but not yet stepped out of the car.

"Is that everything on the PM for now?" he asked.

"For now," confirmed Tina. "I've asked them to send the toxicology report to me when it's ready but for now, I may as well go back to the office."

"You do that," said Nathan. "And when you get there, can you let Gail Hansford know we'll need a forensics team in Bournemouth?"

"I already called her, Sarge," said Meera. "Gavin Larcombe's coming over."

Nathan nodded, impressed. It was almost like they didn't need him.

"Right," he said. "Johnny, what about the photographers?"

A uniformed sergeant was standing outside the car, peering in. Meera got out to speak to him, leaving the phone behind.

"I've spoken to the first fella," Johnny said. "He says it was dark, and he can't be sure, but he thinks he saw a van with three men in, driving up the path to the spot where our guy was found."

Our guy. Nathan realised that Mrs Ashforth was probably waiting for him.

"Tina," he said. "How far are you from Sherborne?"

"Sherborne, Sarge? What's in Sherborne?"

"It's where Mark Ashforth lived. The taxi driver. I've made an arrangement to speak to his wife."

The poor woman. Losing her husband, getting a call from the police… and then the police don't even show up.

"Sure," Tina said. "It'll take me a good hour though. Closer to an hour and a half."

I know. "I'll send you the address. Can you phone ahead and apologise on my behalf? Sorry to ask you to do that."

"OK." Her voice was clipped. "I'll see what I can do."

His phone buzzed: the forensics lab. Meera and the uniformed sergeant were standing a short distance away, occasionally glancing back at him.

"Sorry, Johnny," he said. "Can you message your notes to the case inbox? Both photographers, when you have them. This can't wait any longer."

"Sure, Sarge."

"OK. Thanks, both. Keep in touch." He ended the call, secretly quite relieved the boss hadn't agreed to make him SIO.

CHAPTER FIFTY-FIVE

Lesley knocked on Jill's door and opened it without waiting. She'd already started to hate that particular feature of this building, the way all her team were hidden behind solid, if very trendy, pale oak doors.

Her last office had been surrounded by glass. Sure, it hadn't been great for privacy, especially when she'd been investigating the death of a PSD officer. But it had meant she could see her team and they could see her.

Jill was behind her desk, typing on her computer. She looked up.

"Boss," she said. "I don't suppose the super has softened?"

Lesley resisted a laugh. It was true that Carpenter did soften from time to time. But never on her schedule.

"He's got wall-to-wall management meetings," she replied. "I'm hoping to catch him before the end of the day. Are you busy?"

Jill glanced at her screen. "Filling out the paperwork for my team's performance reviews." A cloud crossed her face. "I know it's not the best use of time when we're in the middle of a big case, but—"

"But you've put your team on background research and the reviews have to be submitted by tomorrow," Lesley said. "I know only too well." She noticed the look on Jill's face and smiled. "Don't worry, yours will be in on time. And it'll be good. No surprises."

Jill smiled. Lesley thought of Hannah; how the hell was she going to submit a performance review for her?

Maybe she wouldn't. Or maybe that would be unwise.

She shook out her shoulders; *worry about that later*. And besides, she should be celebrating.

"There's someone we can go and see without Carpenter's say-so," she said. "And I'm in exactly the right frame of mind for it."

Jill looked intrigued. "Who?"

"Her name's Aurelia Cross, she's a lawyer, and I'm fairly sure she won't tell us anything. But we can at least try."

"Aurelia Cross of Nevin, Cross and Short?"

Lesley frowned. "You're three years out of date. It's Aurelia Cross of Cross and Associates now. Harry Nevin died. And Elsa Short... well, she's ploughing her own furrow."

Jill stood, grabbing her jacket from the back of her chair. "I heard. Good for her."

Lesley didn't feel like discussing Elsa's escape from her old firm, but she grunted in response. "Thanks. Come on, I'll drive."

Forty minutes later, they were climbing the narrow stairs up to Aurelia Cross's offices, which were above a row of shops in Bournemouth town centre. At the top of the stairs Lesley found the same spartan waiting area she'd sat in before.

"Expect a wait," she told Jill. "Aurelia likes to play mind games."

The door to the inner office opened and a young man emerged. He was smiling. That was new.

"DCI Clarke," he said. "We haven't seen you for a while."

Good bloody job, she thought.

"And your colleague is...?"

"DI Jill Scott," Jill said, without mentioning which team she ran.

The man nodded. "Come on in, then. I'm sure Aurelia will be pleased to see you."

Lesley exchanged a look with Jill. What game was Aurelia playing now?

She said nothing, just followed the man through. Aurelia still had the corner office with the most meagre of sea glimpses. Most of the view was of buses pulling up at the row of stops opposite.

Aurelia stood as they entered her office. She rounded the desk as they entered, a hand outstretched.

"Lesley," she said. "You don't mind me calling you Lesley, do you? Only I feel like we're old friends. And this must be DI Scott."

She pumped Jill's hand. Lesley let the woman grab her hand, too, narrowing her eyes as they shook.

What the actual fuck is going on?

"Sit down," Aurelia said. "Harry here will get you coffee." She chuckled. "Harry. Unfortunate name, I know, but he's wonderful at his job. Please, sit down."

Lesley lowered herself into a chair, her movements stiff. Something was most definitely not right here.

"You seem remarkably cheerful, Aurelia," she said. "I assume business is going well?"

Aurelia gave her a quizzical look. "Oh, we lost our biggest client two months ago. So... well, things are a little quieter than they have been."

Lesley frowned. Beside her, Jill shifted in her chair, no doubt wondering what the hell was going on.

"I don't understand..." she began.

Aurelia placed her palms on the table. She cocked her head.

"I know why you're here, DCI Clarke."

"You do?"

"Of course I do. It's always the same thing. The same client. Arthur Kelvin. Vera Kelvin, after his death."

Lesley smiled to herself. "What makes you so sure?"

Aurelia gave a dismissive wave. "Look. I'm a criminal lawyer. I know my firm has plenty of clients you might have an interest in..."

The door opened and the young man – Harry – reappeared with

a tray; a cafetière of coffee, jug of milk and three mugs. And a plate of chocolate digestives.

"Thank you, Harry," Aurelia said. She started to pour. "I know you like the good stuff, DCI Clarke, but I'm not sure about your colleague."

"Milk, no sugar," Jill said. She glanced at Lesley then took a biscuit.

Sensible woman. Take the opportunities to eat where you can get them. Lesley followed suit.

She paused, the biscuit halfway to her mouth. "You were saying, Aurelia? Your biggest client."

"Yes." Aurelia smiled and rocked back in her chair. "Terrible shame. But this client was old-school. She couldn't stand having a woman representing her."

Lesley grunted. "But she would have known you were a woman when she hired you." She was starting to suspect who this client might be.

Aurelia shook her head. "She didn't hire me. Her son did. Well, he hired Kenneth Fogarty and Catherine Lawson, years ago, then the baton passed to Harry, then to your wife after Harry's death." She sighed. "And then to me. At around the same point that the client inherited her business. From her son."

"We're talking about Vera Kelvin?"

"We are." Aurelia's gaze was level.

"She just... fired you?"

"She did. She took advice first, checked that lawyer-client confidentiality would be preserved. Which it is, of course."

"I can imagine why you're relieved. I know that his previous lawyer—"

"Oh, don't talk to me about bloody Elsa Short," Aurelia said. "She left me right in the *merde*, as they say."

Jill leaned forward. "So you can't tell us anything about the Kelvin family? Not even from 1993?"

Aurelia stared at her. "1993?"

"Long story," said Lesley. "Have you—"

Aurelia turned back to her. "I can't believe you haven't cottoned on yet."

"Cottoned on to what?"

Aurelia shook her head. Her hair, in its near-solid updo, moved with her.

"Vera did her research," she said. "She took advice. But I took better advice. Proceeds of Crime Act 2002."

"She's right," Jill said. "If a solicitor suspects their client of money laundering, they're required to submit a report."

Lesley looked at Aurelia. "But that applies while you're acting for the client. Why—"

"Oh, Lesley. Don't be naive. You've seen the lengths your wife went to, to get away from him. Still scared, is she?"

Lesley resisted a nod.

"I bet she is," Aurelia continued. "Well, I'm three years past retirement age and I'm ready to quit the lawyer business. If you can organise protection for me, I'm prepared to submit all the reports you want."

Lesley felt her stomach clench. "So you're saying the Kelvins were involved in money laundering?"

"Oh, darling." Aurelia laughed. "Have you not seen the house she lives in? Every bloody thing the Kelvins do is about money laundering."

CHAPTER FIFTY-SIX

"PS Dillick." The uniformed sergeant held out a hand as DS Strunk got out of the car. "You must be in charge."

The DS took the man's hand and nodded. For a moment, Meera thought he was about to disagree.

"That's right," he said. "DS Nathan Strunk. MCIT. You've been briefed by DC Vedra?"

Sergeant Dillick smiled. "Meera's filled me in, yes." The smile dropped. "Body of an IC1 female, room 229. Possibility that there may be hostiles observing. Waiting for us, or for her partner to come back."

The sergeant nodded. "He already came back last night. As far as I'm aware he didn't encounter anyone." He turned to her. "Meera?"

"Yiannis told me he was in the room for about ten minutes, Sarge. It sounds like he was trying to revive her. That was at two am. He spent the rest of the night wandering the streets of Bournemouth, which was why he couldn't remember where the hotel was."

"Poor fella," said PS Dillick. "So what's the plan, Nathan?"

The DS flinched at the use of his name, then looked around the car park.

"How many officers do you have?" he asked.

"Me and three others."

"Good. Two of you come inside with us, two of you watch the exterior of the building."

Dillick nodded. "That was my thinking. PC Laurence is already on the rear exit, PC Sharma will stay here. Sue – that's PC Jarrett – is already in there. I'll come in with you."

The DS nodded. *Well, get on with it,* Meera thought. *Poor Jackie is lying there, all alone...*

"Let's get to it then," DS Strunk said. He started walking towards the hotel entrance.

Inside were two women wearing purple uniforms, and a man in a grey suit.

"We've cleared out most of the guests," the man said. "There are just sixteen still in their rooms." He licked his lips; he was sweating. "They've hung out the Do Not Disturb signs."

Meera frowned. The power of a piece of cardboard. But she saw no reason to disturb the guests. There'd been no report of Jackie's killer returning.

"We'll show you up," said one of the women. "I'm Rebecca, housekeeping manager. I don't suppose you've found Catalina?"

"Sorry," Meera said. "We haven't heard from her."

A nod. "Poor girl. Must have been such a shock to her." She put a hand to her chest. "I didn't know she was illegal, you know. False papers. Pity. She's a damn good cleaner."

"Let's just worry about the body upstairs," said the DS. "Take us to the room, please."

"Sorry." Rebecca turned and pushed through a door leading to a stairway. "We turned the lights off, just in case."

"You did the right thing," said Meera.

The woman smiled back at her. She hurried up the stairs, pushing through another door on the second floor.

"That way: 229. You can't miss it." She pointed.

A uniformed constable stood halfway along the corridor, presumably outside Room 229. PS Dillick had come up the stairs behind them and remained by the door to the stairwell.

Meera exchanged a glance with DS Strunk, then they moved forwards together. At Room 229 they showed the PC their ID, put on protective suits and overshoes, then went inside.

Lying on the bed, her legs splayed at an awkward angle, was a woman. She was blonde, in her early forties. Meera had half expected the blonde to grow out while Jackie had been in hiding, but it seemed it was natural.

On her neck was a pattern of red marks consistent with strangulation. Pathology would need to confirm, but there was no blood, and no sign of any other fatal injuries.

Meera looked around the room. Two chairs sat under the window; one had been knocked on its side. A bottle of water lay open on the floor, a dark patch of carpet surrounding it. She stepped towards the chair, hoping to see prints.

The sergeant stood by the bed, bent over the body. He pulled out his phone to take a photo, then zoomed in on it.

Meera approached him. "What have you seen?"

He turned to her, eyebrows raised. Onscreen was a close-up of Jackie's hand. Her nails weren't painted, but they weren't short.

And underneath one of them was a long strand of auburn hair.

CHAPTER FIFTY-SEVEN

"I PRESUME she wasn't behaving in character?" Jill asked as Lesley backed her car out of the parking spot.

"Really not," Lesley said. "Aurelia Cross is normally one of the most obstructive, supercilious people I've ever had the misfortune to deal with. Elsa won't believe me when I tell her."

Jill tapped on the passenger door, looking out at the traffic. "Your wife used to be a partner there."

"Not anymore. She found a way out. And she can't provide us with any information about Frank Kelvin." Lesley grimaced. "I already asked."

Jill glanced at her. "Working with your other half. Never easy, is it?"

"I wouldn't exactly say I *work* with Elsa. And most of her clients are in Hampshire now, which makes things easier." She pulled onto Bath Road, narrowly missing a seagull that was sauntering across it.

"Meera's a good DC," she continued. "She interviewed a highly emotional witness this morning and did a very good job of it."

Jill nodded. "How's the Chesil Beach investigation going?"

"Slow, without an ID on the body. But we now have a second victim. And some more leads, thanks to your wife."

"Jackie Kendall."

"Jackie Kendall." Lesley glanced to her right. They were passing Bournemouth station; that Premier Inn wasn't far away. She hoped things were running smoothly there. Maybe they'd finally get a lead that would lead them to the killers.

She turned onto Wessex Way at the roundabout and put her foot down, then raised it again as she remembered this was a forty-mile-an-hour road.

"I need to talk to you about something," she said. "It's potentially sensitive, and it involves a member of the team."

Jill cleared her throat. "It won't go any further."

"Good. When we were in with the super, I asked him about a retired officer who—"

"Eric Chiles."

"Yes. Dennis told me about his history." Lesley glanced at Jill. "I know you never worked with Dennis, and we're only getting this on his say-so, but—"

"But you trust Dennis," Jill said. "I understand that. And if you trust his word, then so do I."

Lesley smiled. If only bloody Hannah Patterson was more like this. "I appreciate that," she said.

Jill shrugged. "You're my boss. I wouldn't have taken the job if I didn't trust your judgement."

Lesley glanced away from the road and eyed the DI. Well, that was something. "So," she said. "I'm assuming that once the super has spoken to whoever he needs to speak to, there'll be an opportunity to speak with retired DI Chiles."

"Not to mention Vera Kelvin," said Jill.

"You're frustrated at not being able to act on your tip-off?"

Jill shrugged. "Yes. I know Stanley is, too. But I get it. You don't just go storming in with a woman like Vera Kelvin."

"Indeed you don't," Lesley said. "And nor do you draw attention to yourself. If she gets wind that we're onto her, she'll move Frank's body."

"What if she doesn't know it's there?"

Lesley shook her head. "She moved house two and a half years ago. I think she'd have noticed."

"Cut a body up, wrap it so it looks like meat..."

Lesley wrinkled her nose. "You really think Frank's at risk of finding himself on the table for Vera's Sunday roast?"

Jill covered a laugh with her hand. "Sorry. To be honest, I don't know what I think."

Lesley sighed. They'd passed through the gyratory without incident and were on Poole Road, which was flowing smoothly for once.

"Anyway," she said, "it means I need you to be the one to speak to Eric."

Jill looked at her. "OK."

"If I do it, it'll get back to Johnny. Possibly Vera, too."

"Eric won't tell Johnny," Jill said. "Not if what Dennis told you is true. And I don't imagine Vera is watching you."

Lesley raised an eyebrow. "Let's not tempt fate. Your biggest case since you took this job was Rowena Sharp. No link to organised crime. You haven't found your way onto Vera's radar yet."

"I certainly hope not."

Lesley nodded. "But you can't speak to Eric about any of his internal investigations, or his knowledge of Frank, until I've got the OK from Carpenter."

"No."

"And," Lesley continued, "given the connection between your two potential informants and the Kelvins, I don't want your team talking to them."

"But we already—"

"I know," Lesley said. "And I'm sorry. But I need you to call them off."

Jill had her phone out and was typing a message already. "Done," she said.

Lesley smiled, imagining the pushback she'd have got from Hannah in the same situation. "They'll be OK with it."

"They'll have to be."

"I'm liking you more and more, DI Scott."

Jill suppressed a grin. "Glad to hear it."

"Right." Lesley licked her lips. "That's that in hand. But there is one person you can speak to. He might be able to give you some more background, and no one will bat an eyelid."

Jill pursed her lips. "Who?"

"Dennis," Lesley said. "I'm going to take you back to HQ, and then I want you to pay my favourite retired DS a visit."

CHAPTER FIFTY-EIGHT

Tina hadn't realised quite how far away Sherborne was. Or bargained for the fact that once she got there, she'd get lost in a complicated town centre road system that felt like overkill for such a small place.

At last she found Anne-Marie Ashforth's house. It was a nondescript mid-century semi on a quiet cul-de-sac. She pulled up outside and checked her face in the rear-view mirror. She knew she had dark circles under her eyes, but a quick pinch of the cheeks made her look a bit less sleep-deprived. For the time being, at least.

The door opened as she walked up the path. A short woman with a long black ponytail stood in the doorway, her expression wary.

Tina gave her a smile; the kind of smile calculated to offer reassurance but not hope. It was a smile Tina had had plenty of opportunities to perfect.

"Mrs Ashforth," she said.

The woman shook her head. "Anne-Marie Mercier." She had a French accent.

"Sorry." Tina was usually the last person to assume a woman had taken her husband's surname. "Can I come in?"

Anne-Marie nodded and turned into the house. She waited for Tina to enter, then closed the door behind them. Without speaking, she led Tina into a living room that ran from the front to the back of the house and perched in the centre of a long leather sofa.

"You have found Mark," she said. It wasn't a question.

Tina took the armchair next to the sofa and turned to face the woman.

"My name's Tina," she said. "DC Tina Abbott. I work in the—"

"You have found Mark." The woman's voice was dull. She didn't look at Tina but instead stared ahead at the ornate marble fireplace. It seemed out of place in the otherwise minimalist room.

Tina swallowed. "We believe we may have found Mark," she said. "But we aren't certain. I need to ask you—"

"Where is he?" Anne-Marie's voice remained flat, her gaze on the fireplace.

"Yesterday morning, the body of a man was found thirty miles south of here, at St Catherine's Chapel above the Fleet and Chesil Beach. We haven't identified the man yet, so we're—"

"You haven't found Mark." Anne-Marie turned to Tina, her brow furrowed.

Tina offered her that smile again. She didn't think it was working.

"I'm sorry not to have more concrete information, Ms Mercier. I can't say for sure if the man we have found is your husband. But it would be very simple to check."

The woman raised her eyebrows. "It would?"

Tina nodded. "We need to compare the DNA. If you have Mark's toothbrush, or his hairbrush..."

A frown. "Not fingerprints."

"We don't have Mark's fingerprints stored, so there would be nothing to compare them to." She was glad she didn't have to explain what had been done to the victim's hand.

Anne-Marie stood up. "One moment." She took a few steps forward then turned, her movements robotic. She walked past Tina's chair.

Tina waited, scanning the room. There was no sign of family photos, no evidence of children living here. She wondered what it must have been like for the woman these past sixteen months. Living here alone, wondering if her husband would ever return.

She jumped at the sound of scratching at the other end of the room. She peered around the furniture and saw a fluffy white cat outside the patio doors. It miaowed at her in silence.

"That cat." Anne-Marie was back. She strode to the patio doors and thumped on the glass, making it shake. "Scoot! Vas-y!"

The cat stared at her for a moment, then slunk off. It seemed less scared of her banging than Tina was.

The woman turned to Tina. She held out her hand; she was holding a hairbrush.

"Here. It is Mark's."

"Thank you." Tina pulled an evidence bag out of her jacket pocket and used it to take the hairbrush. "This will be helpful."

Anne-Marie stared at her. "Good."

Tina pursed her lips. Even if the brush proved their man was Mark Ashforth, it wouldn't tell them how he had died.

"Ms Mercier, am I right in thinking that it was you who reported Mark missing?"

"You have read the report, no? Otherwise you would not be here."

"I have. But I want to hear it from you. Can you tell me more about Mark's activities before he went missing? The people he spent time with, the fares he took?"

A frown. "No."

Tina didn't know what to say. "No?" she repeated.

Anne-Marie shook her head and wiped a tear from her cheek. "I am sorry. I cannot do this again. I made a detailed statement a year ago. I told the police everything I know." She sniffed. "Please, read that. If... if this man on the beach is Mark, come back. Talk to me then."

It wasn't an unfair request. Recounting your last days with the person you loved most would be hard enough once. Tina shouldn't make this woman do it twice.

"You're right," she said. "I'll be back in touch, as soon as we know anything."

Anne-Marie nodded. "You will."

CHAPTER FIFTY-NINE

"THANKS, MATE." Johnny took the offered mug of tea and sipped at it. He needed this.

"My pleasure," said Thomas Wolf, the second of the photographers on Johnny's list. "Always happy to help the boys in blue."

Johnny took another long slurp. This was a good cup of tea. He'd had to wait twenty minutes while Thomas brewed the pot. Probably not the best use of his time, but it was worth it. And the pot was a large one; plenty more tea to keep him going.

"So," said Thomas. He groaned as he took the seat opposite Johnny at a Formica-topped kitchen table that Johnny guessed must be at least fifty years old. "What is it I can help you with, son?"

Johnny gave him a nod. "Good tea."

"Glad to hear it." The man blinked, expectant.

"I gather you're a regular at St Catherine's Chapel," Johnny said.

"That I am. Although it's not much in itself. It's the position that makes it. And it's not much of a walk, from down here." His house was along a narrow lane near Abbotsbury Swannery, a few hundred yards from the Fleet and the beach and less than half a mile from the chapel.

He smiled. "Beautiful. Perfect spot to capture the view down to the lagoon and the beach. I'm no expert, but I'm learning." He tapped the side of his nose. "Never too late to be learning."

Johnny smiled. "I couldn't agree more. Do you regularly go there early in the morning?"

"I do, son. Only yesterday I was there for the sunrise."

Thomas was the first of the two early-morning visitors. He'd been at the chapel at five am.

"Do a lot of people go up there at that time in the morning?" Johnny asked.

Thomas chuckled. "Have you ever been woken up by the dawn chorus?"

The flat that Johnny and Alice had rented in London had had a massive plane tree outside, beloved by wood pigeons and thrushes. "I have."

"Well, imagine that down here. With added swans. Wakes me most days, so I get up and capture the dawn from the top of the hill. Keeps me young." He scratched his chin. "But you're not here 'cos of the views. You're here 'cos of the people I saw."

"I am. Can you—"

Thomas stood up, shaking his head. "No need to waste your time asking me questions about that, son."

Johnny frowned. A wild goose chase. "Oh."

He knew what the problem was already. The old man wasn't wearing glasses. Maybe he needed them.

Damn.

Thomas flashed him a grin. "Why you looking so glum? I've got good news. Gonna help you solve your case."

Johnny looked up. "You are?"

"I am, lad. See, I was testing a new bit of kit while I was at the chapel. High-resolution video camera. Automatic focusing, so whatever it was you lot are after looking at, I'll have it on film... well, on my computer. You know what I mean."

He walked out of the room, no doubt heading for that computer. Johnny followed, wondering if it was appropriate to hug a witness.

CHAPTER SIXTY

THE DOOR OPENED, and a blonde woman wearing an apron over a green silk blouse and navy trousers looked at Jill.

"You must be Lesley's friend," she said.

"Er... not really her friend." Jill held out her hand. "I'm DI Jill Scott. You must be Pam."

Pam gave her hand a surprisingly strong shake and winked. "I imagine you've heard I'm some kind of monster. I'm sure that's what Dennis told his colleagues before he retired." She smiled. "Come in. I've made blueberry muffins."

"Actually, I didn't work with Dennis," Jill pointed out as she followed the woman inside. "I'm new to DCI Clarke's team."

"Good for you," Pam said, ushering her towards a doorway. "So you got my Dennis's job, after his injury?"

Jill froze. Was this what people thought?

"No," she said. "I'm running the Cold Cases team. Different from MCIT. If anyone could be described as having your husband's old job, I suppose it's Nath—"

"Don't worry, dear. I'm very glad to have him at home. Even if it did take some getting used to at first. Are you married?"

Jill smiled, then frowned. She'd been meaning to call Meera, check she was OK after finding Jackie Kendall's body.

"Yes," she said. "To another police officer."

"Well, I bet he runs you ragged." Pam chuckled.

Jill sighed. Every time she had this conversation, it was like outing herself all over again.

"She," she said. "My wife's name is Meera."

Pam raised an eyebrow. "Oh. Another one. Is there something in the water at Dorset Police?" She gave Jill's arm a nudge. "I don't mean anything by it, Jill. You're very welcome here."

Jill pushed down her irritation and gave the woman a nod. She'd experienced worse. Much worse, when she'd joined Uniform.

"Are you giving DI Scott a hard time, Pam, love?" Dennis's voice came from the front room. "Send her in and you can get back to your garden."

Pam shook her head, but she was smiling. "He's in there. Tell him he can help himself to the blueberry muffins." She disappeared through the kitchen and out of a door leading to the garden. Jill wondered if a silk blouse and smart trousers was really gardening wear.

She walked into the living room, steeling herself. She'd never met Dennis Frampton, but she knew him by reputation. The swear box. The tweed jackets with leather elbow patches. The old-fashioned attitudes.

But he was a DS. A retired DS, at that. And the boss, she knew, had learned to trust and respect him.

What's good for DCI Clarke...

The man standing in the bay window was medium height, slim, with thick-framed glasses and a short, neat haircut that showed no sign of the comb-over she'd expected. He wore a very different outfit from his wife; a pair of jeans that looked like they'd come from Marks & Spencer, and a threadbare sweater that was threatening to unravel at any moment. He also looked ten years older than Pam. She wondered if that was the case, or if it was just the effect of blonde hair dye.

Jill approached and put a hand on his arm; a handshake felt too formal.

"Dennis," she said. "It's good to meet you at last."

His eyes creased. "At last, eh? This something you've been fantasising about?"

She laughed. "Well, I wouldn't go that far."

"I should think not, too. The boss told me to expect you, DI Scott."

She eyed him. "Please, call me Jill. But don't tell Nathan Strunk."

His smile dropped. "I won't."

Shit. She'd forgotten; when Dennis had retired, Nathan had been working for Robert Collingwood, the bent DI who'd killed Dennis's friend and mentor Tim Mackie.

Best not to mention Nathan again. Even if there was no evidence he'd known what his old boss was up to.

"So what's this I hear about blueberry muffins?" she said.

The tension in Dennis's body eased. "Ah yes," he said. "Let's see where she's put them..."

He led her through to the kitchen, where the kettle was already boiling. On a worktop sat a cooling rack, with neat rows of muffins resting on it.

"Nice," Dennis said. "Would you like one?"

"Yes, please." Jill wondered if this was the reason the DCI came here so often.

Dennis fetched a couple of plates down from a cupboard and put a muffin on each one. He got two mugs from another cupboard then waved the kettle in Jill's direction, eyebrows raised.

"Tea, please," she said. "No sugar."

"Sensible woman. You're much better off drinking the tea I make than the coffee."

Jill smiled again, wondering what the DCI drank when she came here.

He made two mugs of tea and handed one to her. He put both plates on the worktop between them, then leaned against it, sipping his tea and eyeing her over the top of his mug.

"So," he said.

She took a bite of her muffin. *Wow.*

"So," she said.

"You're the head of the new Cold Cases team, so I'm guessing you're here to ask me about a certain retired desk sergeant."

He was sniffing her out, checking that the DCI had passed her the information she'd given her.

Why the hell else would I be here?

"Not a desk sergeant," she said. "An undercover DI."

He nodded, his body language tight. "I'm not the best person to talk to about this, you know."

She shrugged. "You're the only person I have authorisation to speak to."

"You certainly know how to massage a chap's ego." He sipped his tea, his muffin untouched.

"Sorry, Dennis, but I'm not going to lie to you. DCI Clarke and I went to see Superintendent Carpenter, and he—"

"He told you not to speak to anyone." He shook his head. "Sounds like Carpenter to me."

"I'm getting that impression." Why did she feel like she was playing a game of poker?

Dennis took a long breath. He looked out towards the garden and gave a little wave, presumably to his wife. He looked back at Jill.

"Superintendent Carpenter is a cautious man," he said, "and he often has good reason to be. In this case, he certainly has good reason to be."

"I get that."

"Do you, though?" He leaned back, holding her gaze. "Has it occurred to you that DI Chiles might have been investigating men who are still in the force? Men who are now Anthony Carpenter's contemporaries?"

Jill raised an eyebrow. "Men?"

He waved a hand. "Figure of speech. I have no idea who Eric was investigating. But given that it was the late twentieth century, I imagine there's a fair chance it was men. If not exclusively, then not far off."

She nodded. The statistics supported his assumption. But it was still an assumption.

"So the DCI thinks I can benefit from speaking to you," she said. "That you might be able to remember details that can help me."

He pulled his mouth into a thin line. "This isn't easy for me."

She frowned. "Why not? It's not as if you haven't been involved in uncovering—"

He shook his head. "It's not that. I have no compunction about exposing corrupt officers. They're a blight on the force."

"Good."

"But this is different. It's personal."

"I don't understand."

"Don't you?" Dennis watched her.

She looked at him. "I'm investigating the alleged death of Frank Kelvin. You think that Eric Chiles might have information that could help. I don't see how—"

"It's not the Frank Kelvin thing that's personal. It's the Eric Chiles thing. Have you met his son?"

"DC Johnny Chiles?"

He nodded.

"Briefly," she said. "He's not on my team."

"And that's a very good thing." His gaze left her face and roamed the kitchen for a few moments. At last, it settled back on her. "Johnny is an old colleague of mine. An old friend. I worry about him."

"From what I hear, I don't think you have to worry about Johnny."

Dennis shook his head. He narrowed his eyes, looking at her for longer than felt comfortable. She forced herself not to squirm. After what felt like a lifetime, he sighed and picked up his muffin.

"I don't want Johnny to be brought into this," he said.

"And he won't be." There was no reason for a DC in the MCIT to be brought into the Frank Kelvin investigation, even if there was a family connection.

And she wasn't even sure there was.

"Oh, hell." She slapped her forehead. "How could I forget?"

He had flinched at the *hell*. Surely that wasn't swear box-worthy?

"What have you forgotten?" His voice was tight.

"Nothing. It's not important. The DCI will sort it."

Johnny had been assigned to her team, originally. He'd only spent half an hour with them before being reassigned.

Sure, the DCI could move him across to the MCIT until this case was concluded. But would he wonder why? Especially now they had a cold case to deal with, and a significant one at that?

The DCI would come up with a good reason. Johnny was new; this was how things worked.

"Don't worry about it," she said. "I'll make sure he's not brought into it. But I still need to know what it is *you* know that's prompted the DCI to send me here. Did you encounter Frank Kelvin before he disappeared? Have you got any idea how he managed to avoid a criminal record?"

Dennis nodded. "I don't have any concrete information. But I did see things. And I have a hypothesis."

"A hypothesis? Is that all?"

"It's one I can back up with things I observed. Over the years." He glanced past her, and she looked over her shoulder. Pam was at the far end of the garden, weeding.

"I have to know I can trust you," he said. "And I need to reiterate that you can trust me."

She nodded. "Yes. On both counts. The DCI trusts us both, so..."

"Good. Well, in that case, here it is. You say Frank Kelvin had no criminal record, that he's barely on the system. But I remember him being arrested when I was in Uniform. I remember nothing coming of it."

"I know about that. Shoplifting, when he was sixteen."

Dennis shook his head. "I wasn't in the job then. No, this was later than that, in 1988. And it wasn't shoplifting. It was drug supply. He was arrested for supplying a network of low-level dealers. Presumably part of the family operation."

"So why isn't that on the system?"

"Eric Chiles was undercover as the desk sergeant in the station Frank was brought to. I was a PC, present at the arrest. But I wasn't the arresting officer."

"Who *was* the arresting officer?"

Dennis shook his head. "That isn't what you need to be asking. The question is, what was Eric Chiles's involvement?"

"So what was Eric Chiles's involvement?"

"This is my hypothesis, DI Scott. Jill. I believe that Eric and Frank were working together."

"So Eric was corrupt?"

"No. Frank was honest. He wanted to expose his family for what they were. He was providing Eric with information to assist in that."

She let out a low whistle. "Which would certainly give his family a motive to have him killed."

"It would. And it would give Eric a reason to somehow get the record of Frank's arrest removed from the system."

"Or never added to it in the first place."

He nodded.

She tapped her fingers on the worktop. "I need to know more about this arrest. The one for drug dealing. Would that have been how Frank and Eric met?"

"It could well have been. I'm not aware of any contact between them before that."

"And you were there."

"I was." Why did he look so uncomfortable?

"Dennis," she said. "You avoided this question last time. Who was the arresting officer?"

"Ah."

"Ah? That's all you're saying? I thought we trusted each other."

He closed his eyes. "We do. I do. But... well, this might explain your current roadblock."

She raised her eyebrows.

He nodded. "The arresting officer was a fellow PC. A man who rose considerably higher in the ranks than me."

She looked at him. *Mackie? Collingwood?*

"Who?" she said. "Is he still serving?"

"He is. At the time, he was PC Anthony Carpenter."

CHAPTER SIXTY-ONE

Tina's phone rang as she reached the edge of Blandford Forum. She'd stupidly decided to cut across country instead of taking one of the main roads east to Shaftesbury or south to Dorchester. She was regretting it.

"DC Tina Abbott," she said as she rechecked the road sign. She wanted to make sure she took the bypass rather than finding herself in the middle of town. Blandford might be lovely, but today wasn't the day for a visit.

"Tina," came a woman's voice. "Good to have you back. How are you finding it?"

She looked down at the display: Gail Hansford. *Excellent.*

"Gail," she said. "Just the person I wanted to speak to. I've just visited the wife of a man who may well be our Chesil Beach victim. I've got his hairbrush. Do you have the DNA back from the crime scene?"

"We do," Gail said. "Can you drop the brush off in the lab, in Dorchester? It'll speed things up."

Damn. Why hadn't she taken that route?

She sighed, squinting at the road signs. If she went straight on at the next roundabout, instead of turning right...

"Sure," she said. "I'll be with you in about half an hour."

"Oh, thanks, Tina. That helps us a lot."

She nodded, driving past the turn towards Winfrith. "I hear your team are in Bournemouth, at the hotel?"

"Gav's taking care of things. If the people who killed Jackie Kendall are the same ones who killed Chesil Beach man, they were far less careful."

Good. "Can we match the two?"

"Not sure the forensics will help, sorry, but I expect some of your good old-fashioned policing work will do the trick."

Tina tutted. "Let's hope so. See you shortly."

She hung up just as her phone rang again: Meera.

"Hey, Meera. D'you need me for something? I'm on my way to the lab, with Mark Ashford's hairbrush."

"Oh. That's good. Yeah, I'm calling to bring you in on a conference call."

"Another one?" Tina asked. She knew the DS had something to prove, but...

"The DCI's running this one," Meera said.

"Ah." Tina waited to be put through.

The next voice she heard was DCI Clarke's. "Tina, welcome. Are we all here now?"

There was a chorus of yeses. DS Strunk's sounded particularly disgruntled.

"OK," the DCI said. "We've made a fair amount of progress in the last few hours. Tina, have you heard that the DNA analysis for our victim has come back from the lab?"

"Yes," Tina said. "I just spoke to Gail."

"I'm here, Tina." Gail's voice.

Tina frowned. Why had Gail called her if there was a briefing imminent?

Because she knew as much about that briefing as Tina did, of course.

"Meant to ask you, Gail," she said. "Did the DNA match anyone on the system?"

"No one," Gail replied. "Your victim hasn't got a record."

"Which rules out our theory that he's a member of a criminal gang," said DS Strunk.

"Not necessarily," said the boss. "He could just have been very careful."

"Or been very recently recruited," added Meera.

"Poor bastard," muttered Johnny. There was a moment's silence.

"Well, if it's your taxi driver," said Gail, "we'll soon know enough. And you'll be pleased to know that the second crime scene is covered in forensics."

"Second crime scene?" asked Tina. "So we are assuming the two deaths are related?"

"Jackie Kendall claimed to have witnessed our guy's death," said Meera. "Or at least his final moments. So it makes sense to assume she was killed to prevent her providing information."

"It makes no sense," said Johnny. "Why go to such trouble to delay us identifying Chesil Beach guy, clean him so there are no forensics, and then do the exact opposite when you kill the witness?"

"They'll have been in more of a hurry when they killed Jackie," the DCI pointed out. "They'd only just learned she was back in the country. Maybe they were disturbed."

"Maybe they planned on going back to clean up," suggested DS Strunk. "But couldn't when they realised Yiannis was there."

"Why not just kill Yiannis and be done with it?" suggested Johnny.

"We're looking through CCTV," Meera said. "The hotel has plenty of it, but it's hard to work out what's suspicious and what's not."

"You're picking up number plates?" Tina asked.

"Yes."

"Well maybe we'll find a plate that matches some of the prints or DNA that are supposedly all over the scene."

"Not 'supposedly'," Gail said. "Gav's swimming in forensics. Hotels, too many people."

"OK," said DCI Clarke. "Meera, I want you to come back to HQ and continue where you left off with Yiannis. Nathan, you stay at the hotel. Johnny, how did you get on with your photographers?"

"Bloody brilliantly, boss."

Silence. Was Johnny waiting for a reaction?

Tina rolled her eyes. She was ten minutes from Dorchester now.

"Don't keep us hanging," said the DCI.

"Sorry, boss. Yeah, the second bloke, he was trying out his new camera. High definition, all the bells and whistles. Cost a bloody fortune, he told me."

"I hope this is pertinent to the case," the DCI said. Tina covered her mouth to suppress a snigger.

"Yeah. Very. He got the whole thing on video."

"Come again?"

"I've watched it, boss. Pin-sharp. And I'm sure when Gail's lot have cleaned it up, we'll be able to identify at least some of the killers."

There was a chorus of gasps and splutters.

"Why didn't you say this earlier, Johnny?" DS Strunk asked.

"Because you were all talking about hotels, and hairbrushes, and CCTV. I was waiting my turn."

The DCI laughed. "Send over that footage, will you, Johnny? Send it to Gail's team, right now."

"Doing it as we speak, boss."

Tina sighed. Johnny might have spent the last three years in the Met, but he hadn't changed.

"Right, folks," said the DCI. "You all know what you're doing. We're closing in on these bastards. Hold your focus, and report back as soon as you have more."

CHAPTER SIXTY-TWO

"Sir." Lesley stood in Superintendent Carpenter's doorway, waiting for him to invite her in.

He looked up, his face darkening. "Lesley. I thought you'd be out at your second crime scene."

"That will be my next stop."

"I can imagine." He waved her inside. "But I don't imagine that's why you're here."

"I need to brief you on the progress of the case, Sir. We're closing in on identifying suspects and may be making an arrest very soon."

He raised both eyebrows. "Bloody hell, Lesley. I thought you didn't even know who your victim was."

"We have a potential ID. We're just waiting on DNA."

"And if it isn't who you think it is?"

"Even without an identity for the victim, we're amassing a substantial body of evidence to help us identify suspects. A member of the public has video footage of the body being taken to St Catherine's Chapel, and the Jackie Kendall crime scene is – and I quote – 'awash with forensics'."

"You think it's the same suspects for both killings."

"We think Jackie Kendall witnessed the murder of the St Catherine's victim. We think she was killed to prevent her giving evidence."

"Hmm. Bloody sloppy of them, leaving so much behind. You don't think that disproves your theory?"

"We're working on a hypothesis that they were disturbed, or that they intended to return but were prevented from doing so."

"Some impressive words there, Lesley. Just make sure the case is sound before you make any arrests."

"I will, Sir."

A grunt. The two of them were standing, facing each other across Carpenter's desk. He sat down. She followed suit.

"But this isn't why you're here," the super said. "And I note that you don't have your cold case DI with you, this time."

"She's busy gathering background information."

He twisted his lips together. "Not drawing attention to herself, I hope."

"Of course not." Lesley hadn't heard from Jill since she'd left for Dennis's house, too busy with MCIT. She hoped the two of them weren't coming to blows.

"I embarrassed you in front of her," he said.

She narrowed her eyes. "That's not how I recall it, Sir."

He sighed. "Must we?" He cocked his head.

"I'm sorry, I'm not following. Must we what?"

He shook his head. "You and I have been through too much together to be pussyfooting around each other like this." He clenched a fist on the desk. "It's like that bloody day in 2021 when you arrived here, looking down your nose at all of us."

As Lesley remembered it, Carpenter had been the one looking down his nose at her. "I'm not trying to pussyfoot around anyone."

"I know you didn't trust me, Lesley. I know there was a long period of time when you thought I'd been involved in Mackie's death." He leaned forward. "But then you realised you were wrong, and that I wasn't the crook you thought I was."

Lesley licked her lips. This had been a bad idea. But she wanted to know why he'd reacted so negatively when she'd mentioned Eric Chiles.

"I was wrong, Sir," she said. "And for that, I can only apologise." She forced herself not to say more.

"Hmm. Well, treat me like a colleague, woman. Like someone you trust. Like someone you know for sure, right in here," he thumped his chest, "isn't corrupt."

Lesley took a breath. *Alright, then.*

"When I mentioned Eric Chiles," she said, "your reaction was... more extreme than I'd expected."

"You thought I didn't know what he was up to."

"I don't believe he was 'up to' anything, Sir. From what Dennis tells us, he was deep undercover, investigating corruption."

Carpenter nodded. "He was."

"You knew about it."

He nodded and leaned back. "I knew him, Lesley. I knew him well. I was promoted to sergeant while he was the desk sergeant at Sandbanks Road station in Poole. That station doesn't exist anymore, they turned it into flats. But it was a good one. I have many happy memories of that time. Including my friendship with the supposed Sergeant Eric Chiles."

"You didn't know."

"Not at first, no. But things happened, Lesley. You learn things. Not always things you wish you'd learned."

"Was Eric investigating the Kelvins, Sir? Was he rooting out the officers on their payroll?"

"Yes, Lesley. I don't think it's any surprise if I tell you he was."

"And do you believe he might know things that would help us in the investigation into Frank Kelvin's death?"

"Of course he might know things. I might know things. You might know things. Dennis might know things. Good God, *anybody* might know things."

She'd seen him like this before. She knew the best course of action was to wait.

Carpenter stood up, pushed back his chair and rounded the desk. He stopped next to her and crouched down, looking into her face.

"This isn't about what Eric Chiles might or might not know, Lesley. It's not about me going off and conferring with my senior officers, or with PSD, or with whoever else you think I might be talking to."

Lesley nodded. Was he sweating?

"It's very simple, DCI Clarke. It's about Eric Chiles. A man for whom I have a lot of respect. A man whose own son doesn't know what he did for all those years. A man who, given what it was he did for all those years, is bloody lucky to be alive."

Lesley nodded. She was beginning to understand.

He stood up. "The long and short of it, Lesley, is that if your DI brings Eric Chiles into this investigation, then she could be putting his life, and the lives of his sons and grandchildren, at risk."

CHAPTER SIXTY-THREE

Nathan yawned and scratched his chin under the protective mask.

"You alright, mate?" said the forensic investigator. Gavin. Nathan had met him a couple of times before. He was possibly the tallest man Nathan had ever met, the kind of tall that meant getting up from a chair required unfolding himself and the kind of tall that made Nathan pity the man if he ever had to take a long-haul flight.

"Sorry," Nathan said. "Burning the candle at both ends."

Gavin winked. "Hot date last night?"

"Something like that." Her name was Gemma, and it had been their third date. He'd thought it was ending well when she'd taken him back to her flat. But then he'd discovered the flat contained a boyfriend, and the pair of them were hoping for a threesome.

No chance. He'd been out of the place and in an Uber faster than shit off a shovel.

"At least you're getting some action," Gavin said. "Try being six-foot-five. None of the women are interested in me."

"It can't be that bad. I thought women liked tall men?"

Nathan frowned; how was it he was having this conversation

with the forensics guy, instead of talking about blood spatter and fingerprints?

Gavin snorted. "That's a myth, mate. There's tall, and then there's me. You'd think online dating would be my salvation. But I match with them on the app, I make sure to get to the bar or restaurant first so I'm sitting down. But then as soon as I stand up to go to the bar, or to give them a welcoming hug, that look comes into their eyes."

"What look?" Nathan wasn't sure if this was more interesting than blood spatter, or less.

"The 'Jesus Christ, how the fuck do I get out of here without being a bitch?' look."

"Ah. Yes. I've seen that look." Nathan chuckled. "Although last night, I'm pretty sure I *did* that look." He felt his cheeks flush: *too much information.*

"Anyway," he continued, changing the subject. "How close are you to finishing in here?"

"Oh, miles off," the CSI said. "I'm starting to wonder if the reason there's so much forensics here is 'cos a different person sleeps in here every night." He glanced at the bed. "Imagine."

Jackie Kendall's body had been taken away, but Nathan could still see her in his mind's eye. He didn't want to imagine anything. He didn't need to.

"Don't worry," Gavin added. "It's not really that bad. I'm focusing on the areas that get cleaned between occupants. Bed sheets, bathroom and hard surfaces. I've spoken to the housekeeping manager and identified the cleaning products they use. Knowing that means I can work out which traces were added before the last clean, and which after."

"Impressive," Nathan said.

Gavin winked. "That's forensics for you. It's like its own special kind of magic."

Nathan suppressed an eye roll. He heard movement at the bedroom door and turned to see one of the Uniforms standing there.

"Sorry to bother you, Sarge, but me and Dev – that's PC Sharma – have worked our way through the car park CCTV."

"Well done. Fast work." Nathan gave the CSI a nod and approached the PC. "PC...?"

"PC Laurence, Sarge. Jack Laurence."

"OK, Jack. So did you find anything of interest?"

A nod. "We did, Sarge. You might want to see."

"I do." *Anything to get me out of this room.* It smelled of forensic chemicals, cleaning fluids and decay.

"Great." PC Laurence turned and walked to the stairs, which he descended without looking back. Nathan followed him down the two flights, past the reception desk, and into a small office that held a woman in a purple Premier Inn uniform who he hadn't seen before, along with PC Sharma.

The Premier Inn woman stood up, making the room instantly twice as crowded.

"Hello," she said. "You must be Detective Sergeant Strunk. I'm Pasha Gurtha. I took over as duty manager at two pm."

He checked his watch. "Is it that late already?"

"It's almost five, Sarge," said PC Laurence.

"Yes. OK. Nice to meet you, Pasha. I hear you've been looking through the CCTV."

"The three of us have," she said. "These officers kept an eye on me, I know I'm not supposed to get involved." She drew herself up straight. "I'm a special constable, at the weekends. I do big events: the boat show, the air festival, that kind of thing. So I thought you wouldn't mind."

Nathan winced. *Chain of evidence.* But the video belonged to the hotel in the first place, so...

"Just show me what you've got," he said.

PC Laurence bent over the screen. Pasha sat down again, meaning Nathan could fit into the room. He watched the centre of the three screens ranged on the desk.

"Watch this, Sarge." The PC pointed. The video started moving, and an SUV appeared at the entrance to the car park.

"We have ANPR," Pasha said. "Guests have to register their vehicle."

The SUV's registration plate was highlighted.

"Have you found a match?" Nathan asked.

"Yes, Sarge. Belongs to a woman called Vera Kelvin. Or at least, to a business owned by a woman called Vera Kelvin."

"I looked on the Companies House website," Pasha said. "I hope you don't mind."

Nathan shook his head. "Did you say Vera Kelvin?"

PC Laurence nodded. "Yes, Sarge. I take it you know who she is."

"Everybody knows who she is." He looked between the two uniformed constables. "Don't they?"

The second man, PC Sharma, shrugged. "I've not heard of her."

"Nor me," said Laurence.

Nathan raised an eyebrow. *Blimey*. "Keep playing it," he said.

What the hell were Vera Kelvin's people doing, heading out to kill a woman in a car registered to their boss? And then leaving their DNA all over the scene?

The video started again. The SUV pulled into a space, and three men got out. Two wore balaclavas, and the third was pulling one on.

"Zoom in," he said.

PC Laurence zoomed in on the man. The side of his face was visible.

Visible enough for him to be identified? Probably not.

At the door to the hotel, the men stopped. They turned to each other as if they were having a conversation. Then they removed their balaclavas, bent their heads and walked inside.

Nathan felt his mouth fall open.

Of course. They couldn't walk past the receptionist wearing balaclavas.

"Do you have video from the reception area?" he asked. "And do we know how they gained access to Jackie's room?"

"You can only access the rooms, loft or stairways with a room key," Pasha said. "And they used one registered to a guest who had booked and checked in online. The key would have been on a phone."

"You can do that?"

She looked up at him. "It's a new system. Designed to reduce plastic waste. We lose hundreds of key cards every year."

God, plastic waste. This new system made it easier for criminals to gain access.

Nathan shook his head. "What was the name of the guest? The one who checked in online?"

"Same name as the vehicle, Sarge," said PC Laurence. "Vera Kelvin."

Nathan frowned at him. He was imagining things. "Say that again."

"Say what again?"

"The guest. The name." He was imagining things. Either that, or Vera Kelvin was toying with them.

"Same name, Sarge," the PC said. "The vehicle, and the room. Which room was it?"

"Room 149," Pasha said. "One of the refurbished ones."

"Room 149, Sarge," said PC Laurence. "Registered to a Vera Kelvin."

CHAPTER SIXTY-FOUR

Lesley slumped into her chair and rubbed her eyes. She needed painkillers.

She should be relieved that all this Hannah Patterson nonsense was over. No case to answer.

And even better, she'd had an email from the woman; she was resigning, going back to Devon.

Thank God.

But of course there was no case to bloody answer. She was tempted to raise a complaint herself about the way Hannah had treated her team. Lesley had seen how much more relaxed the MCIT were with their boss away.

And now she had Carpenter being weird, and then not being weird, or at least less weird. Just how much did he know about Frank Kelvin's death? How much did Eric Chiles know?

And was the Cold Cases team's second big case about to get closed down before it had even begun?

She yanked open the door to her mini fridge. *Damn.* It was empty.

She could go out and get food, or she could find a way to calm her nerves. She didn't have time to go out.

She grabbed her phone and dialled.

"Lesley," Zoe said. "Two calls in one week. What have I done to deserve this?"

Lesley rubbed her eye. She bent over and rummaged in her bag for paracetamol.

"Sorry," Zoe said. "That was insensitive. Is everything OK?"

Bingo. Lesley pulled out a packet and cast about her desk. There was the tiniest drop of water in a glass. She put the pills in her mouth and swallowed the water.

"Lesley?" Zoe said. "Are you there? Are you... Who am I speaking to, please? If you've stolen a police phone..."

Lesley clapped a hand to her mouth. She felt her eyes watering, and not from the pain.

"I'm putting a trace on this call as we speak," Zoe said. "It's no use hanging up, my colleagues will already have sufficient data to locate you."

Lesley spluttered out a laugh.

"Hello? Lesley? Are you there?" A pause. "Tell me you're not hurt."

"Oh, Zoe." Lesley could barely speak, she was laughing so much. "Oh God, I needed that."

"What? This is you, right? Tell me you're OK."

"Yes!" More laughter. "I'm fine, Zoe. Shit, you're funny when you panic."

Silence.

"Zoe?"

"I thought that was an appropriate response."

"Tracing my phone as we speak? Not too early to hang up and lose the location? You do know that was total bullshit, don't you?"

"I know that, and you know that. But if someone had kidnapped you... they might not know."

"True," Lesley spluttered. "But bloody hell, it was entertaining listening to you."

Zoe coughed. "Well, I'm sorry you find it funny that I care about your safety."

"Come on, Zoe. Surely you can see the funny side."

"You didn't do that deliberately? You weren't winding me up?"

"No! No, of course not. I'm a DCI, Zoe. D'you really think I would deliberately pretend to have been kidnapped?" She frowned. "And besides, why did you jump to that conclusion so quickly?"

"Your number dialled me, and then there was silence." Zoe's tone lightened. "That's not like you."

"No," Lesley admitted. "That's not like me. I was searching in my bag for some painkillers, and then I was swallowing them. That's all."

"Oh. Well, that's good. Sorry you're in pain, though."

"Oh, just a headache. Par for the course. You wait till you're menopausal."

"I'd like to wait for as long as possible, please."

Lesley laughed. This time it was with her friend, not at her. "Let's start again. Tell me about the Cumbria weather."

This was their routine, their ritual. Compare their weather and their views.

"Guess," said Zoe.

"Rain?"

"Yup... Actually, no. It looks like it's just stopped."

"That's a bonus," said Lesley.

"Hmm. What about you?"

"Mixed. Clouds, some sunshine. No rain, sorry."

"I envy you."

"So do I. Anyway, cheer me up. I've got my super being weird and a DI who's buggering off back to Devon."

"Hannah's leaving? What about her complaint?"

Lesley smiled. "PSD say I have no case to answer."

"Lesley, that's brilliant." The smile was evident in Zoe's voice. "So why the headache?"

"Menopause, remember? That, and a body we can't identify. Not to mention... other stuff."

"Other stuff? Your cold case?"

"Sorry. I'd rather not talk about it." Lesley shook herself out. The headache was easing, just a little.

Laughter. The best medicine.

"But I didn't call to grumble about my day," she continued. "Or to laugh at you thinking I'd been kidnapped. Tell me about your day."

"My day? It's been pretty mundane so far. I've been helping Aaron with paperwork for that human trafficking case I told you about."

"You did good work there, Zoe."

"I had help. Aaron, and Carl, and... I had help."

"Don't let men take the credit for your hard work," said Lesley. "Aaron's a good DS from what you've told me and Carl... well, Carl's your partner. But none of this would have happened without you."

A pause. "Thanks," Zoe said.

"Jesus Christ, woman, will you not take a compliment? At least admit this: you learned from the best."

Zoe laughed. "That I did."

"Thank you."

"I've got more news," Zoe said. "I should have told you on the phone the other day."

"You and Carl are getting married."

"Good God, no. That's about the furthest thing from my mind."

"Things not great?"

"No. I... I did something. Lied about something. I'm not sure if he can forgive me."

"Don't tell me you've got another bloke."

"No!" Another pause. "Euch. Definitely not."

"So what's this news then?"

"It's Nicholas. He's moving down south, to do a master's. After he graduates."

"Ah, yes. Sharon told me," Lesley said. "Exeter's nice. He'll like it." She nodded. "Good for him."

"It's a long way from Cumbria." Zoe's voice was flat.

"He can get the train, can't he?"

"Life isn't like that at his age. He'll be busy. I just need to accept that he's growing up. It was just me and him, for so long..."

"You've got Carl now."

"Yeah." Zoe didn't sound convinced.

Lesley perked up in her seat. "Zoe, I've had an idea. It might be bonkers, and it might not even be possible, but..."

"Go on. Nothing feels too bonkers for me right now."

"OK. I've got a vacancy, with Hannah gone, and you've got a son moving down to the West Country. How about you come and work for me? Head up the MCIT?"

"Surely you've got plenty of great DIs in Dorset who'll bite your hand off for that opportunity."

"I've been thinking about it and to be honest, I haven't."

"I find that hard to believe."

"Well, it's true. I have high standards, Zoe. And you, as you just admitted yourself, learned from the best."

Zoe snorted. "I don't think that's enough."

"You won't even consider it?"

A sigh. "I have things I need to finish off here. Important things. I've got a good team. And I need to give me and Carl a chance."

"Fair enough. I will need to fill this post, so the offer won't be there for long."

"And besides," Zoe said. "It's an inter-force transfer. They're not as simple as all that."

Methinks the lady doth protest too much, Lesley thought.

"You and I have both moved forces," she said. "You know it's perfectly doable."

"I'm flattered," Zoe said. "Very flattered. But I can't. Right now, I can't."

"Very well." Lesley wasn't going to put pressure on her.

But that didn't mean she wouldn't raise the subject again, once Zoe had had time to consider.

CHAPTER SIXTY-FIVE

"I'M WONDERING if I should maybe pinch myself," said Gail. "Or just go home, go back to bed and start the day again."

Lesley was on the stairs leading down to the DIs' offices. She needed to drop her faintly ridiculous idea of bringing Zoe into her team and focus on working with the team she had. Gail had called her just as she'd left her office.

"Maybe it is all a dream," Gail said. "Maybe I'll get out of the shower and all this evidence will turn out to be something my subconscious invented. Like Bobby Ewing in *Dallas*."

Lesley chuckled. "That dates you."

"Oi. I watched it on reruns. I bloody loved *Dallas*. Until they brought the bloke from Lovejoy in, it went downhill from there."

"I remember the night JR was shot," Lesley said. "Proper appointment TV." She stopped outside the row of four closed office doors. "Anyway, what's all this about? What's got your imagination running away with you?"

"That's the thing," Gail said. "I don't think it is my imagination. We double-check things here, of course we do. Triple-check them, if we suspect evidence might be compromised."

"You're thinking that the evidence on Jackie Kendall's murder might be compromised? Or is it the Chesil Beach victim?"

Gail sighed. "The Chesil Beach victim we've already matched. I spoke to Tina about it. The hairbrush she brought me... it's your victim, alright."

Lesley narrowed her eyes, going over what Tina had said about the mispers files. "The taxi driver?" she said.

"Yup. Mark Ashforth. Married, ordinary bloke by all accounts." A pause. "Poor bloke. Poor wife."

"You say you spoke to Tina. Has she told the widow?"

"She was headed there when she left the lab. Quite a drive she's got."

Sherborne, Lesley remembered. "OK," she said. "The taxi driver isn't what we expected. We'll have to find out more about him, see if there's any connection to—"

"To the kind of people who remove a bloke's fingertips and teeth. Not to mention what they did to his eye." Gail winced.

Lesley nodded. "I'm sure we'll work it out. And we've got the video."

Gail grunted. "Let me know if you need it cleaning up or enhancing. I'll get Sunil on it."

"I think Johnny's already speaking to him," Lesley said. She'd received a text update from Nathan after getting off the phone with Zoe.

"But Gail," she said. "None of this explains your sudden fixation with Bobby Ewing. What is it that's spooked you?"

"Yeah," Gail replied. "It's... oh for God's sake, Lesley. I don't know if I even want to tell you about this. No matter how many times I check it, I still think it's wrong."

Lesley gripped the phone tighter. "You never get things wrong. And you're starting to worry me. What evidence are you talking about?"

A sigh. "Don't hate me for this, Lesley. If it is right, and it must be, then it means someone's leading you a merry dance.

Either that or... or someone's acting completely out of character."

"Who? For fuck's sake, will you just tell me?"

Gail snorted. "Don't let Dennis hear you talking like that."

Lesley bit back irritation. "Sorry. Tell me, please."

"OK. But you'll want me to check this again after I've told you."

"I'm sure I won't."

Gail gave out a mirthless laugh. "Oh, you will. That hair you found under Jackie Kendall's fingernails. Long strands. Grey, dyed red. We've got a match."

Lesley jabbed the fingers of her free hand into her thigh. "Who? Who's the match?"

Another sigh. "It's Vera Kelvin, Lesley. That hair you found under the nails of your murder victim belongs to Vera Kelvin."

CHAPTER SIXTY-SIX

Lesley was about to reply to Gail's revelation when the door to Jill's office opened and the DI hurried out.

She almost crashed into Lesley, pulling back just in time.

"Sorry, boss, I... Is everything OK?"

Lesley shook her head.

Vera Kelvin? Vera Kelvin's hair, found on a murder victim?

Vera Kelvin was the matriarch of an organised crime family whose influence spread across Dorset and beyond. Wife of Gerard, mother of Arthur.

Even if Vera Kelvin was responsible for someone's death, there wasn't a red squirrel in hell's chance she'd have turned up at the crime scene herself, much less leave evidence as crude as strands of her hair.

Lesley blinked at Jill.

"Thanks, Gail," she said into the phone. "I don't need you to double-check it."

"Good luck working out how it got there," Gail said.

Lesley frowned. "Is there any other evidence of her being at the scene? Fingerprints? DNA?"

"We're still processing it all. But no, not yet."

"So the hair was planted," Lesley said.

"Not for me to say. I'll let you know if we find anything more." Gail hung up.

"Is everything OK?" Jill repeated. "You look pale."

Lesley shook her head. *Bloody Vera Kelvin.* "I'm fine," she said. "Just some surprising evidence on MCIT's case." She eyed Jill. "You look like you're in a hurry."

"I am. I was." Jill nodded. "I was looking for you, actually. I tried texting, but..."

Lesley looked down at her phone. "Sorry," she said. "I was on a call, didn't..."

"It's fine. You can't be everywhere at once." Jill glanced towards the doors to the two team rooms. "I've got some new information. In the Frank Kelvin case."

"Good."

"It's... it's very sensitive. Can we...?" She jerked her head towards her office door.

"Of course. Lead the way." Lesley followed Jill into the office. Inside, Jill looked awkward for a moment, then rounded the desk and sat down. Lesley took one of the chairs opposite her. With just the two of them, it wasn't quite as cramped as the last time she'd been in here.

"Fire away," Lesley said. "Is this about Eric Chiles?"

Jill gave an uncertain shake of her head, rather a waggle from side to side than a shake.

"Indirectly," she said. "But not really."

Lesley nodded. She was getting used to everything about this case being obscure or complicated.

"Indirectly," she repeated.

Jill nodded. "You know how Frank is barely on the system?"

"Just three mentions," Lesley replied.

"Exactly. I've got Stanley looking into the files around his disappearance. The original report, the claim that he was in Malaga. He's working with the information we were given at the time and trying to square it with any concurrent investigations involving the family."

Lesley nodded. "The Kelvin family."

A nod. "There's not a lot to go on."

Lesley wasn't surprised; the man had disappeared in 1993, after all. "So what have you found that's so sensitive?"

Jill nodded. "The other mention is when Frank was arrested for shoplifting in 1982."

"I knew about that."

"But it wasn't Frank's only arrest, boss. He was arrested again in 1988, for drug dealing."

"That's more serious than shoplifting."

"Dennis thinks he was working for the family."

Lesley frowned. "So why didn't it find its way onto the system?"

"Dennis reckons Eric covered it up, boss."

Lesley looked at Jill. How much had Dennis told her?

"He was working with Eric," she said. "Maybe Eric did that so—"

Jill's eyes were wide. "You knew?"

"Sorry, Jill. The super talked to me."

"He knows about it, too?"

"You saw how weird he was when we mentioned Eric. I reckon he knows more than he's letting on. But Carpenter's not the kind of man who will tell us anything he doesn't want us to know." Lesley shook her head. "What else did Dennis tell you?"

"Dennis was there. He was a uniformed sergeant at the time, and he was tangentially involved."

"Tangentially."

"He wasn't involved in Frank's arrest, but he was working in Sandbanks Road that night. He witnessed it. Or..." She blushed. "I wanted to check out what he told me, given that it was so long ago."

"You thought he might have misremembered."

"People do misremember things all the time," Jill said. "Even police officers."

"It's alright," Lesley said. "I'm not offended and Dennis won't be. It was a long time ago. What is it he told you?"

Jill licked her lips. "Thank you. I managed to find microfiches of the record, from the arresting officer's notebook. Katie went through them. There isn't much detail, but there is a note of an arrest."

Lesley nodded. "Katie's always thorough."

Jill smiled. "She is. She's an asset." She straightened in her chair. "Anyway, I imagine this will alter the way you want to proceed with this investigation."

"How? I'm not getting you."

"Frank Kelvin's arrest, boss. It was 1993. Dennis was still in Uniform. And so was the super. He was the arresting officer."

Lesley sighed. *Sorry, Jill.* "I know."

Jill stopped, her mouth open to speak. "You know?"

"Sorry, Jill. Dennis told me. I wanted to... I'm not sure what I wanted to do. I should have told you."

"Oh."

"This doesn't mean I don't trust you, Jill."

"It's OK. It's the super. You have to be careful."

"I do."

Jill leaned across the table, her voice low.

"What else does he know, boss? Was he part of Eric's operation?"

Lesley scratched her eye. "I'm not sure. But what I do know is that we have to be very, very careful about jumping to any conclusions."

CHAPTER SIXTY-SEVEN

Meera sank into her chair as the DS and Johnny entered the team room together. Interviewing Yiannis again had been exhausting, even if it had been more productive than she'd expected. She'd copied the video from Yiannis's phone, and it was now logged in the case file. But watching the look on Yiannis's face as he'd observed his dead partner speaking... that had been heartbreaking.

The door opened again, and the DCI entered, closely followed by Sunil Shah from the forensics team. Meera had worked with him a few times before on digital forensics; she knew Katie had a crush on him.

Sunil made a beeline for her desk.

"Meera, isn't it?" he said, looking uncertain.

She nodded. "Meera Vedra, that's me. Is this about the video Yiannis Kallas gave me?"

He gave her a wobbly smile. "Well, that and a hundred other things. Your team's keeping me busy today." He glanced at her computer monitor. "Do you have the video now?"

Meera turned to check she wasn't needed by the DS or the DCI.

They stood at the front of the room, deep in conversation. She turned back to Sunil.

"It's on HOLMES," she said. "Correctly logged in the case file."

"He sent it to a police email address?"

"Don't worry. I followed procedure." There was every chance the video would eventually be played in court. It was important to ensure that no one could claim it had been tampered with.

"And you've got the device it was recorded on?" Sunil asked.

She nodded. "I've got both Jackie's and Yiannis's phones and Yiannis's laptop. Those are the only devices they had access to between the video being recorded and it being handed over to me."

"Phew." He visibly relaxed. "You have no idea how many people don't understand how important this stuff is. Chains of evidence work digitally as well as physically, you know."

"I do." Meera had been on a course covering this very subject six months earlier. That, and she wasn't an idiot.

"People reckon you can pass evidence back and forth between phones without it being an issue," he said. He lowered his voice. "I worked with one DCI who even tried using his phone to enhance the photo."

"Er... right. Yeah." Meera was starting to wish the DS would pull her away from this conversation.

"I appreciate you being thorough, though," he said. "Maybe you could talk to some of your colleagues, impress upon them the importance of digital chains of evidence. You can trace which computers a file has been on, you know."

"Yeah. I know. Is that everything?" Meera felt her cheek twitch. Just what did Katie see in this guy?

His expression slumped. "Oh. Oh, yeah." He grinned. "Thanks. I'll let you know if I've got any questions, but it doesn't look like I have." He gave her another smile and headed over to DS Strunk.

Good luck, Sarge, Meera thought. But the DS cut Sunil off mid-sentence, putting a hand on his shoulder and speaking over him. Sunil kept shrugging his shoulder in an attempt to free himself.

Maybe that's what I need to learn, Meera thought. Or maybe it was just rude.

The DCI turned away from the DS to face the rest of the room. She clapped her hands twice.

"Right, folks," she said. "Looks like we've had some breakthroughs on both our cases. Everyone settle down, and let's regroup."

"Shouldn't T be here for this, boss?" Johnny said.

The DCI gave him a look. "T, Johnny?"

His ears went red in that way Meera had begun to notice. "Er... sorry. Tina. DC Abbott. It's what Mike calls her."

The boss sighed. "Not in the middle of a briefing, he doesn't. Not when he's being professional."

The ears were almost fluorescent now. "Yeah. Sorry, boss." He shrugged and turned to Meera with a grin. She shook her head.

What was with him? He'd gone to the Met, presumably not been very successful, and come back. Whose idea was it to bring him back in? And why?

"Tina is driving back from Sherborne," the DCI said. "She passed on the sad news about Mark Ashforth being our Chesil Beach victim to his widow, and she has apparently gleaned some information about his activities before his death that might help us identify why he was killed."

"Are we any closer to knowing who killed him and Jackie?" Meera asked.

The DS stepped forward. "I've been co-ordinating a trawl of traffic cameras and ANPR in the area around the hotel last night. We've got CCTV of three men entering the building during the time Yiannis was away from it. They all wear balaclavas for at least part of the time, and the cameras show them going up to Jackie's room. We also have footage of the same vehicle leaving the hotel and driving towards the A31."

"Leaving the area?" Meera asked.

The DS nodded.

"Wouldn't they have known there were cameras?" Johnny said. "In a place like that?"

The DS shrugged. "You'd think so. But maybe they were desperate. And they used a key card attached to a reservation made online only a few hours earlier."

"After Yiannis and Jackie checked in?" Meera asked.

He nodded. "After they checked in."

"So they were following them," she said.

"Either that," said the DCI, "or they were able to access Yiannis's credit card details."

Yiannis had queried this when Meera had spoken to him. She'd dismissed it; they had to have tracked him and Jackie down another way.

Maybe not.

"How?" she asked.

The DCI looked at her. "How what?"

"How would they be able to trace credit card transactions? That's not the kind of thing your—"

"She's right," said Sunil. "Accessing someone's credit card details means getting through at least three levels of security, depending on the bank. It's something we've only seen when the victim and perpetrator are closely connected."

"Do we think Jackie's killer was connected to her?" asked Johnny.

"No," said the DS. He glanced at the DCI, who nodded. "But we do know there's a connection between the men on your photographer's video and the men at the Premier Inn."

Johnny leaned forward. "Which is?"

DS Strunk raised an eyebrow. "They're the same three men."

Johnny whistled. Meera thought of Jackie and felt her chest clench.

"I'm running facial recognition analysis," said Sunil. "Using AI to identify key aspects of their facial features."

"But I thought they were wearing balaclavas," Johnny said. "And

Thomas's video, it was dark, surely..." He looked around the room as if expecting someone to agree with him.

Meera rolled her eyes, wondering how this kind of thing would have gone down at the Met.

"I've enhanced the video from the chapel," Sunil said. "We'll have to visit your witness again and get the original file from him. Digital chain of evidence, you see."

Meera bit back a smirk. Johnny looked puzzled.

"The point is," said the DS, "that we have three men taking Mark Ashforth's body up there, and the same three men then killing Jackie Kendall."

"Who witnessed Mark Ashforth's murder," Meera added.

Poor Jackie.

The DS smiled at her. "Exactly."

The DCI was shaking her head. "That's not the whole picture, though. We think we know who one of these men is, and we're confident we can identify the others, but—"

"Who?" asked Johnny.

The boss raised an eyebrow. "The first man's name is Billy Miller."

"Say that again," said Johnny. His voice had hardened.

The DCI frowned at him. "Billy Miller. The name's new to me. Is he someone you've come across?"

Johnny opened his mouth. He shifted on his chair. He closed his mouth again.

His ears had reddened, but his cheeks were pale.

"That someone you've heard of, Johnny?" the DCI asked, again. "He's on the system. GBH, five years ago in Southampton. Seems he served a sentence and is now back with us, bigger and more dangerous than before."

Johnny shook his head. "Southampton? No, boss. Sorry, got it wrong. Ignore me."

She grunted. "Well, if your memory comes back, let me know."

Johnny nodded and scratched an ear, then winced.

"Anyway," the DCI said. "I was about to tell you there's an anomaly. Three men entered that hotel and three men left. We've got three uniformed PCs on the premises who've been checking the camera feeds. There's no sign of them having a female accomplice."

"I don't understand," said Meera.

"The hair you and Nathan found. Under Jackie's fingernails."

"Oh. I... I assumed it belonged to one of the men."

The boss shook her head. "It came from a woman. Grey hair, dyed red. We've done the DNA analysis and have a match." She took a breath. "That hair belonged to Vera Kelvin."

Meera felt her limbs tighten. Johnny stood up and crashed straight back down into his chair. DS Strunk watched them with the air of someone who already knew what they were just learning.

"I don't get it, boss," Johnny said. "If Vera Kelvin wasn't there, then she and Jackie can't have struggled, and her hair can't have... Hang on, did they meet earlier in the evening? Before Meera went to the hotel?"

"Yiannis accounted for all their movements between landing at Gatwick and him finding Jackie's body," Meera said. "They didn't meet anyone. They certainly didn't get into a fight."

"So Vera must have been in the hotel," Johnny said.

The DS shook his head. "CCTV doesn't lie."

The DCI watched them think for a moment, then pushed a hand through her hair. "I have a theory," she said.

Meera waited. Johnny, for once, was silent.

"It's not just Vera's hair we have," Lesley said. "The vehicle used by the three men belonged to Vera. The hotel booking was made in Vera's name."

"A woman like Vera Kelvin doesn't stay at a Premier Inn," said Johnny.

"Probably not," agreed DCI Clarke. "But Vera Kelvin isn't stupid. Which is why I believe someone else is responsible for this, and they're trying to frame her."

"That does make sense," Meera said. She glanced at Sunil, who she knew had watched Jackie's video, too. "When Jackie walked in on Mark Ashforth's murder, she heard one of them on the phone. He was talking to 'Mrs Kelvin'."

"Clever," said the DS. "Pin it on her in front of a witness."

Meera shook her head. "Too clever. No one thinks that fast. Jackie took them by surprise. No one expected her to be there."

The DCI's eyes widened. "Unless..."

"Damn," said Meera. "Unless they *did* know she'd be there, and they expected her to go straight to the police and tell us the name she'd heard."

"Wow," said Johnny. "Cunning bastards."

Meera jerked her head towards him. "Don't admire them," she said. "Don't call them clever or cunning. They targeted Jackie. They knew exactly when she'd be preparing for house viewings."

"And then they killed her," DS Strunk said, his voice low. "Why? If they wanted her to see, why kill her?"

"Maybe they decided she was too much of a loose cannon," the DCI suggested. "Running off to Norway and all that. Speaking to police in Cumbria."

"Or she'd served her purpose," the DS said, his voice flat.

Meera felt her eyes prickle. How the hell was she going to tell Yiannis all this? Would she even be allowed to tell him?

"OK," the boss said. "Sunil, keep running the video footage. I want an ID on the other two men as soon as possible."

"Of course." He turned towards the door, but it opened before he got there.

Tina stood in the doorway, looking puzzled.

"Tina," said Johnny. "You took your time."

"I had a bloody long drive, Johnny," she said. "What's going on? Have I missed something?"

"Long story," said the DS. "I'll fill you in."

"Is this about the break-in?" Tina asked.

DCI Clarke stepped forward. "What break-in?"

Tina stepped inside the room and closed the door. "A message just came into the team inbox. There's been a report of a break-in. Stolen car, plus some items from a bathroom and a handbag."

"Why is that relevant to us?" Johnny asked.

Tina looked at him. "Because it's—"

The DCI took another step forward. "Don't tell me. Property in Lulworth."

Tina nodded.

"Just outside town?"

Another nod.

The boss sighed. "And the bathroom items are the kind of things that you'd expect to have hair on them."

Tina frowned. "How did you—"

"The house is Vera Kelvin's, isn't it?" asked the DCI. "Vera bloody Kelvin has reported her car, wallet and something with her hair on stolen."

Tina nodded. "Yes, boss."

"Fuck. OK, we need to follow this up. But the question is, is this a genuine break-in, or something staged by the woman herself?"

CHAPTER SIXTY-EIGHT

"NATHAN, you work with Meera. Find out what happened and report back to me."

Lesley wanted to hoot with exhilaration. She'd spent the whole week trying to work out how to get herself in front of Vera Kelvin. Even better, inside Vera Kelvin's house.

Now she had the perfect excuse.

As Nathan approached Meera's desk and started to confer with her, Lesley beckoned Tina towards her.

"You've missed quite a bit," she said.

Tina shrugged. "The sarge said he'd fill me in."

Lesley nodded. "Long and short of it is we've got video of the same three men going to the hotel to kill Jackie Kendall, and before that moving Mark Ashforth's body to where it was found above Chesil Beach."

"Wow. OK."

"And it seems someone's attempting to fit Vera Kelvin up for it all."

Tina nodded. "Is that related to the break-in?"

"It is."

"Hairs found at the scene, car used by the men, wallet..." Tina frowned. "Wallet used to book a room, so they could gain access? I know how those places work."

"Bang on," said Lesley. Sleep deprivation clearly hadn't impacted on Tina's deductive skills.

"I spoke to Mark's wife, Anne-Marie Mercier," Tina said. "She gave me some information I think might be useful."

Lesley put a hand on her shoulder. "I need a couple of minutes first. Do you mind?"

"Of course not."

"OK. Be in my office in five minutes. Bring Nathan with you, if he's ready to leave Meera looking into the break-in."

"No problem."

"Thanks." Lesley gave Tina a smile and surveyed the room. Nathan and Meera were hunched over her computer. Sunil was heading for the door. Johnny was looking at her, a question on his face.

"You looking for something to do, Johnny?"

"Yeah."

"We still need to ID two of the men. You work with Sunil on it. Sounds like you're best placed to recognise them, you've been around the block a few times."

He chewed his lip. "Not really, boss."

"Really? Don't talk rubbish, Johnny Chiles."

He shrugged and turned to Sunil.

"My software's at the lab," Sunil said. "We've got a much better chance using that."

Johnny wrinkled his nose. "In Dorchester?"

"Sorry, mate."

"Go on, Johnny," Lesley said. "Dorchester's only twenty minutes away. I need you for this."

Come on, Johnny, she thought. *Do your job*. She hadn't missed his reaction to Miller's name, earlier. Knowing who the man was would be fine, good, even, as long as it had nothing to do with the fuck-up that had got him transferred out of Dorset.

Johnny blew out his cheeks, grabbed his suit jacket and followed Sunil.

Lesley turned to Tina. "Five minutes, right?"

Tina nodded.

"And if I'm not there," Lesley said, "just wait. I won't be long."

"OK."

Lesley gave Tina's shoulder a pat and hurried past her. Time to give Carpenter the news.

Two minutes later she was standing outside Carpenter's office.

"He's in," said Carla. "But he's got the ACC with him."

Lesley raised an eyebrow. Were they discussing routine management issues, or a thorny case? Like hers?

Two more minutes later – *sorry, Tina* – Assistant Chief Constable Hawes emerged.

"Lesley," he said. "I hear you've been having some personnel issues."

She forced a smile. "Nothing I can't handle."

"That's what I like to hear." He approached Carla, who jerked her head towards the door, indicating for Lesley to go in.

The super was sitting down behind his desk as she entered, looking troubled. She closed the door loudly enough for him to hear.

He looked up. "Lesley. Not got your DI with you this time?"

Damn. She needed to update Jill. The sooner she recruited a new DI to head the MCIT, the better.

"This is a quick visit, Sir."

"Good. I need to leave for a meeting with the local MPs in..." he checked his watch. "...eight minutes. I don't suppose you fancy deputising for me, do you?"

Lesley smiled. "I'll pass on that one."

"Thought as much." He sat down. "Spit it out, then."

She took the chair opposite his desk. "We've had a report of a break-in at Vera Kelvin's house."

He narrowed his eyes. "The place in Lulworth?"

Lesley nodded. "The items stolen were all involved in Jackie Kendall's murder."

"I don't understand."

"I think someone might be trying to fit Vera Kelvin up for Jackie's murder. And the murder of Mark Ashforth."

"Mark who?"

"We identified the Chesil Beach body, Sir. He's a taxi driver from Sherborne."

"Well, that's unexpected."

Lesley nodded. "And we have video footage from both scenes, showing the same three men. Digital Forensics are—"

"My word, Lesley. The evidence seems to be suddenly dropping in your lap."

"It's the result of good police work, Sir."

He smiled. "I don't mean anything by it. But I know why you're here." He leaned back, surveying her. "Vera Kelvin's report of a break-in means you can go to her house. You can interview her. You can search the property."

Lesley pushed her lips together to keep herself from smiling. She balled her fists in her lap.

"It does," she said.

He sighed. "Has it occurred to you that Vera Kelvin knows all this? That you're the fly, and she's beckoning you into her web?"

"I have considered that, yes."

"Good. Go over there. But do so with your eyes open. She'll have lawyers watching. Do absolutely everything by the book, yes?"

"That's how I work."

"Hmm." He pushed himself forward. "Right, I've got a gaggle of politicians to placate. And you've got a witness to interview."

Lesley stood up. She turned towards the door, then turned back again.

"Sir, can I ask you a question? It's about the Frank Kelvin case."

"Which, unless you find his mortal remains on Vera's property, is barely a case at all."

"The Cold Cases team have done as you instructed, Sir. They've limited their investigation to background research only. No interviews."

"Glad to hear it."

Lesley jabbed her fingernails into her thigh. "And we discovered that Frank Kelvin was arrested, Sir. No charges brought."

Carpenter had been moving around the room; picking up his wallet and a gold pen, fetching his briefcase from a chair to place them in. He stopped, his hand on his jacket, which was hanging from the back of his chair.

"Shoplifting," he said. "Ridiculous, for a young man from a family like that. Amazing that he never got into trouble."

She shook her head "There was another arrest. Not recorded officially. But we found paper records."

Carpenter shook his head. "You and your team, no doubt, will have noticed who the arresting officer was."

Lesley held his gaze. "We have."

"It was me, Lesley. No great secret." He glanced towards the door, which she had closed. "And yes, there's more to this that I haven't told you."

She frowned. "I need to know what that is, Sir."

He grabbed his jacket, shook it out, and put it on. "Not right now, you don't. Keep your conversation with Vera Kelvin to the break-in at her house. You don't want to make her suspicious. Right now, I'm late for my meeting, and you've got another case to run."

"But—"

He rounded the desk and stopped beside her. She could hear his breathing.

"Yes, Lesley. I will tell you what I know. When you've made an arrest in the Ashforth and Kendall cases, come back to me. Bring your DI. I'll bring you up to speed."

CHAPTER SIXTY-NINE

SUNIL SHAH HAD a brand-new VW ID7 that smelled of cleaning fluid and was way smarter than anything Johnny thought a CSI tech would be able to afford.

"Nice car," he said as they glided onto the A35. Johnny thought of the battered old Vauxhall he was driving around. Changing that for something more like this would mean a tricky conversation with his dad.

It would also mean Alice getting a job. Not to mention teaching Brandon not to kick the backs of the front seats or smear sticky fingers on the upholstery.

"Thanks," Sunil said. "I inherited some money last year from my gran. Used it to buy this."

Johnny looked around, marvelling at the crumb-free floor and the fact that there were no toys in the central storage bin.

"Well, count me officially jealous."

Sunil raised an eyebrow. "People think EVs are sluggish. But this does nought to sixty in six and a half seconds and has a range of four hundred and thirty-three miles. And it only costs twenty quid for a full charge. Got myself a special electric vehicle tariff, green energy provider."

"Oh." Should Johnny be polite and ask more questions about the car? Or would more facts and figures send him to sleep? Brandon had woken him and Alice twice last night; he was teething.

Johnny yawned, thinking of his nice soft bed at home. He wouldn't see that for a few hours.

"Here we are," Sunil said. They were leaving the A35, heading into Dorchester. The forensics lab was on the edge of town.

"That was quick," Johnny said.

Sunil patted the steering wheel. "I told you this baby was smooth."

Johnny shrugged. "And we got lucky with the traffic."

Sunil sniffed and gave him a *don't-be-so-sure* look as they turned into the car park. He swiftly manoeuvred into a space – reversing camera, what Johnny would give for one of those – and got out of the car.

Johnny followed him into the building and up a flight of stairs.

"This is where the magic happens." Sunil was grinning as he pushed open the door to the lab.

Are you a bit creepy, or just a geek? Johnny wondered. Probably just a nerd, excited by the minutiae of his work. And he was good at it, or so Johnny had heard.

Gail was in the lab, standing over a container of blue liquid. She looked up as they passed. "Alright, Johnny?"

He nodded. "Hey, Gail."

"Sunil showing you his high-tech wizardry?" She winked.

"This is state of the art kit," Sunil said.

"Oh, I know," she replied. "It came out of my budget. But I hear you're getting closer to identifying the Chesil Beach suspects."

"Let's hope so," Johnny said. Sunil gave him an irritated look.

"Right." Sunil pushed open a glass door to an office off the main space. The room was unlit, the only illumination a bank of computer screens.

"I've been running a new prompt while I was over at HQ." He sank into one of the two chairs. Johnny took the other one. "It should have started cleaning up the images, and at the same time, it's been running a comparison against our database for a facial match." He pointed at the screen. "It uses biometrics, like passport scanning machines. Recognises the shape of people's faces."

"Even in the dark?" Johnny asked.

Sunil sniffed. "There was enough light in both locations for the software to be able to cut through. You don't actually need to manipulate the image. The software can work with the smallest amount of contrast when it comes to video. The multiple angles and frames give it more data to work with."

There were no images on the screens, no video. Just lines and lines of text appearing as Johnny watched, scrolling down the screens.

"Feels retro," he said.

Sunil glanced at him. "The text-based interface gives some people that illusion." He chuckled. "But believe me, this is as far from retro as it gets."

Sunil watched the screen in silence for a few moments, then turned to Johnny. "Can I get you a coffee? This could take a while."

"How long?"

A shrug. "I reckon another hour. Maybe a bit longer. It's narrowing things down."

"How can you tell?"

"Ah, you learn. Coffee?"

"Please."

"Be right back. Don't touch anything."

Johnny lifted his hands in an *I won't* gesture. He stared at the screens as he waited for Sunil to return.

"It's like being in *The Matrix*, isn't it?"

Johnny turned round to see Gail in the doorway, leaning against the doorframe.

"Yeah," he said. "Kinda spooky."

She nodded. "People watch this stuff in movies, they think it takes seconds to get a match. But your video footage... well, it's all a bit shit."

Johnny nodded. "Sunil says the system only needs a little bit of light."

"And it does. Just enough to pick out the biometrics. But to do that, it'll need to look at hundreds of frames. And then it goes through thousands of iterations before it even touches the database. It can't afford to get it wrong."

"No." Johnny gazed at the screens. He could use this to get his kids to sleep. "Sunil's been gone a while," he said.

"Didn't he tell you?"

Johnny frowned. "Tell me what?"

Gail laughed. "He offered you a coffee, right?"

"Um, yeah."

She nodded. "Sunil's a coffee purist. Won't drink the instant we have here, even though Gav insists on the expensive stuff. He won't even go to the Costa round the corner."

Johnny was starting to regret accepting Sunil's offer of coffee. "So where is he?"

"Artisan coffee roasters in the middle of town. Expect a wait."

Johnny sighed. "Right."

"Top tip from me," Gail said.

Johnny smiled. "Never accept an offer of coffee from Sunil."

She pointed a finger. "Bingo. You've learned something today." She withdrew into the main room.

I might have learned something, Johnny thought. *But am I going to learn something useful?*

Like the identity of the killers, for example.

"Hey-ho. Coffee's up."

Johnny turned to see Sunil holding a cup holder with two cups.

"Coffee," he said. "You look like you need it."

Johnny blinked. Had he fallen asleep, staring at the screens?

A glance at his watch confirmed it; he'd lost twenty minutes. He rubbed his chin, hoping he hadn't drooled.

"Is it still hot?" he asked.

Sunil frowned. "Perfect temperature, mate." He held out a cup. "See for yourself."

Johnny took the cup, which was stored inside another cup, and then in an insulated sleeve. A lot of effort, when there was a kettle right next door.

He sipped. "Oh."

Sunil grinned. "Good, huh?"

"Yes. Yes, it is." Johnny drank some more. Maybe this was worth the effort. As long as it was someone else making that effort.

"Thanks," he said. "You'll have to give me the name of the coffee shop."

Sunil gave him a puzzled look, then pointed over his shoulder. "Did you touch anything?"

Johnny turned to see that the text had stopped scrolling. "No," he said. "Swear to God."

But he'd fallen asleep. Could he have slumped onto the keyboard, stopped the programme?

Shit. He could feel his ears getting hot. *Bloody ears.* Thank God this room was dark.

But Sunil was smiling. "Brilliant," he said. "Perfect timing."

"Huh?" Johnny had no idea what was going on. But at least it seemed he hadn't done anything wrong.

Sunil sat in the other chair and leaned towards the screen. "It's done." He turned to Johnny. "And it's given us three names."

"It has?" Somehow Johnny hadn't believed the system would actually work.

Sunil wrinkled his nose and pouted. "Those mean anything to you?"

Johnny looked at the screen. The first name, he was expecting: Billy Miller. Not a name he was hoping to come across again.

But the other two?

He stared at them for a few moments, his heartbeat pulsing in his ears.

He turned to Sunil.

"Yes," he said. "Yes, I know all of those names."

CHAPTER SEVENTY

Tina had been waiting with DS Strunk in the DCI's office for ten minutes now.

She'd been wary of going in without the DCI here, but the DS had said it was ridiculous to stand around in the corridor.

And besides, the boss had told her to go in and wait.

"This is about our Chesil Beach victim, I assume?" the DS said. "You've got a positive ID from the wife?"

She nodded. "The DNA was the main thing. There wasn't much I could show her without giving her nightmares."

He sniffed. "Poor woman. How did she take it?"

"As you'd expect. When I turned up for a second time I could see from her face she knew why. But yeah... She took it hard."

It never got any easier, telling a person that someone they loved had died.

"Sorry to keep you waiting." DCI Clarke closed the door behind her as she hurried in and around her desk. She sat down, then swivelled her chair to reach into a mini fridge on the filing cabinet behind her.

Tina narrowed her eyes. How had she got that past the facilities manager?

The DCI pulled out a pot of strawberry yoghurt, turned back to them, and fished in her desk drawer for a teaspoon.

"Don't mind me," she said. "Still haven't had lunch."

Tina looked at the DS. He nodded. She opened her mouth to speak.

"Ta-dah!" The boss waved a spoon at them. Her expression turned serious. "Sorry, Tina. How was Mrs Ashforth, when you told her?"

"Her name's Anne-Marie Mercier," Tina replied. "She didn't take his name."

"Sensible woman." The DCI peeled back the silver foil on her yoghurt. "Did she seem surprised? Or was part of her expecting it?"

Tina frowned. "Well, I think that given her husband's been missing for a year, it wasn't a huge surprise. And when I turned up for the second time in one day she would have worked it out."

The boss licked her spoon and nodded. "All that makes sense. But did she seem the sort of woman who half expects her husband to turn up dead someday?"

"You mean was her husband a criminal, and was she aware of it?" Tina said.

"It's a fair question," DS Strunk said. "Given the teeth and fingertips."

"Yes," Tina said. "Well, no. But also yes."

The boss cocked her head. "You're not making any sense, Tina."

"Sorry." Tina licked her lips. She grabbed her bag, which she'd stowed under her chair, and pulled out the documents that Anne-Marie had let her take. Bank statements, mainly. A few final demands and overdue debt notices, followed by receipts.

She placed them on the desk. "His wife has spent the last year trying to work out if her husband might have committed suicide. There were financial problems, about six months before he disappeared. And then things were OK again. That was why she was confused."

The DCI started to leaf through the papers. "You say things got better, financially..."

Tina nodded. "There's a bank account. It was in his name only, and she didn't know about it. It was only when she started investigating with her solicitor that she found it."

"She hired a solicitor?" the DS asked.

"Not hired, as such. She's got a friend who works in probate. Good at finding money that's been squirrelled away. And they found this account."

Tina put the bank statement from the savings account on the top of the pile. She pointed at the transactions.

"He opened it with a lump sum of five hundred thousand pounds. There are large withdrawals, mainly in the first month. They correspond with receipts showing overdue bills being settled."

The DCI picked up the sheet. "Does Anne-Marie know where this money came from?"

"She's got no idea, boss. She's got her theories, but she doesn't know."

"And her theories are?"

"He started doing work that took him away overnight," Tina said. "Around a month before this payment."

"Any idea what kind of work?"

Tina shook her head. "He said it was corporate clients. But when she asked him for specifics, he refused to give any."

"And corporate clients don't generally pay in the form of a lump sum of half a million pounds," said the DS.

"No," agreed Tina.

The DCI picked up the pile of papers and tapped it against the desk to straighten it. She laid it down and placed a hand on it.

"This is good work, Tina."

"Thank you."

"And it proves that we were on the right track all along."

"Organised crime," Tina said.

The DCI nodded. "It's going to take more investigation. A closer analysis of Mark Ashforth's finances and activities. ANPR, to find out where he was going in his car."

Tina nodded.

"But I think you're right, Tina. I think maybe our victim was working for a criminal organisation."

CHAPTER SEVENTY-ONE

As Tina and Nathan left Lesley's office, Lesley's phone rang. Nathan turned to look at her with raised eyebrows, but she waved him away.

She could see from the display who it was but decided a bit of formality wouldn't do any harm.

"DCI Clarke," she said.

"Boss, it's Johnny. I'm at the forensics lab in Dorchester."

"How's it going? Is Sunil's explanation of how his facial recognition software works beginning to make any sense yet?"

"It's finished running. It's found a match."

She nodded. "Good. Anyone we know?"

Silence.

"Johnny? Are you OK?"

"No. Sorry. It's no one you'll know, boss, at least I don't expect so. But I've come across them before."

She felt the muscles on her face clench. Only back a few days, and already...

"Is this related to what happened before you went to the Met, Johnny? I saw your face in the team room when Billy Miller's name came up. Please tell me your brother wasn't mixed up with these men."

"No." His words were garbled, his breathing heavy. "It's not that. Quite the opposite, in fact."

"OK. So how do you know them? What are these names, anyway?"

"Billy Miller, Luka Tanner and Mick Donnelly."

She considered. "You're right. They mean nothing to me."

"I arrested them, boss. In London. The three of them were charged with possession of drugs and firearms."

"Firearms? When was this?"

"Three years ago," Johnny said. "In Hayes."

"Did it go to court?"

"Don't know, boss. I was never called to testify."

Shit. She'd been working on the assumption that the three men were disgruntled ex-employees of the Kelvins. Maybe members of a Devon gang, trying to muscle in on Dorset.

But London?

If there was a turf war going on between the Kelvins and a London gang, things could get very nasty indeed. And quite frankly, Vera Kelvin didn't stand a chance.

She sighed. "What else do you know about them? Were they part of a gang?"

"I think so. I was in regular CID, so I didn't get involved in that kind of thing. But yeah, I think they were part of something bigger."

Fuck. "Thanks for letting me know. We have concrete evidence against these men on a double murder investigation, and we'll be making arrests. I'll need you to help liaise with the Met."

"I'm not sure they—"

"Johnny, you know these people, and you know the geography. The Met will make the arrest for us, and we'll need their uniformed teams for backup. But I want you there. How quickly can you be in London?"

"I came here in Sunil's car. I don't have transport."

"A patrol car will bring you back here, and then you can take your car to London."

"Err..."

Lesley clenched her jaw. "What? You're not chickening out, are you?"

"No, boss. It's just that I'm driving my dad's car right now. It's not exactly—"

"Then use a pool car. Bloody hell Johnny, this isn't rocket science."

"Sorry, boss."

"Just get yourself to Wandsworth. You've got three killers to arrest."

She grunted and hung up, shaking her head.

CHAPTER SEVENTY-TWO

London.

If this was happening, Lesley needed to brief Carpenter. She needed to bring the Organised Crime team in.

What if they already knew?

What if this battle had been brewing since Vera Kelvin took over operations from Arthur, three years ago?

The London gangs would see her as a soft touch. A woman in her eighties running an operation the size of the Kelvins' would seem ridiculous to them.

She shook her head. They didn't know Vera Kelvin.

"Stop it," she said to the empty room. Was she beginning to admire Vera Kelvin? Was she starting to feel sympathy for the woman?

Feelings like that could lead a copper down a very dark road. A road like the one her former boss, David Randle, had gone down.

She shuddered. *Thank God I don't have to put up with him anymore.*

She shook herself out and stood up. She had a visit to make.

Jill's office wasn't far out of her way. She knocked twice and put her head round the door.

No sign of the DI. She found her next door, in the Cold Cases team room.

"Jill, are you busy?"

Jill glanced at each of Stanley and Katie then approached Lesley. "Not particularly. Do you need me for something?"

Lesley pursed her lips. "Not sure. Depends if you want to stick your head above the parapet."

"Sounds intriguing."

"Have you heard about the reported break-in at Vera Kelvin's house in Lulworth?"

A nod. "Who hasn't?"

"It's related to the MCIT's double murder. Evidence they found at the suspected crime scene was allegedly stolen."

"That doesn't make sense."

"It might, it might not," Lesley replied. "Anyway, it gives us an in. An excuse to speak to Vera. To search her property. There are two Uniforms and a member of local CID there now, treading water. But—"

"Give me one minute to fetch my coat and my phone," Jill said.

Lesley grabbed her arm before she had the chance to get away. "This is risky, Jill."

"I know that. I wouldn't—"

"No. I know you understand the implications of making yourself known to Vera. I know you're prepared for that. But if you come with me, she'll look you up. She'll see which team you run, and she'll put two and two together."

"Oh." Jill's shoulders slumped. "So why did you come here?"

"I'm sorry, Jill. I was going to give you the option. Make it your choice. But the more I think about it, the more I see that you can't be involved. The break-in is linked to an MCIT case, not a cold cases one. But—"

"But you'll tell me, if anything comes to light?"

"I will."

"Good. That's settled then." Jill smiled. "Good luck."

"I suspect I'm going to need it."

Twenty minutes later, Lesley was crawling along the lane leading to Vera Kelvin's vast house. It was a red brick structure with multiple outbuildings, right at the end of a lane leading eastwards out of Lulworth. Only one way in and out.

Vera Kelvin, you aren't stupid.

The gates opened as she pressed the buzzer, revealing a wide gravel driveway. She parked next to a response car and made for the front door.

A woman in a maid's uniform – black dress, starched apron – had it open before Lesley had even touched the bell. She noticed a camera above her, tucked into the eaves of the open porch.

"DCI Clarke," the woman said. "Please come in."

Lesley frowned. "How d'you know who I am?"

A smile. "Mrs Kelvin watches the camera feeds." The smile dropped. "Especially on a day like today."

"She's expecting me, then."

"She is. Please, follow me."

Lesley followed the woman to a broad sitting room at the back of the house. Glimpses of the sea could be seen through trees.

On one of the three vast, velvet-upholstered sofas, sat a woman. She was short – no more than five foot three – with dyed red hair scraped back from a full face of make-up. Her small eyes traced Lesley's movements towards her. She straightened up as Lesley approached, no part of her back touching the back of the sofa.

"Mrs Kelvin," Lesley said. The last time they had been face to face had been at Poole Hospital after Arthur's death. Vera had been significantly less composed.

"DCI Clarke. Please, sit."

Lesley did as she was told, trying to ignore the fact that she was being spoken to like a dog. She sat in the centre of the sofa, at right angles to Vera, and smoothed out her skirt.

The maid reappeared with a tray: a cafetière of coffee, a china cup. No milk jug, no sugar bowl.

"I hear you like good coffee," Vera said.

Lesley poured her coffee and sipped. It was good, alright.

She nodded. "You forgot the jammy dodgers."

Distaste crossed Vera's face. "Kids' food."

Lesley raised an eyebrow. Sometimes kids' food was the best food.

"I'm sorry about your break-in," she said.

Vera's eyes narrowed. "No, you're not."

"No?"

Vera shook her head. "You're delighted. It gives you an opportunity to get into my house. An opportunity to snoop around my things."

"We need to dust for prints, establish entry points. I've already briefed our best crime scene ma—"

Vera laughed. "It won't work, you know."

Lesley smiled. "I've got no idea what you're talking about."

Another laugh. It was harsh, the laugh of a woman who'd had a smoking habit for much of her life.

"Oh yes, you fucking do," Vera said. "And you won't find a thing."

Lesley shifted her weight to face Vera. "Mrs Kelvin, you reported a break-in. Theft of a car, and other items. We need to—"

"My sponge bag and my brown crocodile-skin handbag," Vera said. "The sponge bag contains a comb, which no doubt has my hair on it." She patted her head. "You'll have discovered that I'm not a natural redhead."

Lesley wasn't about to tell Vera that these items had all been found or seen at the scene of a murder. But she was beginning to have the feeling she didn't need to.

"Have you considered whether anything else might have been taken?" she asked.

"Of course it hasn't." Vera licked her lips noisily. "What are you, fucking stupid?"

Lesley blinked back at her.

"I know who took those things," Vera said. "In time, you'll work it out, too. And they won't get away with it."

Lesley moved along the sofa, towards Vera. "We have sophisticated facial recognition technology and video footage of the men we believe broke into your house. But to be able to prove that in court, we will—"

"You are not searching my house," Vera said. "And even if you do, you won't find him."

Lesley felt her breath catch. She stared back at Vera. She wasn't going to ask the question.

Wait. See what she reveals.

"I know what you're up to, Lesley. You and your DI. The pretty blonde lesbian with the detective constable wife." She wrinkled her nose. "Disgusting."

Vera stood up. Lesley made to rise, too, but Vera pushed her down with the lightest of touches on the shoulder.

"I know about DI Scott's visit to the prison. I know about Lucas Parsons, dumb little arse that he is. I know you've been sniffing around into my past."

Lesley shook her head. She stood up, not allowing herself to be pushed down this time.

"I'm here about your break-in, Mrs Kelvin. You reported it to the police, and we have a duty to investigate."

Vera looked up at her. Even on stiletto heels, she was a good inch shorter than Lesley.

"Frank is in Malaga," she said. "I have documents to prove it. Lucas Parsons is talking bollocks."

"If you can produce additional documentation to verify his whereabouts," Lesley said, "that would be helpful." She paused. "Recent documents."

Vera walked towards the wide windows overlooking the ornate garden and the woods beyond.

"That won't be a problem, DCI Clarke," she said. "Now fuck off out of my house before I have to get my boys in."

CHAPTER SEVENTY-THREE

Meera checked her watch; four minutes before she needed to leave.

"Shit."

DS Strunk looked at her. "You OK?"

She pursed her lips. "Yeah. It's just... I'm sorry, Sarge."

"Why are you sorry?"

She tapped her watch. "I need to head off. Pick my daughter up from school."

"Ah, of course. You're working short hours, since DI Scott came back."

She nodded. It had been almost a year now, but still no one had got used to it.

"D'you think they'll make the arrest tonight?" she asked.

He shrugged. "It's out of our hands now. Johnny's on his way there already."

Johnny had decided to ditch the pool car and have a patrol car take him to Poole station. It made sense, with the rush hour traffic.

"He'll be there in a couple of hours," the sarge said. "I imagine he's hoping he doesn't miss any of the action."

Meera nodded. There had been a detailed briefing between the DS and the Met's armed response unit, with the DCI dialling in on her way back from Vera Kelvin's house.

"Did the boss say how things went at the Kelvin house?" she asked.

She needed to leave. Two minutes ago. But...

The DS was typing into his phone. He looked up. "She wouldn't say anything."

"That sounds ominous."

He grunted. "You're going to be late."

She sighed and headed for the door, giving the team room one last glance before leaving.

God, she loved Suzi. She loved the girl with all her heart. But sometimes it was hard being a parent.

CHAPTER SEVENTY-FOUR

Lesley stood at the front of the MCIT team room. Behind her was a map of Hayes, or at least a section of it. Markers indicated the properties where they expected to find Miller, Tanner and Donnelly.

In front of her were Nathan, Tina and Katie, who'd asked Jill if she could come along and watch. The three of them looked anxious, even Katie, who probably knew next to nothing about what was going on.

Then again, this was DC Katie Young. She'd probably been following the MCIT cases on the system all along.

"DI Ortega," she said, enunciating clearly even though she was confident the microphone hooked over her ear would pick her up well enough. "This is DCI Clarke. Can you hear me?"

"I can," said a female voice. Lesley had spoken with Ortega and her boss DCI Wilton via video call three hours earlier. In the intervening time, the Met had gathered three armed response teams and briefed them all on what to expect.

"Can you hear me, boss?"

"Loud and clear, Johnny."

Johnny had arrived in London fifteen minutes earlier and been whisked to the scene of the operation in a patrol car.

"They're just helping me with my vest, boss," he said. "What do you need me to do?"

"We've agreed that you'll make the arrest," Lesley said. "And verify the identities."

"These men are known to us, Ma'am," DI Ortega said. "We don't need DC Chiles to verify."

Fair enough. But Johnny making the arrest meant that the three suspects would be brought back to Dorset. It meant that she wouldn't have to travel to London to interview them.

It meant that this case, and any other cases that might be related to it, stayed with her team.

"Good," she said.

"DC Chiles," Ortega said. "I need you to stay back until we have the suspects secured. My teams will check for weapons and take the men into custody. Only then do you go near them. Is that clear?"

"Clear, Ma'am."

Lesley's mouth was dry. She hated this; co-ordinating an operation a hundred miles away with no visuals and her only officer on the scene still an unknown quantity.

But he'd been part of the Met. He'd worked with them, he knew their procedures. He was the best placed officer to be there.

She just had to learn to trust him again.

"All units," said DI Ortega. "Are you in position?"

"Yes," came a voice.

Lesley turned and gave her team a thumbs-up. Jill had joined them; she gave the DI a nod.

Did none of these people ever go home?

"Yes." Another voice.

"Yes." A third.

"Roger that," said Ortega. "Command, we are ready to go."

"Authorisation to proceed." A voice Lesley hadn't heard before. She willed the butterflies in her stomach to stop.

"Roger, Command," said Ortega. "DCI Clarke?"

"Go," she said.

Ortega's tone changed, from calm, to clipped and punchy.

"Go, go, go!" she snapped.

Lesley closed her eyes.

Johnny, don't fuck up.

CHAPTER SEVENTY-FIVE

TINA YAWNED as she pushed open the door to the team room. She hadn't got home till gone ten last night, and Mike had been waiting up for her.

"Was it exciting?" he'd asked as she fell onto the sofa then snuggled into the crook of his arm.

"Yeah. Weird, not being able to see anything. But yeah." She put a hand on her chest. "Got the adrenaline going."

He kissed her. "Good. Speaking of which..."

She put a hand to her forehead. "Oh, I'm sorry love. You were expecting me home sooner."

He smiled. "It's fine. I'm knackered, too. Daisy screamed all the way to Swanage on the steam train. I don't think she liked the way it moved."

She grimaced. "Sounds rough. You took one for the team there."

"I bloody did. And tomorrow night, I expect my reward..."

"You OK, Tina?"

Tina jolted out of her reverie to see DS Strunk giving her a puzzled look. Oh, God. Had she been talking to herself?

"Sarge. Sorry. Yes, I'm fine. Tired, but that's normal."

He nodded and turned back to his desk. Not for the first time, she wondered if he had a family.

He was a dark horse, was Nathan Strunk.

The door opened and DCI Clarke entered, followed by DI Scott, Stanley and Katie. Stanley and Katie hovered at the back of the room and the DI followed the DCI to the front.

Tina hung her jacket over her chair and sat down, hoping this was going to be good news. She glanced sideways at Johnny, who gave her a flash of the eyes. His blond hair looked like it hadn't been brushed and his eyes were ringed with dark circles.

And... yes, he was wearing yesterday's suit.

"Morning, everyone," the DCI said, her gaze working across the room. They were all there, MCIT and Cold Cases teams. All except DI Patterson. And Mike.

"Sorry it's a bit of a crush with everyone in here," DCI Clarke continued. "But I wanted to get you all together. Bring you up to speed on a few things."

There were nods, and a few grunts. From Katie, a 'shush'. Tina bit back a smile.

"So you'll all know about last night's arrests." The DCI looked at Johnny, who gave a sheepish grin. "Johnny here managed to conclude his first case back in the MCIT by arresting three thoroughly nasty bastards."

More murmurs. The DS turned and gave Johnny a nod.

"We have a significant quantity of highly damning evidence against these men, especially regarding the murder of Jackie Kendall." The DCI paused for a moment. "But we'll be working with the CSIs to strengthen what we have for the Mark Ashforth murder. And working through records relating to Mr Ashforth's activities and finances to get a clearer picture."

"Have you worked out where the money came from?" Tina asked.

The DCI nodded. "We're building a more comprehensive

picture. It looks like he solved his financial problems by taking on some very lucrative driving work for our three suspects."

"Not for the Kelvins?" Meera said. "What Jackie heard..."

"I know Jackie heard them mention the Kelvins. But we'll never know the context."

"Not unless one of the three musketeers tells us," said Johnny.

The boss raised an eyebrow. "Is that what we're calling them now?"

Johnny shrugged.

"What about Yiannis?" Meera asked. "Is he safe?"

"He is. We'll wait and see if he's in real danger before we can make any more decisions there. With our 'three musketeers' in custody, I'm hoping he won't be at risk."

Meera nodded. "Poor man."

The DCI cocked her head. "We've arranged counselling for him, too. At your suggestion."

"Thanks," Meera muttered.

DCI Clarke cleared her throat. "This is all going to keep the MCIT pretty busy until this case comes to trial. And with Johnny having played a key role, he'll be remaining as a member of that team."

"That means there'll only be two of us," Stanley said. He spotted DI Scott's look. "Three, sorry."

"I understand that," the DCI said. "But your caseload is quieter right now. The case DI Scott was working on appears to have ground to a halt."

"Really?" Stanley said. "But Katie and me, we were..."

He stopped talking at a look from the DI. Tina wondered what was going on there.

"And I have other news," the DCI said. "Personnel-related news."

Silence. This would be about DI Patterson, Tina thought. Was she seriously ill?

"Firstly," the boss said, "good news." She glanced at Tina. "Mike will be back in three months and will be returning to the Cold Cases team. So you'll get your numbers back up, Stanley."

"Sorry, boss."

She threw him a smile. "It's OK. I can see why you think it's unfair. But that's how these teams are supposed to work. People will be expected to move across, when caseloads require it."

Katie shot up a hand. The DCI shook her head.

"Yes, Katie," she said. "I'm sure you'll get a chance to experience both teams."

Katie grinned and put down her hand.

"The second piece of news is less positive," the boss said. "DI Patterson won't be returning to us when her sick leave is over. Instead, she'll be returning to Devon."

Silence. No one looked disappointed. Tina imagined she wasn't the only one trying not to show relief.

"Right," the DCI said. "So it means there's a vacancy. Someone to lead the MCIT. I'd secretly love to do it myself, but I imagine the super would have things to say about that."

There were a few laughs. DS Strunk was standing very still, his gaze boring into the boss.

Really? thought Tina. She was just a DC, but even she knew the sarge wouldn't be getting that job.

But who would?

"You'll all be speculating, I imagine," the boss said. "But I'm afraid I can't answer any questions yet, as I don't have anything confirmed. But I can tell you that the person I have in mind is an excellent DI. I've seen her solve some far tougher cases than we get here, and I know for a fact she's a bloody good boss."

Tina turned to Johnny, whose brow was also furrowed. She couldn't think of any DIs matching that description.

"Thank you, everyone." The DCI put a hand on the table in front of her. "And well done. We had a body whose killers wanted to make it impossible for us to identify, but we identified him. And them." She looked down. "And we've achieved justice for Jackie Kendall."

CHAPTER SEVENTY-SIX

"THANKS FOR WAITING," Lesley said, approaching Carpenter's office. "But you didn't have to."

Jill, who'd been chatting with Carla, shrugged. "You were the one who went to see Vera. I assume you want to bring the super up to speed."

Lesley stopped in her tracks. "I'm so sorry, Jill."

"What for?"

"I've been all over the place the last few days, what with trying to identify our Chesil Beach victim and Vera Kelvin leading us a merry dance."

"You don't have anything to apologise for. And what do you mean, leading us a merry dance?"

"What are you two doing out here kicking your heels? I'm waiting."

Carpenter was in his office doorway, one hand on the half-open door and another on the frame. He looked like his day wasn't going well so far.

"Sir," Lesley said. "Of course." She waited for him to turn back inside and gave Jill an apologetic shrug. The two of them followed him inside.

He stood behind the desk, hands splayed on its surface, fingertips white from the pressure. "So I hear DC Chiles's trip to London was successful."

"Very, Sir," Lesley said. She and Jill stood opposite him, not touching the desk. "The full report is on the system, and I've sent you a summary. My team are—"

"That's not what you're here to talk about," he said.

"It's not," confirmed Lesley.

Jill cleared her throat. "Given the nature of what we're here to discuss, would it be appropriate to make ourselves a little more comfortable? And move away from the door?" She gestured towards the corner seating by the window.

Carpenter turned his gaze on her, one eye enlarging. Lesley was reminded of the kestrels Sharon had taken her to see at Corfe Castle last year.

"You're right," he said. "Please, lead the way."

Jill walked past Lesley and took one of the armchairs. Lesley waited for Carpenter to follow then took a seat herself.

Carpenter was smiling at Jill. "I've heard good things about you. From Serena Harper at Poole CID."

"Detective Superintendent Harper was an excellent boss, Sir."

"But still you came here instead of back to Poole, when your parental leave finished."

Jill stuck out her jaw. "The Cold Cases team had just been created. It felt like a unique opportunity."

He grunted. "Yes, it's that alright." He turned to Lesley. "So, tell me about your little pow-wow with our friend Vera Kelvin."

"I wouldn't call it a pow-wow." Lesley wasn't sure what she *would* call yesterday's conversation. Certainly not a witness interview.

"How was she?" He leaned back in his chair, body slumped a little to one side. Not his usual stiff posture.

"Not good, I'm afraid." Lesley sighed. "She knows everything."

"Everything? Be more specific, DCI Clarke."

Lesley went over the conversation in her head. Something she'd done repeatedly in the early hours of this morning, Elsa sleeping beside her. She ticked off the points in her mind.

"When I said we'd need to search her house for evidence relating to the break-in, she refused. She told me... She told me we weren't going to find Frank there."

Jill gave an involuntary sound. The super grunted.

"She mentioned Frank Kelvin by name?" he said.

"Did she know about Lucas Parsons?" Jill asked.

Lesley looked at Carpenter. "She did. She mentioned him by name, too. She repeated her claim that Frank's in Spain." She turned to Jill. "And she knows that you and your team have been looking into this."

"Shit," Jill muttered.

"So do you still think Frank is dead?" Carpenter asked. "Or do you think this was all a distraction? Maybe to keep us busy instead of identifying your Chesil Beach victim."

"Mark Ashforth," Lesley and Jill said in unison. Lesley gave Jill a tight smile.

Lesley shook her head. "But he was killed by members of a London gang."

"A London gang that was sending a message to Vera," Jill said. "The break-in, the car, the hair..."

Lesley turned to her. "You've been following along."

A shrug. "I like to know what's going on."

"I like that in a detective," Carpenter said. "You never know when a connection will arise between cases investigated by different teams."

Jill nodded. "And my team's cold cases can have links in places that aren't immediately obvious."

He rubbed his chin. "You're right there. DI Scott, what's your take? Do you think we should still be treating Frank Kelvin's disappearance as suspicious?"

Jill chewed on a fingernail for a moment, considering. "Well, normally a cold case begins with a body. Clearly, we don't have one here, and we certainly aren't going to find Frank in Vera's freezer, even if he was there." She pulled in a long breath through her nostrils. "But it's not uncommon for a cold case to begin with a tip-off, Sir. I don't know who Lucas Parsons got his information from, but he certainly believed he was telling the truth."

The super nodded. "And we've seen no concrete evidence of Frank Kelvin being alive and well and sunning himself on the beach in Málaga."

"There was documentation from the local police," Lesley said. "In 1993."

He waved a hand. "Twenty-two years ago." He hesitated, looking between them. "And besides, I happen to know that Vera and Arthur Kelvin would have had a very clear motive for killing Frank."

Lesley looked at Jill, who'd straightened in her chair, and then at the super. "You do, Sir?"

This would be related to his arrest of Frank in 1988. It had to be.

He glanced over towards the door, then twisted to look behind him, towards the building site that might someday become a garden. Finally, he turned back towards Lesley and Jill. He shuffled forward in his chair.

"I'm going to share this with the two of you," he said. "But it goes no further. Jill, not to your team. Lesley, not to Dennis."

They both nodded. Lesley wondered if perhaps Dennis already knew what the super was about to tell them.

Carpenter cleared his throat. "Jill, has Lesley told you that when Frank Kelvin was arrested for drug dealing in 1998, I was the arresting officer?"

"She has."

He smiled. "Good. Not that anyone who took the trouble to look into the relevant records couldn't find out."

Jill was very still, watching the super. She said nothing.

"So when I arrested him," Carpenter said, "he'd been drinking. Some whisky he'd nicked from his dad's office. I can tell you, he was far more scared about that being discovered than about the arrest."

"His dad was Gerard Kelvin," Lesley said.

"Indeed," the super agreed. "If you thought Arthur was a nasty piece of work... Anyway, the booze made him talkative. He told me a great many things about his family that he really shouldn't."

"Not a wise move," said Lesley.

"Indeed. And then he did the self-same thing with the desk sergeant, who was Eric Chiles." Carpenter looked from Lesley to Jill.

"Who was an undercover Vice officer," Jill said.

"Exactly," replied Carpenter. "Frank sobered up during the hours he spent in a cell. He realised what he'd done, and he was scared."

"I don't blame him," said Lesley.

"Am I right in thinking..." Jill began.

"Go on," said the super. "Tell me where your mind's going."

"Eric Chiles told Frank he could protect him," Jill said. "He recruited him as an informant, and he told him he could keep him safe."

Carpenter nodded. "That's exactly what happened."

"And this was five years before Frank disappeared," Lesley said. "Was he an informant all that time?"

Another nod.

"Wow," Lesley said.

"That would explain why he wasn't arrested again," Jill added.

Carpenter shrugged. "Personally, I think that was a bad move on Chiles's part. Frank Kelvin never crossing paths with the police, well, it was suspicious."

"Which is how they worked out what he was doing," Jill said.

Lesley looked at Carpenter. "Sir, can I ask how you knew about all this?"

He locked his lips. "You're forgetting that Frank talked to me, too. In the car, on the way to the station. He told me things he didn't tell Eric. Which is why Eric brought me into his operation."

Lesley's mouth hung open. "You worked undercover?"

"I did, Lesley. It was a long time ago, and I was just a uniformed constable. Easy to fly under the radar. Eric was a sergeant. A man I respected. I couldn't say no to him. Of course, I then learned he was actually a DI."

Lesley opened her mouth, then closed it again. She didn't know what to say.

"We need to speak to Eric," Jill said. "He'll know what happened to Frank."

"I've thought about that a lot over the years," Carpenter said, "and I think there are three possibilities."

"Which are?" Lesley asked.

He raised his hand and held up his forefinger. "One, Frank did exactly what Vera told us. He emigrated to Spain, under his own steam. The most likely reason would be that his family were onto him, so he decided to get away."

"They would have followed him," Lesley said. "They would have found him."

"Exactly," Carpenter replied. "Which is why I don't think that theory holds water. Vera Kelvin is lying to us. She won't be able to prove that he's alive and well and still in contact with her."

"So you think he's dead," Jill said.

"Three possibilities, remember." He held up a second finger. "But yes, my second theory is that Frank was killed in 1993. Maybe his remains spent time in his mother's freezer, maybe not. Maybe he went abroad before he was killed, maybe not."

Lesley shuddered. "She's a thoroughly evil woman."

Carpenter raised an eyebrow. "It's one of three possibilities, Lesley. And if it's true, then there's every chance that Arthur Kelvin is the one who ordered his death."

He was right. Especially with Arthur inheriting the operation from Gerard only weeks later.

"What's your third theory?" Jill asked. "Sir."

He smiled. "This one involves Eric. Frank learned that his family knew he was working with the police. Frank told Eric. And Eric arranged for Frank to disappear."

Lesley shook her head. "A DI couldn't do that on his own." She thought of her last super. David Randle, the corrupt boss who'd given evidence against the gang he'd worked for and then disappeared into witness protection.

Where was Randle now? Alive or dead? Still dodgy? Did she care?

"How likely do you think the third theory is, Sir?" asked Jill.

"Could Frank still be an informant?" Lesley added. "Working with PSD? Organised Crime?"

"I think that's unlikely," Carpenter said. "But there's only one way to find out about the other part of the theory."

"Eric Chiles," Lesley said.

He nodded. "I certainly can't speak with him. And Lesley, I think it would be unwise for you to have contact with him."

"I'll do it," said Jill.

"What if the Kelvins are watching him?" Lesley said. "What if they think he knows where Frank is? Jill, I don't want—"

"That's only one of my three theories," Carpenter said. "And I think it's unlikely they know about Eric's operation, given that nothing's happened to him in all this time."

He was right. "All the more reason to be careful," Lesley said.

"And I will be," Jill told her. "You think I'd put myself at risk, with my family to think about? You think I'd put Eric at risk, with Johnny and his family?"

Lesley gave her a long look. "Tell me how you'll approach him."

"I don't know yet. I need to work out a plan. But I'll be careful. I promise."

"It's the only way to know if we have a cold case or not," Carpenter said.

Jill was still looking at Lesley, her breathing shallow. She was excited.

"Very well," said the DCI. "But for God's sake, be careful."

CHAPTER SEVENTY-SEVEN

"Dad!" Johnny called out, closing the front door behind him. He'd always had a key to his dad's house, but he'd only recently started using it.

"In here," came the reply.

Johnny followed Eric's voice. The man was in the living room on his favourite armchair, the one positioned perfectly for the TV. Johnny didn't recognise the programme.

"What are you watching?" He sat down on the sofa and shrugged off his coat. His dad didn't keep the house warm enough for him to take off his suit jacket, too.

"Huh?" Eric turned to him.

Johnny waved towards the TV. "I don't recognise the show."

Eric frowned. "It's not a show, Johnny. It's a TV programme. A classic." He smiled.

"That still doesn't tell me what it is."

Eric shook his head. "It's John Thaw, son. *Inspector Morse.*" He pointed at the TV. "Don't you recognise it?"

"It must be thirty years old, Dad. No, I don't recognise it. Or him." Johnny wrinkled his nose. "Besides, I thought you hated cop shows? You never let us watch them, back when—"

"That was different. I'm not in the job anymore, I can enjoy it." He winked. "And there are thirty-three episodes of this, which should keep me busy for a while."

"Isn't your new friend Veronica going to keep you busy?"

Eric blinked. "Veronica?"

"You know, your neighbour. The woman from two doors down who gave you a lift to ours the other day."

"Oh, her." Eric didn't take his eyes off the TV, nor did he pause it. Johnny was a bit miffed to be ignored, but it was better that his dad didn't stand on ceremony.

Eric turned to Johnny, finally. "I don't know why you've got all excited about Veronica. She's married."

"Oh." Johnny hadn't been expecting that.

"You angling to get yourself a new mum, Johnny?"

"No." Johnny felt his ears redden. "God, no. No one can replace Mum."

"Well, that's correct. She was a hell of a woman." Eric stared ahead of him with a smile.

"She was," Johnny said.

Eric nodded. The two of them sat in silence for a moment, remembering.

The programme ended and the end credits rolled. Eric heaved himself up from his chair, plodded over to the TV set, and turned it off.

Johnny wanted to laugh. "You can use the remote for that, Dad."

Eric turned to him. He stood in front of the TV, his gaze on Johnny.

He shook his head. "Uses too much power. Always switch it off properly."

Johnny grunted. Like he'd ever do that.

Eric approached him. He put both hands on Johnny's shoulders. Johnny sat still, willing himself not to slide out of his dad's grip.

"I've got a question for you, son."

Johnny nodded. What the hell was this about?

"Which team is it you're in? Over at that fancy new HQ building they've got."

Johnny frowned. He hadn't been expecting this. "Well, I was supposed to be in the Cold Cases team. Covering Mike Legg's parental leave. You remember Mike?"

A nod. "Supposed to be, you say?"

"Yeah. They moved me, on my first day. DCI Clarke did, I mean. Apparently she often moves people between her teams."

"So now you're not in the Cold Cases team."

Johnny shrugged. "No. I'm in the MCIT."

"MCI what?"

"MCIT. Major Crime Investigations Team. They investigate—"

"I know what they investigate, son. So that's where you are now?"

"Yes." Why was this important? "DCI Clarke said I'm staying put, for now."

Eric brightened. He seemed to collect himself. "And do you like it? Do you enjoy the work?"

His dad was concerned about him, that was all. Maybe he worried about Johnny coming back to Dorset to keep an eye on him.

"I'm much happier back here than in the Met," Johnny said. "I know it wasn't what we were expecting, but... Well, it's turned out for the best."

"And Alice? The kids?"

"I was dreading the thought of sending them to a London school. I've arrested too many kids who were still in those schools." Johnny shrugged. "And Alice will find a job soon enough. Her parents are here, too."

"Good," said Eric. He turned back to the TV and switched it on. He strode back to his chair and gave Johnny a furtive look.

"Let's watch an episode together. You'll enjoy it."

"OK," said Johnny. Alice would be wondering where he was, but spending time with his dad was important.

CHAPTER SEVENTY-EIGHT

"You're early," Lesley said. She had her key out to unlock the front door, but Sharon had opened it before she got a chance.

Sharon's smile dropped. "You don't mind? I haven't disrupted your plans?"

Lesley stepped inside and wrapped her daughter in a hug. "Of course not. This is a bonus. And besides, it's perfect timing."

"How so?" Sharon was smiling again. Her face looked washed-out under the blue hair, but Lesley wasn't about to tell her so.

Let her make her own mistakes. That was what being nineteen was all about.

"I just wrapped up a case," Lesley replied. "Well, not entirely wrapped up. There are still i's to be dotted and t's to be crossed. But I can spend some time with you tomorrow."

Sharon's eyes widened. "Take me to Castle Point? I need some new clothes, my jeans are worn out and—"

"Castle Point?" Lesley said. It was a vast retail park just outside Bournemouth. "Isn't that a bit mainstream for a girl with blue hair?"

"It's not entirely blue." Sharon twirled a strand of hair in her fingertips. "And I'm getting bored of it anyway. I bought some new dye on the way here."

Thank God for that. Lesley smiled and nodded.

"OK," Sharon said. "Maybe not Castle Point. Let's go to Westbourne. You can spend money on me." She bit her bottom lip, a question in her eyes.

Lesley ruffled the offending hair. "It'll be fun. Not too much money, though. I have no idea how much fixing this roof is going to cost."

Sharon screwed up her face. "Fair enough. So what d'you think about Nick coming to Exeter?"

Lesley eyed her. "Have you got a thing for Nick or something?"

"Don't be ridiculous. He's gay. But he's a friend, and I know you like his mum. Besides, I've got Pel."

"Who I'm hoping to meet at some point. When are you going to bring him home to Bournemouth?"

Sharon pushed herself out of the hug. "Calm down, Mum. It's not like we're getting married..."

"What's that I hear about Sharon getting married?"

The front door opened and Elsa entered, smiling at Sharon.

"Elsa!" The girl threw herself at her stepmum for a hug.

"It's lovely to see you," Elsa said. She looked over Sharon's shoulder at Lesley. "You OK?"

Lesley grabbed Elsa's hand and kissed it. "I'm better than OK. I have my daughter home, we've solved the Chesil Beach case, and DI Hannah Patterson is going back to Devon."

Elsa's smile widened. "She is? And the complaint?"

"PSD say I have no case to answer."

Elsa grinned. Sharon turned to Lesley.

"PSD, Mum? That's bad news, isn't it?"

"Not this time, love. It was a malicious complaint, and fortunately, PSD didn't take it seriously. It seems like they do know what they're doing, after all."

Elsa nodded. "But that means you have a gap in your team. Again."

"It won't be hard to fill. And I've got someone in mind."

"Who? Not Nathan Strunk, surely?"

Lesley laughed. "What's with everyone and Nathan Strunk? No, not him. Nothing's official yet, and this person might not take up my offer. But I'm working on her."

"Her?" said Sharon. "Who?"

Lesley winked. "You'll see, love. You'll see."

CHAPTER SEVENTY-NINE

"Did you really make this?" Jill looked from the painting to her daughter.

"Yeah. Look." Suzi pointed at the first of the three blobs on the paper. "Mama."

Jill raised an eyebrow at the yellow blob. Now she knew, she could see that it was vaguely person-shaped. "That looks just like me. Well done. Which one's Mummy?"

Suzi pointed to the brown blob across from the yellow one. This one was smaller and kind of spiky. Jill decided to assume that didn't mean anything.

She wasn't sure how she felt about her being yellow and Meera being brown, though. Sure, it reflected their hair colour. But was that how Suzi saw her family?

Judging by the colour of the blob in the middle, probably not. This one was bright orange.

"And that's you?" she asked.

Suzi nodded vigorously and drilled her finger into her chest. "Su-su."

"I think it's very good," said Meera, who was hauling a bag of shopping in through their narrow hallway. "Unlike the process of getting shopping into this house. Do you know how far away I had to park?"

Jill grabbed her hand. "Sorry, sweetheart." They lived in a four-hundred-year-old cottage that Jill loved. She knew Meera didn't. "You should have asked me to move my car."

"I would have had to park somewhere to come and tell you." Meera shook her head. "It's fine. Gives me a workout." She raised her arms and flexed her muscles. "Mummy strong!"

Suzi giggled. Jill considered telling Meera she could have messaged her from the car, but decided it would be a bad idea. They'd argued about parking before. And the damp, and the steepness of the stairs. The electrics. And the plumbing. The list went on.

"Are you OK with Suzi for fifteen minutes while I make a phone call?" she asked Meera.

Meera shrugged. "Still on the clock?" It was only 4pm; hours before Jill was normally home on a Wednesday.

"Something like that," Jill said. She didn't want to make this call from the office. In fact, she didn't want to make it from her own mobile phone.

"That's fine," Meera said. "I'll put the shopping away. Biscuits in the freezer, right Suzi?"

"No!" the girl cried. "Ice cream in freezer!"

"Of course, silly Mummy." Meera looked at Jill. "Go on. The sooner you're done, the sooner we can eat."

"I'm going to go outside," Jill said. "Better signal." She wasn't wrong; the solid walls of their ancient house weren't conducive to mobile signal.

Meera nodded, rooting through the shopping bags.

Jill gave Suzi a kiss on the top of the head, prompting a squeal, then left the house. She turned right into the village. Luckily theirs was the kind of old-fashioned community that still had a phone box.

She pulled a piece of folded-up paper out of her pocket and

looked around her before dialling. Everybody knew everybody else here. If someone saw her using the phone box, they would ask why.

She had an excuse, their terrible mobile phone signal. She knew that if you took the footpath past the church and across a field, you could make a call. But people didn't have to know that she knew.

There were some benefits to living in the kind of village that mounted a spirited protest every time an attempt was made to erect a mobile phone mast.

She dialled the number the super had given her.

"335624, hello," came the answer.

Jill smiled. She didn't know there were people who still answered the phone like that.

"Mr Chiles?" she said.

"Yes. Who am I speaking to, please? Because if you're trying to sell—"

"I'm not a salesperson, Mr Chiles. I'm a police officer. My name is DI Jill Scott. I work for DCI Lesley Clarke in Dorset Police's Cold Cases team, and I'm calling you from a public phone box."

"Very thorough," he replied. "I was wondering if I might get a call from you eventually."

"You're aware of the Cold Cases team?"

"I am. And I'm also aware that my son very nearly became one of your number."

"Very nearly, Mr Chiles."

"Please, call me Eric."

"Eric. It's fortunate that Johnny was moved across to the MCIT to work on the Chesil Beach case. Because only a few hours later, we started working on a case, which is the reason I'm calling you."

"Frank."

She smiled. "I feel like there's nothing I can tell you that you don't already know."

He laughed. "Oh, I'm sure that's very far from the truth. But given that you're calling me from a phone box, I imagine this isn't a social call."

"It isn't. I'd like us to meet, but I'm aware you might not feel comfortable with that."

"I've worked very hard to stay out of the firing line, DI Scott. Jill. Even my family still think I was a desk sergeant. Only two people knew the truth. My commanding officer in Vice, and... Well, only two people. You work at the new headquarters in Winfrith Newburgh, is that correct?"

"Yes." How long could she stay in this phone box without one of her neighbours noticing? "My superintendent is Detective Superintendent Anthony Carpenter."

"Ah."

"It was Carpenter who asked me to call you," Jill said.

"So, he told you. That surprises me." A pause. "Good. I don't like secrets."

Jill resisted a laugh. Eric Chiles, the desk sergeant who was really an undercover DI, not liking secrets?

"Is that a joke?" she asked.

"It isn't. Look, I know what you must think. But I never lied to my family about what I did. Every single thing I told them about the routine of my police work was true."

I bet you didn't tell them everything, though, she thought.

"How would you feel about meeting?" she said. "We can use a location of your choosing, and I'll take measures to—"

"Has Anthony Carpenter told you about his three theories?"

So, no meeting then. "About Frank's disappearance?" she said.

"Yes."

"He has."

Eric sighed. "The first one clearly isn't true. If Frank was alive and well and living the high life in Malaga, we'd know. We'd have evidence. The police officer, who certified his visit to a local station? He was bribed."

"By whom?"

"I don't know. The officer didn't know. But he 'retired' shortly after."

"And the other two theories?"

"The third one... that's the one that involves me, am I right?"

Jill thought back. "Yes."

He grunted. "That one is quite obviously ridiculous. I was clever enough to hide the fact that I was working undercover for all those years. But I certainly wasn't clever enough to make Frank disappear all by myself. And I'd have exposed my operation if I'd attempted to involve other departments in doing so. I haven't been hiding a fugitive Frank Kelvin all these years."

She nodded. "Which leaves..."

"Occam's Razor. The most obvious answer is that Frank died. That his family learned what he was doing and had their revenge." He sounded sad.

"You liked the man."

"I did. I thought what he did was incredibly courageous. The most courageous thing I witnessed in all my time in the job." He sighed. "Which is why I will help you, DI Scott. Jill."

She felt her heart rate pick up. "You will?"

"I will. But please, don't make me regret it. Find a location that's suitably secure, and I'll tell you what I know about Frank Kelvin."

Thank you for reading *The Chesil Beach Murders*. If you'd like to read more about Lesley and the team you could download a free ebook or audiobook called *The Lyme Regis Murder* from my website at www.rachelmclean.com/lymemurder

And keep reading for a bonus Q&A about *The Chesil Beach Murders* and the next book in the series, *The Beach Hut Murders*.

Happy reading! Rachel.

READ THE DORSET CRIME SERIES

The Corfe Castle Murders

The Clifftop Murders

The Island Murders

The Monument Murders

The Millionaire Murders

The Fossil Beach Murders

The Blue Pool Murders

The Lighthouse Murders

The Ghost Village Murders

The Poole Harbour Murders

The Chesil Beach Murders

The Beach Hut Murders

...and more to come

Buy from book retailers.

ALSO BY RACHEL MCLEAN

The DI Zoe Finch Series – buy from book retailers.

Deadly Wishes

Deadly Choices

Deadly Desires

Deadly Terror

Deadly Reprisal

Deadly Fallout

Deadly Christmas

The McBride & Tanner Series – buy from book retailers.

Blood and Money

Death and Poetry

Power and Treachery

Secrets and History

The Cumbria Crime Series by Rachel McLean and Joel Hames – buy from book retailers.

The Harbour

The Mine

The Cairn

The Barn

The Lake

The Wood

The Port

The Marsh

Read the London Cosy Mystery Series by Rachel McLean and Millie Ravensworth – buy from book retailers.

Death at Westminster

Death in the West End

Death at Tower Bridge

Death on the Thames

Death at St Paul's Cathedral

Death at Abbey Road

The Jurassic Coast Mystery Series by Rachel McLean and Millie Ravensworth – buy from book retailers.

The Swimming Club

The Empty Easel

The Shattered Bauble